STAR TREK®
Science Logs

An Exciting Journey to the

Most Amazing Phenomena

in the Galaxy!

Andre Bormanis

POCKET BOOKS

New York   London   Toronto   Sydney   Tokyo   Singapore

For my Mother and Father, with love

Acknowledgments

Many thanks to the producers, writers, cast, and crew of *Star Trek*. Special thanks to Doug Drexler, Mike and Denise Okuda, Rick Sternbach; Margaret Clark at Pocket Books; and, of course, Jeri Taylor.

Many experts in many fields (including several members of my immediate family) help keep me informed of the latest developments and discoveries in the real world of science and medicine, and have reviewed parts of this book: Dr. Peteris and Debra Bormanis, Peter and Cindy Bormanis, Dr. John Bormanis, Dr. Scott Bormanis, Bill Belisle, Dr. Bruce Betts, Max and Irene Bray, Gary Brent, Dr. Alan Dressler, Dr. Louis Friedman, Dr. John Glassco, and Dr. Randa Kutob. Any mistakes in the text are, of course, mine alone.

Lastly, I would like to thank my parents, family, and friends for the support and encouragement they've given me over the years as I've pursued my own personal and sometimes peripatetic Trek.

An *Original* Publication of POCKET BOOKS

POCKET BOOKS, a division of Simon & Schuster Inc.
1230 Avenue of the Americas, New York, NY 10020

ISBN: 0-671-00997-4

First Pocket Books trade paperback printing March 1998

10   9   8   7   6   5   4   3   2   1

POCKET and colophon are registered trademarks of Simon & Schuster Inc.

Book design by Richard Oriolo

Printed in the U.S.A.

Preface

When I was deposited in the middle of the Star Trek universe eight years ago, I felt as though I'd been plunged into an alternate dimension. The immensity of the task ahead of me—getting up to speed with a phenomenon that had millions of passionate fans all over the world, fans who scrutinize literally every word of a script—was overwhelming. I'd largely managed to avoid science during my education, scraping by with one introductory course in zoology. How was I ever going to grasp the principles of physics and astronomy that lie at the heart of science fiction?

The good news: I didn't have to. Gene Roddenberry had realized years ago that solid, informed, and creative science advisors were a necessary component in the making of *Star Trek*. We have been fortunate, over the years, to have had several such consultants upon whom we've relied heavily.

Andre Bormanis came to us four years ago, and we quickly realized that he was that rare and nearly perfect combination of the scientific and the creative. He is a veritable encyclopedia of knowledge in many disciplines, particularly astronomy. Need a real star system near Earth? Easy. Barnard's Star, Ross 154, Epsilon Indi, or Vega would all fill the bill. He also has the ability to come up with fresh and interesting nomenclature for as-yet-undiscovered tenets of science. Need an alien ore? No problem. Psilminite, topaline, mizinite, or astaline will do nicely.

But perhaps Andre's greatest strength lies in his understanding of dramatic necessity. Some advisors have been all but fascistic in their insistence that science is rigid and unyielding. Andre sees it in vaster terms: a flexible, evolving discipline that is limitless in its possibilities. Even as people of the middle ages couldn't have conceived of computers, people today can't set arbitrary limits on what might be discovered or accomplished in the future. Andre's wide-ranging imagination provides us with spatial anomalies, medical advances, alien capabilities, time travel—whatever we need to make a story work.

But all of this is done within the framework of plausible science, one foot firmly planted on factual ground, even if the other is dancing through whimsy. This combination of abilities makes Andre a potent and valuable member of the *Star Trek* team, one I'm grateful to have worked with. Andre—thanks for making all of us look so much smarter then we are.

—Jeri Taylor
Los Angles, CA

Contents

Making the Incredible Credible:
The Science of *Star Trek*

As Science Consultant for *Star Trek: Voyager* and *Star Trek: Deep Space Nine*, I have the job of helping the shows' writers and producers create plausible representations and descriptions of future sciences while remaining true to established science as it is understood today.

My involvement with a *Star Trek* episode typically begins with the first-draft teleplay (script). I read the teleplay with an eye toward scientific concepts and technical language. *Star Trek* writers typically have a good sense of the kind of language that should be used to describe stars, planets, sensor readings, and so on. If the writer isn't sure of the best terminology for a particular scientific phenomenon or twenty-fourth-century technology, the word "tech" will appear in the script. This is my cue to suggest appropriate language. Occasionally writers will call me to discuss and clarify scientific concepts or technical language before they begin writing a script.

After I finish reading the teleplay, I write a set of technical notes and fax them to the *Star Trek* offices at Paramount. The writer reads the notes and selects the tech suggestions he or she feels will work best in the context of the story. This process continues through the various script drafts and draft revisions.

One of the most challenging aspects of creating technical language for *Star Trek* is that the majority of the technical jargon must be *descriptive*, not explanatory. Excluding commercials and credits, each *Star Trek* episode runs about forty-three minutes. Forty-three minutes is barely enough time to tell a complete and interesting story, let alone to explain the physics of an exotic spatial phenomenon or the cause of a breakdown in the warp core's magnetic containment field. But viewers who watch the show closely will see that there is a high level of consistency in the technical language featured in *Star Trek* episodes. Over the years, the writers, producers, and various advisors and consultants have developed a kind of twenty-fourth–century scientific lexicon that, we hope, gives our audience a sense of the science behind the science fiction.

Because the current *Star Trek* series take place nearly four hundred years in the future and depicts technologies far beyond the capabilities of present-day science, the producers of *Star Trek* must occasionally create some "twenty-fourth–century science" to provide a plausible foundation for *Trek* technologies and the extraordinary phenomena our crews encounter in space. Since I am trained in late-twentieth–century physics, this was one of the hardest things for me to get comfortable with when I started working for the show. When a writer creates an interesting space phenomenon for a story, for example, my initial impulse is to try to explain it in terms of present-day physics and space science. Sometimes this just doesn't work.

For example, in the *DS9* episode "Paradise," Sisko and O'Brien are stranded on a planet where none of their devices (phasers, combadges, tricorders, etc.) function. O'Brien concludes that there must be some kind of naturally occurring "field" on the planet that shorts out their instruments. But what kind of field? Magnetic fields are probably common on planets like Earth. Intense electromagnetic pulses can disrupt electronic circuits; maybe the planet's magnetic field was somehow generating such pulses. But one would think that twenty-fourth–century space equipment would be well shielded against such phenomena. And if the planet's magnetic field was so intense that our shielding was ineffective, it would probably have an adverse and possibly dangerous physical effect on Sisko and O'Brien. On the other hand, rapidly fluctuating magnetic fields with occasional, intense but brief, "spikes" might interfere with instruments without hurting people....

In my technical notes I suggested all sorts of wordy language that might explain the nature of the strange "damping field" on the planet; tongue-twisting phrases along the lines of "rapidly fluctuating electromagnetic field spikes." But O'Brien had to refer to this field several times in the script; the term he used for the field therefore had to be short and easy to say in dialogue. I finally invented the term "duonetic field," which derives from the term duotronic circuitry, established in the original *Star Trek* series as the basic "electronic architecture" for the *Enterprise* control circuitry.

When I work on a *Star Trek* script, I always first try to find something in real science that fits the dramatic needs of the story. If I can't find anything appropriate, I try to use a theory or idea on the "cutting edge" of present-day science and extrapolate it into the twenty-fourth century. And if all else fails, I invent new "science." I strive to keep the invented science in the realm of the plausible by using analogies to known science. For example, a few neutrons injected into a pile of uranium can initiate a chain reaction that ultimately raises the temperature of the pile by several thousand degrees; this is how nuclear fission power plants operate. By analogy, a beam of fictitious nadion particles from the *Enterprise*'s phaser banks might initiate a chain reaction that raises the temperature of a planet's core several thousand degrees (see the "Inheritance" science log for more discussion on this).

One thing I will *never* knowingly do is use an established term from present-day science in an inappropriate way. If, say, "inertia" isn't the correct word in the given context, I won't use it, even if it might sound good to a lay audience.

Star Trek can't be *Nova* (the acclaimed PBS science series); its purpose has never been to teach science, but I certainly hope it stimulates interest in science and a desire among our audience to learn more about science and technology, and perhaps even to pursue careers in the sciences or related fields. The writers, producers, and stars of the various *Star Trek* series have received countless letters from fans describing how *Star Trek* was an important factor in motivating their desire to pursue careers in science and engineering.

Certainly a big part of my fascination with space exploration, and my subsequent degrees in physics and science policy and my work for NASA can be traced to watching *Star Trek* at the age of seven, wide-eyed with wonder at the prospect of exploring strange new worlds.

—Andre Bormanis
Los Angeles, CA

Federation Science Logs

Starfleet Archives, Central Science Database

Please note: Stardates correspond to the date a given log entry was transmitted to Starfleet Command, not the date when the events described within the log took place.

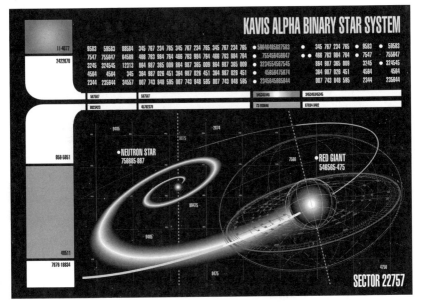

KAVIS ALPHA BINARY STAR SYSTEM

•NEUTRON STAR
756685-867

•RED GIANT
546565-475

SECTOR 22757

DOUG DREXLER

Binary stars are common in our Milky Way Galaxy, and presumably in other galaxies as well. *Neutron stars* are the cores of stars that have ended their lives in a violent explosion called a *supernova*. The stellar core that survives this massive explosion will take one of two forms: a compact ball of neutrons, some ten to fifteen kilometers in diameter—a neutron star; or an even more extraordinary celestial beast, a *black hole*.

Within a neutron star, atoms are compressed to such high pressures that their constituent protons and electrons are crushed together. The positive charge of the proton cancels the negative charge of the electron, resulting in an electrically neutral particle: a neutron. Matter in a neutron star is so dense that a teaspoon of it would weigh as much as a mountain. The term *neutronium* has been coined to describe matter that has been compressed to the point that protons and electrons squeeze together into neutrons. In *The Original Series* episode "The Doomsday Machine," Spock determined that the hull of the doomsday machine was composed of neutronium; even the formidable *Enterprise* phaser banks weren't powerful enough to penetrate such a dense material.

The first neutron star was discovered in 1967. A radio telescope in England detected a radio signal from space that repeated in a remarkably regular pattern: once every 1.3 seconds. The surprising clocklike regularity of the signal led the astronomers who first identified it to wonder if the source might be artificial. They jokingly designated the object LGM-1—Little Green Men 1! They soon determined that their mysterious radio source was a rapidly rotating neutron star. Radio waves beamed into space by the spinning neutron star were sweeping past the Earth every 1.3 seconds, like the beacon of a lighthouse. A rotating neutron star that generates a periodic radio signal is called a *pulsar*

When a star more than about eight times the mass of the Sun explodes, the neutron star remnant is just a brief stepping-stone on the way to an even more remarkable object: a black hole.

T Tauri stars are young, hot stars, typically surrounded by a shell of gas and dust. Strong stellar winds, blowing at speeds on the order of one hundred kilometers per second, radiate from the surface of a T Tauri star, pushing the surrounding gas shell outward. Some T Tauri stars are encircled by disks of gas and dust that may be planetary systems in the making. By the time the material in this protoplanetary disk settles into a retinue of planets and moons, the T Tauri star would have entered the *main sequence* of stellar evolution. The main sequence marks the longest part of a star's active life, during which the star is continuously fusing hydrogen atoms into helium atoms in its core, and shining at relatively constant luminosity. It would therefore be extremely unusual for a star in the T Tauri stage to be accompanied by a Class-M planet.

T Tauri stars are thought to be relatively low-mass stars, ranging from 0.2 to 2.0 times the mass of the Sun. They range in age from ten thousand to ten million years (just kids, by astronomical standards), and tend to be found in the dark *molecular clouds* where most stars are born.

Supernovae
("The Q and the Gray"; *VGR*)

Starship *Voyager* Science Log, Stardate 50351.3. Captain Kathryn Janeway recording.

The Voyager *crew has been witness to a truly remarkable phenomenon: a series of supernova explosions in the same sector, occurring within moments of one another.*

At first I suspected that a single supernova event had triggered the other supernovae, perhaps through some as-yet

Star Clusters ("A Taste of Armageddon"; *TOS*)

Starship *Enterprise* Science Log, Stardate 3197.7. Science Officer Spock recording.

During our diplomatic mission to Eminiar VII, Enterprise sensors recorded routine cartographic and radiometric data on the star cluster NGC 321.

Largely unremarkable in appearance, Cluster NGC 321 contains a smaller proportion of interstellar dust than other open star clusters in this region of the galaxy, perhaps indicative of a greater than average age for this cluster, or the presence of unusually strong stellar winds.

NGC is short for the New General Catalog of Nebulae and Clusters of Stars. The *NGC*, an actual book, lists the coordinates and classifications of all known "nonstellar" objects—star clusters, nebulae, galaxies, etc. NGC 321 is actually not a star cluster, but a roundish galaxy that lies far beyond our own galaxy, the Milky Way. One could argue that by the twenty-third

Globuar Cluster 47 Toucanae. COURTESY OF EUROPEAN SOUTHERN OBSERVATORY.

century the *NGC* would have been revised to focus on nonstellar objects within the domain of the Federation, i.e., the Milky Way Galaxy.

The New General Catalog was first published in 1888. It currently lists over 13,000 objects. The first comprehensive catalog of nonstellar objects was compiled by the French astronomer Charles Messier in the late 1700s. Messier's principal astronomical interest was comets. Faint galaxies and nebulosities sometimes look like comets in small telescopes, briefly fooling comet-hunting astronomers into thinking they've bagged a new one. Messier compiled his catalog to avoid repeatedly mistaking these objects for comets.

Star clusters come in two major forms, open and globular. Open clusters are relatively loose associations of stars, from a few dozen to several thousand, herded into a volume of space several or more light-years across. The Pleiades, or Seven Sisters, is an open star cluster (see photo page 17). Open clusters are found throughout the spiral arms of the Milky Way. Globular clusters are composed of much more tightly bunched stars; thousands of stars are sometimes packed into a volume only three or four light-years across (see photo)! Globular clusters exist outside the arms of our galaxy, forming a kind of halo around the Milky Way. Many other galaxies are also surrounded by globular clusters.

Inhabitants of a planet within a globular star cluster would be treated to a truly spectacular sight. Every night the sky would be filled with hundreds of stars, every one of them brighter than the brightest stars visible from Earth. Their combined light would be several times brighter than the light of the full Moon.

T Tauri stars ("Clues"; TN

Starship *Enterprise* Science Log, Stardate 44505.9. Second Office recording.

The *Enterprise* has encountered what appeared to be planet orbiting a T Tauri star. Federation astrophysic suggests that the evolution of habitable planetar ments should not begin until after the T Tauri phas evolution has ended. Investigations of this system v nated when the *Enterprise* encountered an unstable and was catapulted clear of the system.

tars, like people, are born, grow old, and die. cloud collapses, its core becomes hotter and h tually reaching a temperature and pressure wh fusion is possible. Before a young *protostar* settles atively sedate life of stellar middle age, it exists as a

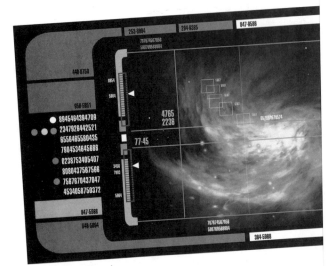

DOUG DREXLER

unknown subspace shock-wave mechanism. The "mechanism," however, proved to be none other than the opening volleys of a staggering civil war within the Q continuum.

A supernova is the granddaddy of all stellar explosions. A star undergoing a supernova explosion will increase in brightness by a factor of *billions*. When a star explodes in a supernova, it radiates more energy in its first few seconds than that of every star in our galaxy and in the universe *combined*. Over the course of the next several days, the supernova's energy output can equal the energy output of a ten billion stars.

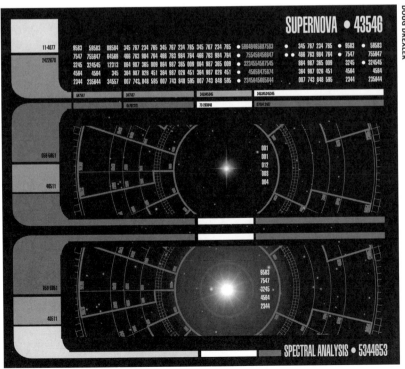

Astronomers recognize two distinct types of supernovae. In a Type I supernova, a *white dwarf* (a small, dense, and very old star, rich in the element carbon) accumulates mass from an orbiting companion star, typically a red or blue giant. Eventually the white dwarf cannot support the weight of all that extra mass, and it collapses in a catastrophic implosion. The core of the white dwarf is heated to a temperature sufficient to rapidly fuse the carbon atoms there into nickel, cobalt, and iron, resulting in a massive explosion of energy.

A Type II supernova occurs at the end of the life of a star at least eight times as massive as the Sun. The process of nuclear fusion has nearly run its course. Most of the lighter elements within the star's core have fused into iron atoms. The core of the star is essentially an iron cinder. Iron atoms cannot fuse into heavier elements under the conditions that normally prevail within a star's core; iron is thus the end product of *stellar nucleosynthesis*, the process that creates heavier elements out of lighter constituents. When the mass of the iron core exceeds 1.4 times the mass of our Sun, the core's internal pressure can no longer support its weight. The core suddenly collapses: in less than *one second*, all of the electrons and protons in the core merge into neutrons. The outer layers of the star fall onto the solid neutron core and rebound outward in an immense shockwave effect that produces the supernova explosion.

If either type of supernova happened in our neck of the Milky Way (that is, within a few dozen or so light-years from the Sun) the consequences could be devastating. Gamma radiation from the stellar explosion would be so intense that most life on Earth would be at risk of extinction. In addition, the Earth's ozone layer, which protects our planet from damaging ultraviolet light from the Sun, would almost certainly be destroyed by the radiation from a nearby supernova. Fortunately, there are no local stars massive enough to explode in a supernova.

Alpha Quadrant Black Hole
("Tomorrow is Yesterday"; TOS)

Starship Enterprise **Science Officer's Log, Stardate 3116.4. Science Officer Spock recording.**

The Enterprise *has experienced a near-catastrophic encounter with a black star, a collapsed star with essentially infinite density.*

Skirting the event horizon of the black star at warp 4 not only catapulted the Enterprise *126 light-years in space, but also propelled the ship three hundred years backward in time.*

Computer analysis of the Enterprise *trajectory during the black star encounter suggests that there is an entire class of hyperbolic warp trajectories capable of effecting time travel. The key is a close encounter with a large gravitational source, such as a black star. Normal stars, such as Sol or the Vulcan primary, can also be utilized for temporal travel, but much higher warp velocities and extremely precise orbital calculations are required.*

The "black star" encountered by the *Enterprise* in "Tomorrow is Yesterday" is an example of what we today call a *black hole*, or possibly a *naked singularity*.

Most black holes are created in the aftermath of a supernova explosion. The core of the exploded star collapses until the strength of gravity at its surface is so great that even light, traveling at three hundred thousand kilometers per second, isn't moving fast enough to escape its gravitational grip. Like a ball tossed in the air, a photon leaving the surface of a black hole simply arcs back down into the black hole, forever lost to the universe.

The strength of a gravitational field decreases with dis-

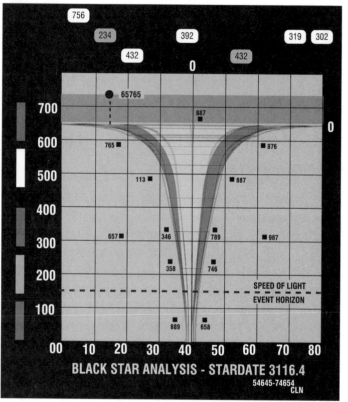

DOUG DREXLER

tance. At some distance from the surface of a black hole, the escape velocity is exactly equal to the speed of light. This distance defines the black hole's *event horizon*.

More and more evidence for the existence of black holes has been gathered in recent years. Black holes cannot be seen directly, but their presence can sometimes be inferred by their effects on other objects. The first likely black hole candidate was called Cygnus X-1. Cygnus X-1 is a star in the constellation Cygnus that strongly radiates X rays. Astronomers suspect that the source of this intense X-ray emission is a star orbiting a black hole. The fierce gravity of the black hole constantly pulls matter away from the orbiting star. As stellar matter is Hoovered into the black hole, it heats up from friction. This intensely hot gas is the source of the X rays.

Super-massive black holes probably exist at the center of many galaxies, including our own. These black holes presumably begin in supernova explosions, but later draw in other stars, and perhaps even other black holes, so that over time they accumulate tremendous amounts of mass. The Hubble Space Telescope has captured images that strongly suggest the presence of black holes in the cores of several nearby galaxies. The masses of these galactic black holes may be on the order of billions of times the mass of the Sun, and may be the power source of *quasars*.

A rotating black hole could provide a means for time travel. Einstein proved that time and space are intimately linked. Under certain circumstances, time and space essentially become interchangeable. If a black hole rotates quickly enough, the time dimension can replace a space dimension in the black hole's frame of reference. A starship on a trajectory passing near the black hole could conceivably move through the time dimension, traveling into the past or future. A black hole rotating quickly enough to create this effect will "shed" its event horizon and become a naked singularity.

The Mutara Nebula
(*Star Trek II: The Wrath of Khan*)

Starship Enterprise **Science Log, Stardate 8140.4. Commander Hikaru Sulu recording.**

During what was expected to be a routine cadet-training mission, the Enterprise *was forced to take refuge in the Mutara Nebula following an attack by Khan Noonien Singh, the late-twentieth–century warlord revived from stasis by Captain James T. Kirk on Stardate 3141.9.*

The details of Khan's remarkable but tragic life, and his death in the battle with the Enterprise *at Mutara, are well chronicled (see James T. Kirk, Starfleet Captain's Logs Archives, reference index Khan Noonien Singh). The unusually energetic plasmas and electromagnetic fields of the Mutara Nebula deprived Khan of the tactical advantage he enjoyed after his initial surprise attack on* Enterprise.

Roughly ovoid in shape, the Mutara Nebula spans 8.7 billion kilometers in its longest dimension. Average mass density within the nebula is approximately $3 \cdot 10^6$ a.m.u. per cubic centimeter. The composition of the nebula is unremarkable, but the presence of a nearby O-type star radiating strongly in the ultraviolet generates high levels of photo-ionization and secondary fluorescence. Principle nebular constituents are ionized hydrogen; helium; carbon; argon; xenon; and interstellar silicate dust grains.

EM spectrum sensor arrays had extremely limited range within the nebula; on the order of 100 hundred meters in the visible, UV, and soft X-ray bands. Infrared and microwave sensors provided some penetration of nebular dust clouds, but were frequently rendered inoperable due to excessive thermal noise from colliding plasma fields. Admiral Kirk anticipated this effect, and used it to ensure tactical parity in the final battle between the Enterprise *and the* Defiant: *both ships had limited sensors and navigational capacity due to interference from the nebular ionization. Captain Spock also recognized that Khan, an inexperienced space traveler, tended to think in two dimensions.*

Nebulae are vast clouds of gas and dust in interstellar space. Most of the gas in a typical nebula is hydrogen, the simplest and most abundant element in the universe.

Astronomers classify most nebulae into two basic types: *emission* and *absorption*. Emission nebulae are illuminated by the light from stars within or close to the nebula. The Great Nebula in Orion, located some fifteen hundred light-years from Earth, glows mostly due to the ultraviolet light from a single

Great Nebula in Orion. ANDRE BORMANIS.

Horsehead Nebula. COURTESY TONY & DAPHNE HALLAS OF ASTRO PHOTO.

star (see photo). Gases within the nebula absorb high-frequency ultraviolet light from this star, and re-emit that light at lower, visible-light frequencies, a process called *fluorescence*. Interstellar hydrogen mostly emits red light. The greens and blues visible in color photographs of the Orion and many other emission nebulae come from atoms of oxygen and dust particles. The Mutara Nebula in *The Wrath of Khan* is a somewhat stylized emission nebula, with a few lanes of dark dust.

Absorption nebulae are nebulae so thick with dust that they tend to absorb most of the light from nearby stars. A striking example is the Horsehead Nebula (see photo above). The horse-head-shaped silhouette is a cloud of dust within the red lanes of hydrogen. The distance from the "nose" to the "mane" of the Horsehead is roughly three light-years.

A less common type of nebula is the *reflection nebula*. Gas and dust clouds in space will sometimes scatter light from nearby stars, reflecting some of that light in our direction. In the Pleiades star cluster several swaths of reflection nebulosity are clearly visible (see photo, following page).

The average density of hydrogen in interstellar space is around one atom per cubic meter. In an emission nebula, the density of hydrogen atoms rises to some 10^9 atoms per cubic

Pleiades Star Cluster and Reflection Nebula. <small>COURTESY TONY & DAPHNE HALLAS OF ASTRO PHOTO</small>

meter. This may sound like a lot, but it's a virtual vacuum compared to the number of oxygen and nitrogen molecules in a cubic meter of air near the Earth's surface: about $50 \cdot 10^{18}$.

The Badlands
("The Maquis, Part I"; *DS9*)

Deep Space 9 Science Log, Stardate 47792.9. Science Officer Jadzia Dax recording.

Following the abduction of the Cardassian military officer Gul Dukat by Maquis freedom fighters, Commander Sisko commanded a rescue mission into the "Badlands" territory near the Bajoran system.

The Badlands is an extensive and extremely dynamic nebular complex, spanning over twelve light-years of space. From a distance, the Badlands is one of the most incredible sights in the quadrant (but I wouldn't place it high on my list of favorite vacation spots). As with most electromagnetically active nebu-

lae, sensors are essentially useless within the Badlands. Microwave masers, ranging in power from 10^9 to 10^{14} watts, are common within the Badlands, posing both navigational and thermal hazards.

Navigation and flight vectoring are further complicated by the propagation of plasma shock waves within the Badlands. Rogue waves, generated by the chaotic interaction of nebular electromagnetic fields with the galactic magnetic field, pose a particularly dangerous hazard. I strongly recommend a series of automated probes be dispatched to more fully characterize this intriguing phenomenon.

In some molecular clouds, concentrations of water and other molecules act as natural amplifiers of radio waves, in much the same way that lasers amplify light. These regions, called *cosmic masers*, are typically found in the vicinity of giant stars or deep within molecular clouds (the birth sites of stars). Radio-telescope observations of cosmic masers are used by astronomers to calculate distances to nebulae with great precision.

It may seem odd to talk about shock waves in space, but they do occur, most commonly in nebulae. A shock wave is a high pressure wave in a gas, liquid, or solid that travels faster than the speed of sound within that medium. The "sonic boom" produced by a jet airplane as it breaks the sound barrier is the result of a shock wave.

Rogue waves in the ocean have been witnessed by surfers, sailors, and other ocean travelers. These gigantic waves can seem to arise out of nowhere, tossing surfers off their boards and even toppling large ships. Rogue waves probably occur when several smaller waves interact in such a way that they are suddenly amplified to several times their normal height. Similar effects might occur within plasmas. This is currently speculation, but provides at least some basis for how our starships might be knocked around by plasma waves within nebulae. Despite a nebula's lovely appearance, future starships should probably avoid probing deep into their hearts.

Delta Quadrant Supernova Remnant ("Alter Ego"; VGR)

Starship Voyager Science Log, Stardate 50464.3. Ensign Harry Kim recording.

Voyager *has encountered what appears to be an evolved supernova remnant. Measuring some 1.6 light-years in extent, the remnant appears to be surrounded by a damping field, of unknown nature, capable of suppressing chain reactions within the strands of plasma that comprise the remnant.*

Extrapolating backward in time from the present velocity and extent of the plasma filaments, the supernova that generated this nebula occurred some sixty thousand years ago. Strangely, sensors have detected neither a neutron star nor a black hole, the bodies that typically remain following the core-collapse of a supernova explosion.

Starship Voyager Science Log, Stardate 50465.2, supplemental. Captain Kathryn Janeway recording.

We have discovered that this supernova remnant is being artificially preserved by an advanced alien race as a kind of natural park. They posses a technology that suppresses nuclear chain reactions that are sometimes initiated within the filaments of the nebula. The current "curator" of this nebular preserve abducted Lieutenant Tuvok, motivated by an intense desperation borne of isolation and loneliness. Fortunately, my close friend and confidant was able to return to the ship unharmed.

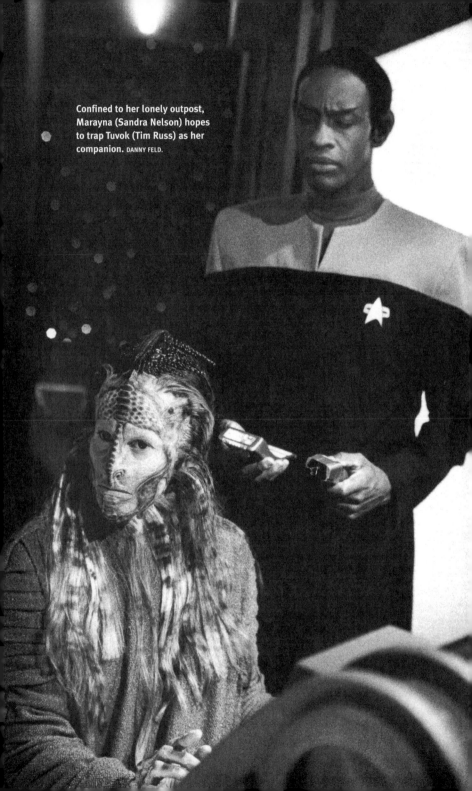

Confined to her lonely outpost, Marayna (Sandra Nelson) hopes to trap Tuvok (Tim Russ) as her companion. DANNY FELD.

Supernova explosions are rare; perhaps one occurs in a typical galaxy every century. After the initial explosion, material from the progenitor-star's atmosphere hurtles into space, spreading away from the supernova core in all directions. As noted above, the resulting nebulosity is called a supernova remnant.

The Crab Nebula, located some two thousand parsecs away in the constellation Taurus (the Bull), is a prime example of a young supernova remnant (see photo). It was born in a supernova explosion witnessed in the year AD 1054. We know the exact year because astronomers around the world (except in medieval Europe) recorded the presence of a new star near the crescent Moon in the spring of 1054. The spindly filaments of the Crab remnant were first observed by Lord Rosse in 1844. The center of the Crab Nebula is extremely bright, implying that something there is generating enough radiation to energize the nebulosity into a glowing cloud. That something is a pulsar.

The gases that comprise the Crab Nebula are still expanding into space. After many thousands of years, the Crab will grow into an extended supernova remnant such as the Vela supernova remnant. Such nebulae are sometimes called *evolved supernova remnants.*

Hydrogen and helium, the two lightest elements, comprise over ninety percent of the mass of the visible universe.[*] The process of *nuclear fusion* generates most of the elements heavier than hydrogen and helium, but supernovae are responsible for synthesizing the heaviest elements present in the universe. Elements such as uranium, thorium, and lead are in fact forged in the shock waves generated by supernova explosions.

---

[*] Most of the mass of the universe appears to be in the form of "dark matter"; astronomers are still puzzling over the nature and composition of dark matter, as discussed in the "Cathexis" science log, page 25.

Crab Nebula. April Labreque. Mt. Wilson Observatory 24" TIE Reflector.

The idea of "fire" in space may seem unlikely, given the near-vacuum environment of space. How can a fire burn without oxygen? On the other hand, stars are, in a sense, "fires" in space. And fires can even burn under water; underwater fuses are impregnated with oxygen-bearing compounds to provide the oxygen necessary for combustion. Many nebulae contain oxygen; it's conceivable that under appropriate circumstances a nebula could, in some sense, "burn."

Vala Supernova remnant. COURTESY OF EUROPEAN SOUTHERN OBSERVATORY

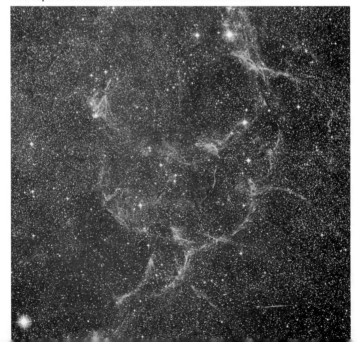

The Nekrit Expanse
("Fair Trade"; VGR)

Starship Voyager Science Log, Stardate 50775.6. Captain Kathryn Janeway recording.

Voyager *is taking on provisions at the Nekrit Supply Depot before entering a region of space known as the Nekrit Expanse.*

Even Mister Neelix's knowledge of this strange region of space is limited. Preliminary scans indicate that the expanse is peppered with exotic stars, including T Tauri and Wolf-Rayet stars. Stellar winds from these bodies shock the interstellar medium, raising the temperature and producing photoionization and secondary radiation effects. High concentrations of interstellar dust clot the expanse, mostly in the form of Bok globules, but filamentary dust lanes also appear to be common. The expanse will place significant stress on Voyager's

DOUG DREXLER

shields and particle deflectors. It is unlikely we will be able to sustain velocities above warp 3 until we have cleared the expanse. The physical boundaries of the expanse are beyond the range of our sensors; no one we have encountered at the supply depot can say with any confidence how far the region extends, or what we may encounter within it.

Bok *globules* are dark knots of dusty matter in space (see photo). They were first discovered by the Dutch-American astronomer Bart Bok in 1947. Bok globules are collapsing lumps of gas and dust in the process of creating stars. Stars form when clumps of matter in molecular clouds aggregate through the action of gravity, forming dense nodules billions of kilometers in diameter. As the clouds continue to contract, they become hotter and hotter. Eventually, the heat and pressure at the center of the cloud becomes so great that hydrogen atoms fuse into helium atoms, producing energy in the process, and thus a star is born.

On a personal note, I'm happy to say that "Fair Trade" was my first teleplay for *Star Trek*, based on a story by Ronald Wilkerson and Jean Louise Matthias.

Rosette Nebula. COURTESY OF EUROPEAN SOUTHERN OBSERVATORY.

The Black Nebula
("Cathexis"; *VGR*)

Starship Voyager Science Log, Stardate 48735.1. Captain Kathryn Janeway recording.

Commander Chakotay sustained serious head trauma during a shuttle reconnaissance of a dark-matter nebula. All neural activity in his cerebral cortex has ceased. We are heading for the nebula in an effort to determine the cause of the commander's injury and hopefully effect a cure.

Starship Voyager Science Log, Stardate 48737.3. Lieutenant Tuvok recording.

Voyager *has encountered the dark-matter nebula Commander Chakotay and I scouted in our shuttlecraft. Sensor readings are inconclusive. The nebula appears to be composed of a form of dark matter unfamiliar to Federation science.*

Starship Voyager Medical Log, Stardate 48738.7 Chief Medical Officer recording.

In a brilliantly improvised fusion of modern medical science and Native American healing techniques, I have successfully reintegrated Commander Chakotay's wayward consciousness with the neural architecture of his cerebral cortex.

On a clear summer night, far from city lights, the Milky Way stretches high across the celestial sphere. Careful observation with the naked eye will reveal lanes of dark material cutting into the Milky Way, particularly in the vicinity of the constellations Cygnus and Sagittarius. In the southern hemisphere, a markedly dark patch of sky is apparent in the constellation Crux, also called the Southern Cross. Commonly known as the "coal sack," this nearly starless patch of space is several times larger in our sky than the full Moon. Before the invention of the telescope, some astronomers wondered if these regions were in fact "holes" in the sky. Eventually it became clear that the coal sack and similar structures are vast clouds of interstellar dust that block light from more distant stars.

In the 1930s, Mount Palomar astronomer Fritz Zwicky studied the structures and motions of several nearby galaxy clusters. He discovered that the rotation rates of the clusters were much higher than expected; in fact, the rates were so high that the galaxies should not be in clusters at all. There simply was not enough stellar mass in the galaxies comprising the clusters to hold them together through the force of gravity. Zwicky concluded that there must be some sort of "dark matter" within these clusters, invisible to telescopes, providing the gravitational glue necessary to maintain them. Unlike interstellar dust, however, the presence of this dark matter cannot be inferred by the absorption of starlight. More recently, astronomers have discovered that the observed rotation rates of individual spiral galaxies are also influenced by some form of dark matter.

Astronomers have been trying to determine the nature of this dark matter ever since. It is now generally accepted that ninety to ninety-nine percent of the matter in the universe is dark. Various forms of dark matter have been proposed, including several forms of ordinary matter, such as brown dwarf stars and Jupiter-mass planets. Some scientists believe that subatomic neutrinos have a slight mass; even though their mass would be extremely small, neutrinos are so numerous they could account for much of the universe's missing mass. Exotic subatomic particles, such as *Weakly Interacting Massive Particles (WIMPs)* and planet-scale *Massive Compact Halo Objects (MACHOs)* have also been proposed, but these are theoretical entities only, and have not yet been observed in the laboratory or space. It may be that there are many forms of dark matter.

The concept of "neural energy" is a fictional device, used in several *Star Trek* episodes to rationalize the idea of a disembodied consciousness. Human consciousness probably arises from the extraordinarily complex ensemble of electrochemical activity in the brain, as opposed to residing in a specific part of the brain, but science has yet to create a comprehensive model of consciousness.

Subspace Eddies ("Real Life"; *VGR*)

Starship *Voyager* Science Log, Stardate 50625.4. Captain Kathryn Janeway recording.

Voyager *has discovered yet another exciting new spatial phenomenon in the Delta Quadrant. Twisting vortices of turbulent energy are somehow being generated in the interphase layer between space and subspace. If we weren't so far from home, I'd spend a month exploring every nook and cranny of this strange realm. The Delta Quadrant offers so much we have never before seen.*

When I read the first draft of this script, my initial reaction was, "Tornadoes in space? No way!" But truth often proves to be stranger than fiction. A few weeks after Jeri Taylor finished writing "Real Life" (based on a story by freelance writer Harry "Doc" Kloor), the Hubble Space Telescope produced an extraordinary image of a funnel-shaped structure in the Lagoon Nebula, an extensive cloud of gas and dust five thousand light-years away in the direction of the constellation Sagittarius. A hot O-type star within the nebula pours out ultraviolet light that heats and ionizes gases on the surfaces of nebular clouds.

In a process similar to tornado formation on Earth, the temperature difference between the hot surface and cool interior of the nebular clouds generates a fierce wind. This wind, combined with the pressure of starlight, twists and shears the cloud into the funnel-shaped structure visible in the Hubble image.

Murasaki 312
("The Galileo Seven"; *TOS*)

Starship *Enterprise* Science Log, Stardate 2824.2. Science Officer Spock recording.

Per Starfleet General Orders, the Enterprise *has interrupted its mission to deliver medical supplies to Makus III to investigate a quasi-stellar phenomenon, Murasaki 312. The core of the phenomenon appears to be a late-stage red giant star generating an exceptionally dense and high-speed stellar wind, with strong bipolar outflows. Ionization levels within the surrounding nebulosity exceed ninety percent. The magnetic field generated by the parent star is also extremely strong, measuring 10^5 gauss.*

Quasi-stellar objects, or *quasars*, were first discovered by the Dutch-American astronomer Martin Harwitt in the early 1960s. Quasars typically lie far beyond the Milky Way Galaxy. They are thought to be the bright cores of distant galaxies, galaxies near the edge of the known universe. In a typical quasar, energies equivalent to hundreds of billions of stars emanate from a region roughly the size of our solar system.

The source of this prodigious energy was a mystery for

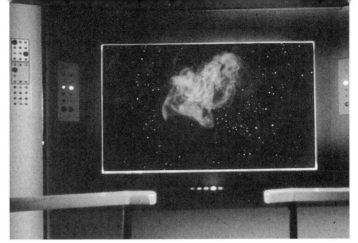

First discovered in 2267, Murasaki 312 remains an enigma.

many years. Various lines of evidence now seem to point to black holes as the engines of these cosmic powerhouses. The theory is that a super-massive black hole at the center of a galaxy gobbles up nearby stars and interstellar matter. As this material spirals into the black hole, it gathers into an *accretion disk*. Heated by friction, the disk releases tremendous stores of energy, from radio waves to X rays. The accretion disk is so hot that jets of gas are sometimes blown back into space along its axis of rotation, forming *bipolar outflows* that can be detected by radio telescopes. Some bipolar outflows are bright enough to be visible in optical telescopes as well.

Many quasi-stellar objects, however, exist within our own galaxy. Like extragalactic quasars, a Milky Way denizen called X-ray Nova Scorpii 1994 spews jets of plasma, at speeds that appear to exceed the speed of light. This "superluminal" velocity is an illusion; the jets travel almost along our line of sight. Line-of-sight velocity measurements are very difficult to make, and sometimes produce the illusion of velocities exceeding the speed of light. Like its extragalactic cousins, the plasma jets in Nova Scorpii are probably created by matter falling into a black hole. The swirling gases seen in *Star Trek's* Murasaki 312 could be generated by an object of this kind, but the likelihood of a habitable planet existing within such a maelstrom is small.

The Merkoria Quasar
("The Pegasus"; *TNG*)

Starship Enterprise Science Log, Stardate 47458.2. Second Officer Data recording.

Before being diverted to a rendezvous with Starship Crazy Horse *in sector 1607,* Enterprise *sensors were able to collect 22.46 megaquads of radiometric data on the quasi-stellar phenomenon known as the Merkoria Quasar.*

Sensors measured emissions from two distinct bipolar flows collimated by an intense magnetic field generated in a circumstellar torus.

L ike Murasaki 312, the Merkoria Quasar is a local quasi-stellar object, that is, an object located within the Milky Way Galaxy.

Astronomers have long suspected that a massive black hole lurks at the center of our galaxy. Not large enough to constitute a quasar, it nevertheless produces observable effects, such as intense radio emissions.

The Compton Gamma Ray Observatory, as the name implies, is devoted to the detection of gamma rays from space. Orbiting high above the Earth, Compton has recently detected gamma rays coming from the center of our galaxy with energies of 511 MeV (million electron volts). This is precisely the energy produced when an electron and its antimatter counterpart, the positron, collide and annihilate one another. Astronomers have concluded that a fountain of positrons emanates from the center of the Milky Way, probably produced as stars, falling into the massive galactic black hole are torn apart by *tidal forces*.

Even though the gamma-ray emissions of the positron fountain are sufficiently intense to be detected by Earth-

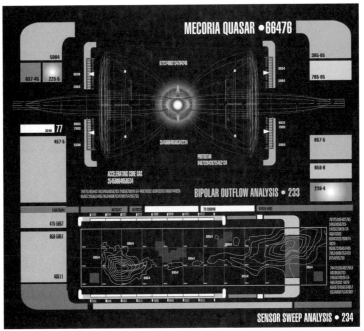

DOUG DREXLER

orbiting telescopes, the density of particles in the antimatter jet is probably fairly small, perhaps one positron per several hundred cubic meters of space. If the Earth were to pass through a low-density positron cloud, the effect on our planet from positron-electron annihilation events would be very small; every day the Earth absorbs billions of times as much total energy from another astronomical object: our Sun.

Ngame Wormhole ("Clues"; *TNG*)

Starship Enterprise **Science Log, Stardate 44507.1. Second Officer Data recording.**

As the Enterprise *began to investigate an unusual planetary system orbiting a T Tauri star , we encountered an unstable wormhole that displaced the ship 0.54 parsecs. Given the dangerous and unstable nature of the wormhole, Captain Picard decided not to resume exploration of the T Tauri system, and has recommended Starfleet command issue a Federation-wide advisory warning all starships to avoid this system. The first officer and second officer concur with this recommendation.*

Traveling across the country by car can be a lot of fun, but it takes time. Driving the twenty-five hundred or so miles from Washington, D.C., to Los Angeles takes at least a few days, even if you only stop for food, gas, and sleep. But what if you could find a route from D.C. to L.A. only one or two miles long? You could ride your bike and make the trip in twenty minutes. Finding *wormholes* in space would do for space travel what a two-mile long road between D.C. and L.A. would do for cross-country travel.

Theoretical physics, in the form of Einstein's general theory of relativity, provides a basic framework in which to understand the nature of wormholes, which are closely related to black holes.

In 1963, a New Zealand mathematician named Roy Kerr realized that black holes should be rotating, since the stars that formed them would've been rotating prior to their collapse. Much as a twirling ice skater spins more and more quickly as she pulls in her arms, black holes should in fact be rotating extremely rapidly; so rapidly, in fact, that the black hole is shaped into a ring. The highly curved region of space within the ring forms a tunnel-like "shortcut" connecting two widely separated points in space (and potentially, two different universes). Like the tunnel a famished worm bores through an apple, this celestial shortcut provides a much quicker way to travel between regions of space on opposite sides of the wormhole.

Traveling through a wormhole would be an interesting experience, to say the least. Looking into the mouth of the wormhole, you would see stars in another part of space, potentially billions of light-years away from your present location, as if a window to another part of the universe were simply hanging in space before you. As your spaceship plunged into the wormhole, an outside observer would see your ship disappear, nose to tail, as you hurtled toward the region of space at the opposite end of the wormhole.

Bajoran Wormhole ("Emissary"; *DS9*)

Deep Space 9 Science Log, Stardate 46380.1. Science Officer Jadzia Dax recording.

An extraordinary discovery has been made at DS9: a stable wormhole, created by an advanced alien race that lives outside the normal boundaries of space and time.

The wormhole and its alien residents were discovered by Commander Benjamin Sisko, recently assigned to command Deep Space 9. In addition to its immense scientific importance, the wormhole also holds spiritual significance to the people of Bajor, a Class-M planet virtually on the wormhole's doorstep. This places Commander Sisko in a somewhat sensitive position: as the discoverer of the wormhole, Commander Sisko is himself considered a spiritual leader of Bajor, much to the chagrin of Starfleet Command, and the commander.

Traversing the entire length of the wormhole requires approximately thirty seconds. The distance traveled is, however, over fifty thousand light-years; half the length of the entire galaxy! The importance of this phenomenon to Federation science and galactic exploration cannot be overstated.

The construction of an *artificial* wormhole would require a material capable of distorting the fabric of space to an extraordinary degree. Maintaining a space warp of this magnitude would not be an easy task. The *tensile strength* needed to prevent a wormhole from collapsing (that is, to keep it "propped open") has been shown to be roughly ten to the seventeenth power (10^{17}—a one followed by seventeen zeros!) times the density of the material used to construct it. No substance known to modern science possesses this property (a typical steel rod, by comparison, has a tensile strength approximately ten to the fifth power greater than its density). It is possible, however, that "exotic" materials may exist that could possess the required properties; in the *Star Trek* universe a particle called the *verteron* has been tailor-made for this purpose. It has been demonstrated theoretically that matter with *negative* mass (this is something different from antimatter) would have the required tensile strength. Verterons, presumably, are negative-mass particles. A few physicists think that negative-mass particles may exist in nature, although at present they are as hypothetical as *tachyons*, particles alleged to travel faster than the speed of light.

Stephen Hawking has demonstrated that a black hole emits subatomic particles at a rate proportional to its surface area through the quantum-mechanical mechanism of *pair*

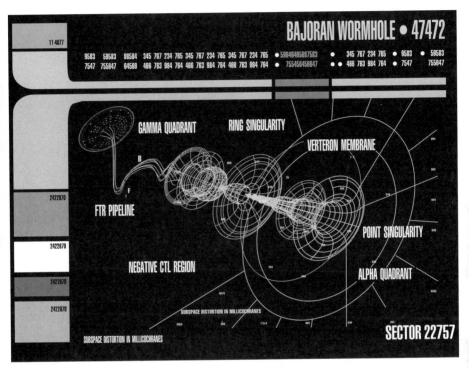

BAJORAN WORMHOLE • 47472

GAMMA QUADRANT
RING SINGULARITY
VERTERON MEMBRANE
FTR PIPELINE
POINT SINGULARITY
NEGATIVE CTL REGION
ALPHA QUADRANT
SUBSPACE DISTORTION IN MILLICOCHRANES
SUBSPACE DISTORTION IN MILLICOCHRANES
SECTOR 22757

DOUG DREXLER

production. Simply put, empty space is not really empty. The Heisenberg uncertainty principle states that an exactly zero energy state cannot exist, since pairs of matter and anti-matter particles are constantly being created and destroyed throughout space. Quantum-level fluctuations in empty space spontaneously create and absorb particles and their antimatter complements. Because these particles are quickly created and destroyed, this apparent "something out of nothing" phenomenon does not violate the law of conservation of mass and energy. Conservation of mass and energy would also be satisfied if one of the particles had positive energy and positive mass, while the other had negative energy and negative mass.

Since the pair-production phenomenon occurs throughout space, pair productions will occur near the event horizons of black holes. Occasionally, one member of the pair will fall into the black hole while the other escapes, appearing to an outside observer as radiation emitted by the black hole (now called *Hawking radiation.*) Perhaps occasionally one of these sub-atomic defectors will have negative mass. A sufficiently advanced technological civilization (such as the Bajoran worm-hole aliens) could in principle harvest and utilize such particles to create stable wormholes.

The idea of a particle with "negative" mass is a tricky thing to imagine. If I overdraw my bank account, I have a negative balance; in other words, I'm in debt. But what does it mean to have negative mass? When matter and antimatter collide, the result is mutual annihilation in a blast of energy. But if equal quantities of matter and negative matter collide, they simply cancel each other out of existence, and produce not a trace of energy. Strange indeed.

The Big Bang
("Death Wish"; *VGR*)

Starship Voyager Science Log, Stardate 49301.4. Captain Kathryn Janeway recording.

Voyager *has received an unexpected and unwelcome visit from the entity Starfleet refers to as Q. The details of his latest escapade are recorded in the Captain's Log, Stardate 49300.2. My interest as an astrophysicist was stimulated when the Q entity allegedly took* Voyager *back in time to an era a few microseconds after the Big Bang. Naturally I question the reality of everything connected with an encounter with Q, but the few readings* Voyager's *sensors recorded during our ostensible visit to the birth of the universe are utterly fascinating.*

Modern *cosmology*, the study of the large-scale properties and history of the universe, asserts that the universe has not always existed, but was born in a massive explosion some fifteen to twenty billion years ago.

Two major lines of evidence support the Big Bang theory. In the early 1920s, astronomer Edwin Hubble, working at the Mount Wilson Observatory in California, discovered that virtually all other galaxies in our universe are moving away from our galaxy. In addition, the farther the galaxy, the more quickly the galaxy is moving away from us: the entire universe appeared to be expanding. Hubble realized that in the distant past, all galaxies must have been closer together. Run the clock back far enough, and all of the stars and galaxies in the universe were crammed together in a "primeval fireball." This event marked the birth of the universe as we know it today.

Albert Einstein visited Mount Wilson shortly after Hubble made his historic discovery. Einstein had developed the general theory of relativity a few years earlier. The initial version of the theory predicted that the universe couldn't be gravitationally stable: it must either be contracting or expanding. Einstein, like everyone else at the time, assumed that the universe was static, that is, neither contracting nor expanding. He therefore introduced a term into the equations of relativity that he called the "cosmological constant," a kind of cosmic "fudge factor" that kept the universe from shriveling up or ballooning out. Had Einstein simply trusted his equations, he might have predicted the expansion of the universe; Hubble's later discovery would then have been yet another stunning confirmation of a prediction made by relativity theory. Einstein subsequently referred to his introduction of the cosmological constant as "his greatest blunder."

The second major piece of evidence for the Big Bang is the *cosmic microwave background radiation*. In the early 1960's, two radio astronomers, Arno Penzias and Robert Wilson, working at the Bell Laboratories in New Jersey, were attempting to track down the source of a persistent radio static that was interfering with their study of radio waves from the Milky Way. The noise was extremely uniform in the sense that no matter where in the sky the astronomers pointed their radio antenna, the level of the mystery static was the same. They eventually discovered that the source of the noise was residual energy left over from the Big Bang. As the primeval fireball that gave birth to the universe expanded, the radiation from the explosion shifted to lower and lower wavelengths, and currently peaks in the microwave portion of the electromagnetic spectrum. This is the source of the noise that Penzias and Wilson discovered: the cosmic microwave background radiation.

The first few minutes following the birth of our universe was a tumultuous time. The four fundamental forces of nature came into being during this period, along with the fundamental particles that make up ordinary matter. After several thousand years of continuing expansion, electrons were captured by atomic nuclei, forming the first simple atoms. At this stage the universe also became transparent to light. Several million more years would pass before atoms began to congregate into stars and galaxies; our own Milky Way Galaxy probably came into being about a billion years after the Big Bang.

2. Nuclear and Space Physics

"If, in some cataclysm, all of scientific knowledge were to be destroyed, and only one sentence passed on to the next generation of creatures, what statement would contain the most information in the fewest words? I believe it is the *atomic hypothesis*, that all things are made of atoms..."

—Richard Feynman, twentieth-century physicist.

"People like us, who believe in physics, know that the distinction between past, present, and future is only a stubbornly persistent illusion."

—Albert Einstein, twentieth-century physicist.

Antiprotons and Positrons ("The Doomsday Machine"; *TOS*)

Starship *Enterprise* Captain's Log, Stardate 3724.4. Captain James T. Kirk recording.

The Enterprise *has managed to neutralize the deadliest weapon of mass destruction every encountered by the Federation. A robotic device, some fifteen hundred meters in length, capable of firing beams of pure antiprotons at energies as large as 700 TeV.*

The Federation Starship Constellation, *commanded by Commodore Matt Decker, was destroyed by this "doomsday machine." Remorse over the loss of his ship and crew ultimately led Commodore Decker to pilot a shuttle into the maw of the weapon. Explosion of the shuttlecraft's fusion engine caused a small but measurable loss in the weapon's energy output. It occurred to me that a larger fusion explosion, triggered by the impulse engines of the crippled* Constellation, *might destroy the alien weapon.*

Antimatter has played an important role in the *Star Trek* universe since the debut of *The Original Series*.

The existence of antimatter was first postulated in the late 1920s by the Nobel prize–winning physicist P.A.M. Dirac. The first confirmed detection of a particle of antimatter was made in 1932 by Carl D. Anderson, then a graduate student at the California Institute of Technology. Anderson was using a *cloud chamber* to study the tracks of electrically charged subatomic particles. He noticed a track that corresponded to a particle with the mass of an electron, but a positive electric charge: a positron. Antiprotons were discovered twenty-three years later using the Bevatron particle accelerator at the University of California, Berkeley.

When a particle of antimatter encounters a corresponding particle of matter, the result is mutual annihilation. All of the mass of the two doomed particles is converted into energy in the form of *gamma rays*, the most energetic photons in the electromagnetic spectrum. When electrons and positrons collide, the result is a burst of gamma rays whose energy is 511 million electron volts (MeV). The Compton Gamma Ray Observatory, an Earth-orbiting gamma telescope, recently discovered a fountain of 511-MeV gamma rays streaming out of the center of our galaxy, very probably the result of electron and positron collisions (as noted on page 30 in the Science Log describing the Merkoria Quasar).

The possible development of antiproton and other particle-beam weapons was investigated by the Strategic Defense Initiative (SDI) program conducted in the 1980s by the U.S. Department of Defense. A number of high-energy laser weapons were also designed and tested. Much of this research remains classified. Work on exotic, space-based weapons has largely ceased since the end of the Cold War.

Berthold Rays ("This Side of Paradise"; *TOS*)

Starship Enterprise Science Officer's Log, Stardate 3420.8. Science Officer Spock recording.

Long-range probes confirmed the presence of lethal levels of berthold radiation on Omicron Ceti III. Contrary to the landing party's expectations, however, all of the members of the colony were alive and in perfect health.

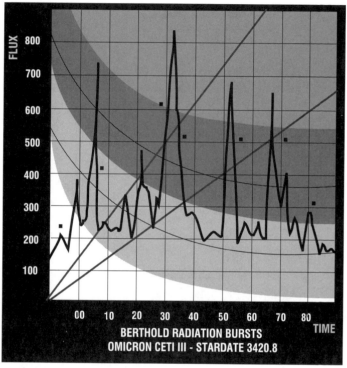

FLUX

800
700
600
500
400
300
200
100

00 10 20 30 40 50 60 70 80 TIME

BERTHOLD RADIATION BURSTS
OMICRON CETI III - STARDATE 3420.8

DOUG DREXLER

The reason for their survival was soon discovered. A benign spore had invaded each of the colonists, providing protection against berthold rays as well as an extremely euphoric state of mind. After the entire Enterprise crew—myself included—had abandoned ship to join the colony, Captain Kirk discovered that violent emotions would drive out the spores. By transmitting a low-frequency but highly irritating acoustic signal through the crew's communicators, the captain and I were able to stimulate feelings of hostility and rage among all of the crew and colonists. No longer protected, the entire Omicron Ceti colony must be evacuated. Recommend the Federation

Science Council investigate the biomolecular properties of the spores for possible medical applications.

Berthold rays are another *Star Trek* invention; prolonged exposure to berthold rays is deadly. Most of what are called "rays" in modern physics are really composed of some form of *electromagnetic radiation*, although some "rays" are streams of atomic nuclei and subatomic particles.

Life on Earth evolved in an environment containing several sources of radiation. All life on Earth is exposed to some level of naturally occurring radiation; indeed, evolution through natural selection is in part driven by radiation-induced mutations. There are three major sources of this *background radiation*: cosmic rays from the Sun and the far reaches of outer space; radioactive elements, such as radium, in the Earth's crust; and various *radionuclides* naturally present in living organisms, such as potassium-40. The atmosphere protects us from most of the radiation that arrives from space, but people who live at high altitudes are generally exposed to higher doses of cosmic rays. Citizens of Denver, Colorado—the Mile High city—receive about twice the dose of cosmic rays as people living in Paris, France.

Biologically significant radiation dosages are typically measured in units called *roentgens*, an absolute unit of radiation energy; or *rems* (roentgen equivalent man), a unit that takes into account the fact that living tissue responds differently to different kinds of ionizing radiation (other radiation-related units are discussed in more detail below). Combining both natural and man-made sources (from dental or chest X rays, for example), the average person is exposed to about two hundred millirems (thousandths of a rem) per year. It would take a minimum of about ten rems to trigger detectable changes within cells in human tissue. A dosage of around one hundred rems is sufficient to induce mild radiation sickness in most people. Exposure above ten thousand rems would result in death within a few hours; several dozen technicians and rescue workers died from radiation poisoning in the immediate aftermath of the Chernobyl nuclear-power-plant disaster in Russia.

Star Trek has frequently speculated on the existence of new kinds of radiation, such as delta rays (see page 47). It is not inconceivable that new forms of radiation may someday be discovered. Today we recognize that infrared, visible light, ultraviolet, X-ray, and gamma radiation are all different forms of electromagnetic radiation. *Cosmic rays*—energetic beams of radiation from space discovered early in the twentieth century—are highly energetic subatomic particles moving at velocities close to the speed of light.

Omicron Ceti is a star in Cetus, the Whale, a constellation whose name has been passed down from the ancient Greeks. Omicron Ceti is the fifteenth brightest star (as viewed from Earth) in the constellation Cetus (see the Basic Science Primer at the end of the book for information on star-naming conventions). Omicron Ceti III is presumably the third planet in the Omicron Ceti system.

In the past two years, several new planets have been discovered orbiting nearby, sunlike stars. Who gets to decide what they will be named? The names of astronomical objects are formally determined by the International Astronomical Union (IAU). The IAU General Assembly met in Kyoto, Japan, in August 1997, and for the first time considered the question of naming planets orbiting other stars.

Cosmic Strings ("The Loss"; *TNG*)

Starship Enterprise **Science Log, Stardate 44358.2. Second Officer Data recording.**

The Enterprise *has discovered one of the most remarkable life-forms ever encountered in the Milky Way Galaxy. Existing in a two-dimensional plane, these spacefaring entities appear to feed on the energy emanations of a cosmic string fragment.*

Traveling in a vast school, like a species of fish, the two-dimensional life-forms were drawn to the power emissions of the Enterprise *warp drive. Feeding on the ship's warp-power output, the creatures posed a serious threat to the function of the ship. Strangely, they also had a detrimental effect on Counselor Troi: the presence of the life-forms completely inhibited her empathic capacity.*

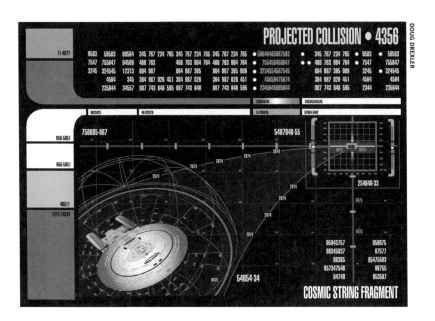

We were eventually able to free the ship from the grip of the life-forms by stimulating harmonic oscillations in a nearby cosmic string fragment using the Enterprise's *deflector dish. The string fragment may be a natural feeding ground or perhaps even a "home" of the two-dimensional creatures.*

According to the Big Bang theory, the universe was born some fifteen to twenty billion years ago in an extraordinary cosmic fireball that eventually gave birth to all of the galaxies, stars, and planets that inhabit the universe today.

One problem with the Big Bang theory is that it doesn't seem to explain the observed "lumpiness" of the universe. Galaxies aren't uniformly spread throughout space, but are aggregated into great clusters and sheets of galaxies.

One possible explanation for this uneven distribution of matter is an effect similar to what happens when you make ice cubes in your freezer. As water freezes into ice, it undergoes what physicists call a *phase transition*. A phase transition is simply the term for a change in the state of matter, from gas to liquid, or liquid to solid. When liquid water freezes into solid ice in a freezer tray, defects—cracks, fractures, striations, and so forth—often form in the resulting cubes.

Some astrophysicists think that something similar happened shortly after the Big Bang. As the infant universe expanded, it cooled and underwent a phase transition. Defects in the fabric of space accompanied this transition. The defects became cosmic string fragments, extremely thin segments of space-time with extraordinary density. A one-meter-long snippet of cosmic string only 10^{-31} meters in diameter would weigh 10^{19} kilograms.

The *Enterprise* and other starships are advised to steer clear of cosmic strings. The gravity generated by a string fragment is so great that the one-meter segment described above, floating down a Los Angeles freeway at rush hour, would suck up every car for miles around at nearly the speed of light. (Hmm, there may be a solution to gridlock in here somewhere....)

Delta Rays ("Menagerie"; *TOS*)

Starfleet Headquarters Science Log, Stardate 1710.4. Lieutenant Commander Alisa Farrell recording.

In an accident aboard a class-K cadet trainee vessel, a plasma explosion in the engineering section ruptured the aft warp core baffle plate. Delta radiation quickly flooded the compartment. Radiation levels exceeded four thousand rems. As a result of damage from the explosion, containment fields failed to energize.

Fleet Captain Christopher Pike effected the rescue of twelve cadets, heroically carrying each of them out of several compartments of the ship. In the process, Captain Pike was exposed to a lethal dose of delta radiation.

Remarkably, Captain Pike survived. Only a man in the extraordinary physical condition of Captain Pike could have survived the radiation levels measured in the compartment. Sadly, the severe radiation exposure completely debilitated Captain Pike's motor cortex.

Delta rays were created in the original series episode "The Menagerie"; prolonged exposure to delta rays rendered Captain Christopher Pike totally paralyzed and mute, able to communicate only "yes" and "no" answers to questions through a flashing light mounted on his wheelchair. Severe strokes can sometimes lead to this condition, called *locked-in syndrome*. A celebrated French journalist, Jean-Dominique Bauby, suffered from this condition for the last two years of his life. Only able to make his left eye blink, he nevertheless dictated an entire book about his condition using a specially devised "blinking alphabet."

One is also perhaps reminded of the incredible life of Dr. Stephen Hawking. Confined to a wheelchair, barely able to move his hands, and unable to speak, Dr. Hawking still conducts research in theoretical physics, communicating his ideas and theories to the rest of the world through a computer. Using a joystick, Dr. Hawking composes sentences and equations from lists of words and symbols displayed on his computer screen. A voice-synthesis program "reads" what Dr. Hawking has written.

I was fortunate enough to attend a lecture Dr. Hawking gave at the California Institute of Technology in 1996. I definitely felt a kind of electricity in the air when he entered the lecture hall, probably not unlike the excitement Albert Einstein generated in his public appearances.

Metreon Radiation ("Jetrel"; VGR)

Starship *Voyager* Science Log, Stardate 48835.1. Chief Engineer B'Elanna Torres recording.

Voyager agreed to assist in an experimental procedure developed by the Haakonian scientist Ma'Bor Jetrel. Jetrel was the principal architect of the metreon cascade, a deadly radioactive cloud employed as a weapon in a war between the Haakonians and Talax, Mister Neelix's home world.

The Talaxian moon where the cascade was unleashed still retains a blanket of metreon fallout and biogenic matter from the cascade's victims. Jetrel believed that by utilizing Voyager's *transporter system he would be able to reanimate Talaxians who had been obliterated by the metreon cascade, through a process called "regenerative fusion," wherein scattered bio-*

matter is matched to a genetic template and reconstructed into a whole, living organism—a dubious idea at best.

Attempts to reintegrate victims of the cascade, using records of their genetic structure as transporter templates, ultimately failed. Jetrel himself died a few days after the experiment, due to long-term exposure to metreon radiation.

Since the detonation of the atomic bombs at Hiroshima and Nagasaki, Japan, in 1945, the harmful effects of *radioactive fallout* have become shockingly clear. Many of the victims (perhaps as many as fifteen percent) of the atomic bomb were injured or killed not by the blast of the bomb's explosion, but by the subsequent blanket of radioactive material that spread across the two cities in the explosion's wake.

Radioactivity was first discovered in 1896 by the French physicist Henri Becquerel. Experimenting with various uranium salts, Becquerel happened to leave a crystal of potassium uranyl sulfate on top of a photographic plate wrapped in heavy, light-tight paper. When he later developed the photographic plate, he noticed it contained a black spot, as if it had been exposed to light. Becquerel surmised that the uranium salt emitted some form of radiation invisible to the eye that could pass through heavy paper and other opaque materials. The *becquerel* has become a unit of measurement in atomic physics, corresponding to a radioactive decay rate of one nuclear disintegration per second.

Fallout consists primarily of radioactive metallic oxides that form in the aftermath of a nuclear explosion, as well as various forms of nuclear radiation (gamma rays, alpha and beta particles, and neutrons). The oxides condense into fine particles that float through the air like chimney smoke. These materials eventually "fall out" of the air, often in rain or snow, and can remain radioactive for months or years.

Radiation can also heal. Focused beams of X rays, thousands of times more powerful than those used for diagnostic purposes, can be concentrated onto cancerous growths in order to destroy them. In a new and experimental technique, small quantities of radioisotopes are attached to *antibodies* that bind to tumor cells. As the radioisotope decays, the resulting radiation destroys the tumor. Medical researchers are also exploring "internally delivered" radiation as a treatment for some forms of arthritis and coronary artery disease.

Duonetic Field ("Paradise"; *DS9*)

Deep Space 9 Science Log, Stardate 47577.9. Science Officer Jadzia Dax recording.

Commander Sisko and Chief Engineer O'Brien have been rescued from a Class-M planet orbiting Orellius Minor.

The planet appeared to possess an unusual duonetic field that interfered with the operation of all electrical devices, but, curiously, had no obvious effect on electrical activity within the humanoid brain and nervous system. Commander Sisko subsequently discovered that the duonetic field was artificially created by Alixus, the leader of a human colony that had been established there some ten years earlier. Alixus embraced a rather primitive contempt for modern technology, and used the duonetic field to prevent the operation of transtator-based devices.

Electromagnetic fields of high intensity can have profound effects on human beings. When physicists first began to build large-scale particle accelerators in the 1930s, a few adventurous souls occasionally stepped inside the accelerator's powerful electromagnets to experience an interesting

Alixus (Gail Strickland) explains why she has spurned Federation technology. ROBBIE ROBINSON.

visual sensation: the intense magnetic field would affect their optic nerves in such a way that they would see rainbows around bright lights, and other optical illusions. There is some concern today that low-level electromagnetic sources, such as cell phones and power lines, might promote the growth of cancer, but there is no scientific evidence as of yet to support this contention.

As noted in the introduction, the challenge for me in this episode was to find some kind of "tech" field that would compromise our twenty-fourth–century equipment but not harm our away team physically. Intense, repeated bursts of electromagnetic energy might do the trick, but it would be hard to explain how something like this might occur naturally and not be potentially harmful to people. Something like a nearby neutron star could also have produced the desired effect, but would affect ships in orbit even more than equipment on the ground (where the planet's atmosphere and magnetic field would provide some protection). I ultimately decided that a fictional device, the duonetic field, was the best choice for this script.

Almost certainly, many new subatomic particles and fields will be discovered in the future. It may be unlikely that anything with the particular properties of the duonetic field will be discovered in nature, but it seems possible to me that such a field could someday be created through artificial means, as proved to be the case in "Paradise."

Neutrinos ("Rivals"; *DS9*)

Deep Space 9 Science Log, Stardate 47399.8. Science Officer Jadzia Dax recording.

My poor friend Quark. An entrepreneur named Martus Mazur nearly put him out of business by opening a rival bar across the Promenade from Quark's.

Mazur's patrons seemed to have extraordinary luck playing a certain gambling device of unknown alien origin. Quark's customers, on the other hand, were having nothing but bad luck at the dabo wheel and quickly defected to the Ferengi's rival's establishment. Needless to say, I smelled a vole. Analysis of neutrino spin states ultimately revealed that the alien devices were altering the laws of probability throughout the station.

In "Rivals," subatomic particles called *neutrinos* gave Dax the clue she needed to deduce that somehow the laws of chance were being altered on the station. Neutrinos are the most ephemeral of subatomic particles, barely more substantial than shadows. A wall of lead several light-years thick would stop only about half of the neutrinos passing through it. The extraordinary penetrating power of neutrinos makes them extremely difficult to detect.

Martus Mazur (Chris Sarandon) relates to Dax (Terry Farrell) and Sisko (Avery Brooks) how his luck has suddenly changed. ROBBIE ROBINSON.

Trillions upon trillions of neutrinos are produced by the nuclear reactions that power the stars. Billions of them are passing through your body at any given moment, a fact that author John Updike found quite rude. In his poem "Cosmic Gall," Updike writes, "neutrons....At night, they enter at Nepal / And pierce the lover and his lass / From underneath the bed— you call it wonderful; I call it crass."

The existence of the neutrino was hypothesized in 1930 by pioneering quantum physicist Wolfgang Pauli. Scientists observing a form of radioactive decay called *beta decay* had discovered that the sum of the energy and momentum of the decay products were typically less than their energy and momentum before. This seemed to challenge one of the most cherished laws of physics: conservation of energy and momentum. Rather than accept the toppling of a pillar of modern physics, Pauli suggested that an as-yet unseen particle, the neutrino, was carrying off the extra momentum. Pauli's prediction was confirmed when the neutrino was experimentally detected in 1956 by a group of physicists from the Los Alamos National Laboratory in New Mexico.

Neutrinos may or may not have mass. Some physicists think they may have just the slightest bit of mass (equal to a few *electron volts* worth of energy, at most), but this has yet to be established experimentally. But if neutrinos do have mass, they may account for much of the so-called "missing mass" of the universe, simply because there are so many of them. (An interesting side note: if neutrinos have mass, it follows that protons eventually decay. The average lifetime of a proton would be unimaginably long, something like 10^{30} years. If the universe doesn't collapse in a "Big Crunch" before a substantial number of protons decay, at some point in the very distant future stable atoms will no longer exist in our universe.)

Author and theoretical physicist Lawrence Krauss has pointed out that neutrinos can exist in only one spin state, the left-handed spin state (antineutrinos, however, are in the right-handed spin state), and therefore Dax could never have discovered a "statistically unlikely" left-handed alignment of whirling neutrinos. This was simply a mistake on my part; I thought neutrinos had multiple spin states like other subatomic particles, and didn't double-check. Well, as Spock noted in *The Wrath of Khan*—nobody's perfect.

Omicron Particles
("The Cloud"; *VGR*)

Starship Voyager Science Log, Stardate 48546.8. Captain Kathryn Janeway recording.

Sensor readings of an unusual nebula have detected high concentrations of omicron particles. Chief Engineer Torres believes that shipboard power systems could be readily modified to utilize omicron particles as an energy source.

If we can collect omicron particles in sufficient quantity, replicator rations could be increased substantially for the crew. I am eagerly looking forward to having a good cup of coffee every morning.

Starship Voyager Medical Log, Stardate 48547.2. Chief Medical Officer recording.

In yet another medical first, I have managed to repair the damage Voyager *inadvertently inflicted on the space-borne entity that proved to be the source of the omicron-particle readings. Wielding a nucleonic beam like a laser scalpel, I was able to simultaneously close and cauterize the wound opened in the creature's "tissue" by the ship. Captain Janeway, unfortunately, will have to do without her morning cup of coffee until an alternative energy source can be located.*

Omicron particles are another invention of the *Star Trek* universe. Although a starship's powerful warp engines generate enormous amounts of energy, only some of that energy can be siphoned off to provide electrical power for the ship. As *Voyager* makes its way through the Delta Quadrant, Captain Janeway is constantly keeping her eyes open for potential backup and alternative energy sources.

But where exactly does energy come from? Most of the forms of energy we take for granted in the modern world begin as *potential energy* stored in atoms or molecules. You can think of the bonds between atoms within molecules as if they were tight springs. In a chemical reaction, the bonds between certain atoms are broken. In some reactions, potential energy is released as the springs (i.e., chemical bonds) "snap." Potential energy has thus been converted to another form, typically heat or electrical energy.

Nuclear energy works on a similar principle. Protons and neutrons are bound together in the nuclei of atoms through nuclear forces. These forces constitute the "tight springs" that hold together the atomic nucleus. A nuclear reaction can break some of these bonds, liberating extraordinary amounts of energy. Pound for pound, nuclear reactions typically release a million times as much energy as chemical reactions.

Polarons ("Faces"; *VGR*)

Starship Voyager Science Log, Stardate 48660.2. Captain Kathryn Janeway recording.

The Kazon-Nistrim sect use an unusual cloaking system that makes their ships appear to blend in with background scenes: stars, planetary atmospheres, etcetera.

We have discovered that it is possible to "unmask" Kazon-Nistrim vessels with an active polaron beam, configured to induce an overload in their cloaking circuitry.

Physics is a science that attempts to explain everything we see in the world around us in terms of a set of fundamental particles interacting through a set of fundamental forces. An apple is a collection of molecules, which in turn are made up of atoms that bond to one another through electromagnetic forces. Atoms are themselves made up of smaller particles: protons, neutrons, and electrons. Protons and neutrons are bound together in the nucleus of the atom through the action of something called the *strong nuclear force*. Protons and neutrons are made up of smaller particles still, called *quarks*.

Physics has been extremely successful at developing mathematical formulas that precisely define the manner in which subatomic particles interact. But the equations of physics that can be solved exactly through the application of mathematical techniques, such as the methods of the calculus, apply only to extremely simplified situations involving the interaction of just two particles at a time.

Sometimes this is enough. The orbit of the Moon around the Earth can be computed with great precision by treating the Moon and the Earth as idealized pointlike particles. Many important phenomena in the real world, however, simply cannot be reduced, in any meaningful way, to the interaction of two particles. And so, physicists have developed a number of clever techniques for solving problems involving ensembles of particles.

In some circumstances, subatomic particles behave in a collective, coordinated manner. For example, electrons in a *semiconductor* material, such as silicon, influence and constrain one another's motion. An electron and the polarized electric field it generates within a semiconductor or other similar media can be treated as a large-scale "quasi-particle" called a *polaron*. The stability of the electron and its field can be thought of as the "lifetime" of the associated polaron.

Tachyon Particles
("Redemption, Part II"; *TNG*)

Starship Enterprise Science Log, Stardate 45026.3 Second Officer Data
recording.

*Lieutenant Commander La Forge has developed an extremely
innovative and valuable technique for detecting the presence of
cloaked Romulan warbirds.*

*Utilizing a network of interlinked tachyon generators, the
technique exploits the fact that tachyons display a marked
reduction in superluminal velocity when they encounter the
field of a cloaked ship.*

Ever since Albert Einstein convincingly demonstrated in
1905 that nothing with nonzero *rest mass* can travel at or
faster than the speed of light, physicists have been trying to
invent ways for material particles to break the "light barrier."
Breaking the sound barrier was essentially an engineering challenge. Aircraft designers needed to find ways to make *ailerons*
and other airplane control surfaces stable under the extreme
stresses and turbulence a plane encounters when it approaches the sound barrier. Unlike the sound barrier, however, the
light barrier is a fundamental property of the physics of the universe, not just an engineering challenge.

In the special theory of relativity, Einstein showed, and subsequent experiments with subatomic particles have confirmed,
that as an object increases its velocity, its mass also increases.
This effect is so small at low speeds that it is not measurable.
But close to the speed of light, relativistic mass increases
exponentially. For example, at a speed of 1000 kilometers per second
(kps), a one-kilogram mass weighs in at 1.0000056 kilograms
(kg), just a fraction over its rest mass. At ninety percent the

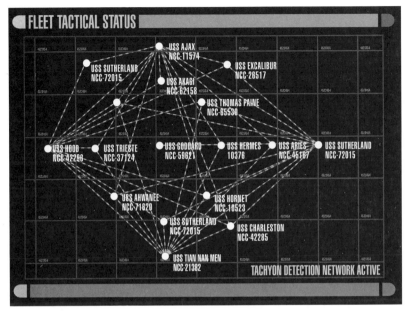

FLEET TACTICAL STATUS

USS AJAX
NCC-11574

USS SUTHERLAND
NCC-72015

USS EXCALIBUR
NCC-26517

USS AKAGI
NCC-62158

USS THOMAS PAINE
NCC-65530

USS HOOD
NCC-42296

USS TRIESTE
NCC-37124

USS GODDARD
NCC-59621

USS HERMES
10376

USS ARIES
NCC-45167

USS SUTHERLAND
NCC-72015

USS AHWANEE
NCC-71620

USS HORNET
NCC-10523

USS SUTHERLAND
NCC-72015

USS CHARLESTON
NCC-42285

USS TIAN NAN MEN
NCC-21382

TACHYON DETECTION NETWORK ACTIVE

DOUG DREXLER

speed of light (270,000 kps), the mass increases to 2.29 kg. At ninety-nine percent the speed of light, the mass increases to 7.09 kg. Notice that mass is increasing exponentially as we get closer to the speed of light. It turns out that as the velocity of a moving object gets closer and closer to the speed of light, its mass approaches infinity. Since it would require an infinite amount of energy to accelerate an infinite mass, a material object can never reach the speed of light.

Tachyons are hypothetical particles, conceived by theoretical physicists, that can *only* travel faster than light. Tachyons have never been observed in nature, but they do not violate the special theory of relativity, as long as they never travel at or slower than the speed of light. In some ways tachyons "mirror" the properties of ordinary matter. For example, when a tachyon loses energy it actually speeds up. If a tachyon were accelerated to infinite velocity, its energy would drop to zero. Tachyons also have the curious property that they travel backward, not forward, in time. To the mind of a theoretical physicist, this bizarre conjecture isn't necessarily that hard to swallow. Richard Feynman once noted that from the point of view of the laws of physics, antimatter particles could be thought of as ordinary matter moving backwards in time; i.e., a positron can be treated as an electron traveling backward in time.

Verteron and Graviton Particles ("Emissary"; *DS9*)

Deep Space 9 Science Log, Stardate 46381.9. Science Officer Jadzia Dax recording.

The stability of the wormhole connecting the Alpha and Gamma Quadrants appears to be a consequence of a unique scaffolding composed of verteron particles. Verterons are among the most extraordinary particles ever discovered in nuclear physics. Most strikingly, they possess negative mass, which accounts for their ability to maintain the extreme spatial curvature necessary to sustain a wormhole. The verterons are bound together in an elaborate geometric matrix that provides a traversable spatial conduit some five hundred meters in diameter.

As noted above, verterons are fictional subatomic particles invented by the writers of *Star Trek* to provide the forces necessary to keep the Bajoran wormhole propped open.

Modern physics asserts that particles are responsible for all of the fundamental forces in nature.

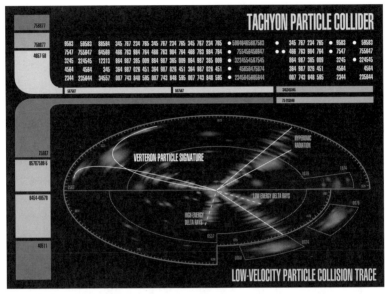

DOUG DREXLER

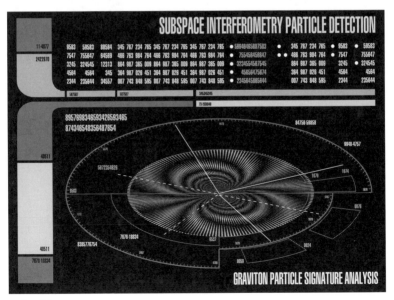

DOUG DREXLER

According to the principles of quantum theory, forces are mediated by the action of particles, called *exchange particles*. A repulsive force between two magnets, for example, is created by the constant exchange of *photons* between the magnets. This idea gives rise to a simple mental picture. Imagine two skaters standing on a frozen lake. If they toss a baseball back and forth, they will slowly begin to move away from one another due to recoil as they alternately toss and catch the ball.

Attractive forces can also be understood in terms of the exchange of particles, although the "mental picture" is not quite as simple as two ice skaters playing catch. Photons are particles of *electromagnetic radiation* that serve as the exchange particles for electromagnetic forces, both attractive and repulsive. *Gravitons* are particles of *gravitational radiation* that serve as the exchange particles responsible for the force of gravity. It may strike you as ironic that gravitons are thought to have no mass.

Einstein's general theory of relativity suggests that gravitational radiation, in the form of *gravity waves*, should propagate through space at the speed of light. Gravity waves have not yet been detected, but several experiments have been designed to look for them. Most of the experiments involve suspending massive weights in isolated, underground chambers, and monitoring the motion of these test masses with ultrasensitive laser equipment. The hope is that a gravity wave traveling through space, perhaps produced by the collision of two neutron stars or some other gravitationally cataclysmic event, will strike the test mass and cause it to move. Because gravity is such a weak force compared to the other fundamental forces, the degree of motion would be extremely small. Great care must be taken to ensure that the test masses will not be disturbed by air currents, ground tremors, electromagnetic fields, or other forms of interference. Many physicists are nevertheless optimistic that gravity waves will be detected sometime in the next few years.

Psionic Field
("Persistence of Vision"; VGR)

Starship Voyager **Science Log, Stardate 49201.6. Captain Kathryn Janeway recording.**

While traveling through a sector of the Delta Quadrant controlled by a race known as the Bothans, members of my crew, including myself, began to experience strange and disturbing hallucinations.

At first we suspected a biological agent, possibly a food supply contaminant or psychogenic compound encountered during an away mission. We eventually discovered the source of the hallucinations to be far more sinister: the Bothans were staging a psionic attack on Voyager.

With the help of Kes, the Doctor and Lieutenant Torres were able to neutralize the Bothan psionic field.

Mental telepathy has been a *Star Trek* staple since the debut of *The Original Series*. There is, however, no scientific evidence for the existence of telepathic abilities in people or animals. The word telepathy is typically used to describe the ability to read other people's thoughts, but the term actually means "to feel at a distance"; this is closer to how one might describe Counselor Troi's empathic capacity.

In order to suggest a rational, scientific basis for telepathy, *Star Trek* has coined the phrase "psionic" field. A psionic field is

One by one the crew is falling into the psionic trap, but Captain Janeway (Kate Mulgrew) hopes to free Tuvok. ROBBIE ROBINSON

presumably the "medium" through which unspoken thoughts and feelings are communicated through space. Some humanoids can tap into this field through a kind of sense organ located in the brain (in the case of the Betazoid race, of which Counselor Troi is a member, I invented the term *paracortex* for this region of the brain). In the same manner that human eyes can sense portions of the electromagnetic field, telepaths can presumably sense portions of the psionic field. This strikes me as a some-what dubious proposition, but then I thought the notion of twisters in space was silly.

Many-Worlds Interpretation of Quantum Mechanics ("Parallels"; *TNG*)

Starship Enterprise Science Log, Stardate 47393.5. Second Officer Data recording.

The Enterprise *has unwittingly discovered what appears to be stunning confirmation of the "many-worlds" interpretation of quantum mechanics.*

En route to the Enterprise *after a short leave of absence, Lieutenant Worf's shuttle collided with a quantum fissure. The encounter only minimally damaged the shuttle. Mister Worf, however, entered a state of quantum flux. For Worf, the dimensional barriers among the infinite number of alternate universes predicted by the many-worlds theory had broken down. All that was needed to propel him into an alternate universe was the proximity of a narrow-band energy emission. The emissions from Lieutenant Commander La Forge's VISOR provided the required energy trigger.*

Once the conundrum of Mister Worf's interdimensional translocations was understood, the Enterprise *of each parallel universe proceeded to the location of the quantum fissure. As Worf traveled through the fissure on a reverse trajectory, his state of quantum flux stabilized. Then each* Enterprise *used its primary drive system to generate a broad-spectrum warp field that effectively sealed the fissure.*

Physics at the turn of the twentieth century—what we today call "classical" physics—conceived the universe to be a comfortable, predictable sort of place. The laws of physics could readily forecast the motions of the stars and planets as well as a falling stone. The universe seemed to run like an ele-

Swept up in quantum fissure, Worf (Michael Dorn) now finds that he is a commander aboard an *Enterprise* in an alternate universe. ROBBIE ROBINSON.

gant clock, and everything in nature behaved according to a set of straightforward rules. Many physicists believed that there wasn't much work left to do in basic physics except fill in a few minor details.

When the theory of *quantum mechanics* was developed to explain the behavior of atoms and subatomic particles in the late 1920s and early 1930s, it produced much excitement and no small degree of agitation in the world of physics. Experimental predictions based on the theory were remarkably accurate. But the foundation of the theory rested on principles that scientists who came of age in the late nineteenth century found extremely hard to accept. According to quantum mechanics, a subatomic particle can sometimes be in two places at the same time; electrons can "tunnel" through otherwise insurmountable energy barriers; two particles separated by light-years of space can somehow recognize each other's quantum states without communicating. Neils Bohr, one of the pioneers of quantum theory, once said, "Anyone who isn't shocked by quantum mechanics doesn't understand it."

Quantum mechanics upset the classical order by asserting that the fundamental particles that make up all matter obeyed a set of rules that were essentially statistical in nature. Quantum theory makes mathematically precise predictions, but they are predications about probabilities. For example, quantum theory can predict with great precision the *probability* that an electron will carom off in some particular direction after a collision with another particle, but it cannot predict *which* direction the electron will actually move after the collision. Albert Einstein was particularly disturbed by the probabilistic nature of quantum theory. He summed up his objectives to the theory in his oft-repeated phrase, "God does not play dice with the universe."

The many-worlds interpretation of quantum mechanics was an attempt to restore strict determinism to the world of physics. For simplicity, let's say there is a fifty-fifty chance of an electron having one of two distinct energy values (let's call them A and B), and we measure the electron's energy and discover it is B. Then, according to the many-worlds theory, there is *another universe* where the energy of the electron is measured as A. This universe is in fact created when we measure the energy of the electron. It might look like God has simply tossed a coin and it came up A, but in this parallel universe he also tossed the coin and it came up B.

This is a pretty strange assertion, but it does remove the probability aspect of quantum theory, because all possible outcomes for a measurement or experiment do in fact occur. They just occur in other universes.

Critics of *Star Trek* like to point out that quantum-mechanical effects can almost never be observed in the world of "macroscopic," or human-scale, objects, and therefore Worf's universe-hopping odyssey could never happen. But this criticism misses the point. In a wonderful book written in the 1940s, *Mister Tompkins in Wonderland*, pioneering nuclear physicist George Gamow describes the strange adventures of a hapless character named C.G.H. Tompkins. Tompkins finds himself in all manner of strange "alternate universes," where fundamental constants of nature, like Planck's constant, have values substantially different from their values in our universe. The point of these stories was to introduce the reader to basic ideas in quantum physics. Gamow knew that, taken literally, the settings of the stories were impossible; if Planck's constant really were a very large number, the universe as we know it simply wouldn't exist. But by granting himself a little dramatic license, Gamow was able to give his readers, in a charming and entertaining way, some sense of the meaning of these new and exciting ideas in physics. "Parallels" and several other *Star Trek* stories were written in much the same spirit.

Alternate Universes ("Mirror, Mirror"; *TOS*)

Starship Enterprise Science Log, Stardate 3848.6. Science Officer Spock recording.

A landing party beaming up from the surface of the Halkan homeworld during an intense ion storm was transported into a parallel universe remarkably similar to our own universe in terms of individuals and technology, but ethically ruthless. The

*landing-party counterparts from the alternate universe simulta-
neously appeared in our transporter room.*

*Fortunately, Chief Engineer Scott, a member of the landing
party, was able to re-create the parameters of the transporter
accident using power from the alternate Enterprise's warp
engines. The landing party returned safely to the ship, as their
counterparts beamed back to theirs.*

One of the problems with the many-worlds interpretation of
quantum mechanics is, how could this idea ever be tested? No one has yet devised an experiment that could prove or
disprove the validity of the many-worlds concept. Many physicists (myself included) question whether a theory is meaningful
if it can't be tested. The idea that parallel universes are constantly spinning off from our universe at every quantum turn is
interesting, but until we can find a way to "access" those other
universes, or convincingly show that they don't exist, the many-
worlds idea will remain little more than interesting speculation.

Most scientists today have come to accept the statistical
aspects of quantum theory, despite Einstein's lament about
God not playing dice. *Chaos theory*, a theory that examines the
behavior of complex phenomena such as whirlpools in rivers,
suggests that the apparent randomness one often encounters in
nature may in fact belie an underlying order. And as the mathematician Ian Stewart notes in his book, *Does God Play Dice?*, if
God did play dice, he'd win.

The Guardian of Forever ("The City on the Edge of Forever"; *TOS*)

Starship Enterprise Science Log, Stardate 3221.3. Science Officer Spock recording.

The Enterprise *has discovered one of the most awesome alien powers in the known galaxy. Calling itself the Guardian of Forever, it claims to be neither organism nor machine, but it is extraordinarily intelligent and immensely old. Its main function is to serve as a porthole into the past, to any number of worlds, in any era.*

The story of "The City on the Edge of Forever" is based on a classic time-travel paradox: if you traveled back in time and killed your grandfather when he was a young man, you would never have been born; therefore, you couldn't have traveled back in time to kill your grandfather. This paradox has long been used to refute the idea that time travel is possible.

The many-worlds interpretation of quantum mechanics, however, may provide a loophole in this paradox. If alternate universes are constantly splitting off from our universe, a trip backward in time could land you in an alternate universe—ever so slightly different from the past recorded in the history books, but a different universe nonetheless. Killing your grandfather in this universe would not have any effect on your birth in the universe you started from; you would simply never be born in the universe where your grandfather was killed. Science fiction writer David Gerrold (who wrote *The Original Series*'s episode "The Trouble With Tribbles") explored this idea in imaginative detail in his novel *The Man Who Folded Himself*.

Another possible means of time travel was recently discovered by Kip Thorne, a physicist specializing in relativity theory at

The Guardian generates ripples in time that can be scanned from orbit.

the California Institute of Technology. Dr. Thorne has been studying the physical properties of wormholes for many years. He has
determined that if one end of a wormhole were accelerated to
close to the speed of light, then brought back through space to
a position close to the other end of the wormhole, the wormhole
would become a time machine. *Time dilation* would slow the
rate at which time flows at the accelerated end of the wormhole;
that end would essentially "move forward" in time at a slower
rate than the other end of the wormhole, and perpetually exist
in the past of the other, stationary, end. Traveling through the
wormhole and coming out the end that had been accelerated
would therefore take you into the past. You could not, however,
travel further into the past than the time at which the wormhole
had been accelerated. Suppose, however, an advanced alien
race, millions of years ago, constructed and accelerated wormholes. In principle, these wormholes could be used to travel millions of years into the past.

Causality Paradox
("Time and Again"; *VGR*)

Starship Voyager Science Log, Stardate 48483.6. Captain Kathryn Janeway recording.

Kes has reported a strange but powerful sensation that something unusual, perhaps involving a temporal paradox, has occurred on a Class-M planet in a nearby red-dwarf system. Scanners, however, have failed to register any unusual temporal signatures. The system is inhabited by a prewarp technological society, and I have therefore decided to avoid contact.

In this episode, the crew of the *Voyager* became trapped in a "time loop" that repeated several times, each repetition resulting in a disastrous explosion on the surface of the planet that caused the deaths of several *Voyager* crew members and

Lieutenant Paris (Robert Duncan McNeill) and Captain Janeway try to find a way back to their own time line. ROBBIE ROBINSON.

many other people. The situation was somewhat similar to the premise of the movie *Groundhog Day*, where a man keeps living the same day over and over again. By the end of this episode, however, none of the crew members can recall setting foot on the planet, although Kes has an intuitive sense that some sequence of events on the planet has been set right.

Going back in time once or many times to alter events that have "already" happened (or to change the course of "future" events, depending on how you look at it) raises the same kind of causality-paradox issues discussed in the previous log. Physicists seek to explain the workings of the universe in rational terms, and causality paradoxes are inherently irrational.

Physicist Stephen Hawking once dismissed the idea of time travel this way: If time travel were possible, we would find ourselves inundated by tourists from the future.

Traveling into the Future ("A Matter of Time"; *TNG*)

Starship Enterprise Science Log, Stardate 45353.2. Second Officer Data recording.

En route to Penthara IV, the Enterprise *has taken aboard an unusual human claiming to be from the twenty-sixth century.*

Arriving in a time-travel pod, Doctor Berlinghoff Rasmussen explained that he was an historian interested in observing how the Enterprise *coped with a planetary disaster that was incompletely recorded in standard history texts. We eventually discovered that Doctor Rasmussen was in fact from the twenty-second century and had stolen the pod from a time-traveling scientist. He then had exploited relativistic effects to travel forward in time to the twenty-fourth century. Doctor Rasmussen was attempting to return to the twenty-second century after*

Rasmussen (Matt Frewer) believes he now has collected the ultimate technology from the future: Data (Brent Spiner). ROBBIE ROBINSON.

stealing various medical and scientific devices from the Enterprise, in the hopes of making a fortune by "inventing" those devices in that earlier era. Doctor Rasmussen has been remanded to the authorities on Starbase 214.

Unlike traveling into the past, traveling into the future is done all the time. We're all doing it right now! But traveling into the *far distant* future is also possible. We even know how to do it, and the technique is demonstrated in particle accelerators all over the world every day.

In the special theory of relativity, Einstein showed that if a spaceship were to be accelerated to a substantial fraction of the speed of light, clocks aboard the spaceship would appear to run more slowly than clocks on the Earth (from the point of view of an observer on Earth; to someone aboard the spaceship, time would appear to proceed normally). This effect is known as *time dilation*. Time runs more and more slowly the closer the ship travels to the speed of light.

Experimental verification of time dilation can be observed in particle accelerators, the giant machines that physicists use to "smash" atoms. A number of subatomic particles, such as *muons*, have very short life spans, typically fractions of a second. Muons and other short-lived particles are frequently created in particle accelerators when protons and other particles ram into one another at high speeds. Most of this subatomic flak is also traveling at high speed, often close to the speed of light. Measuring how long these particles live, physicists have discovered that they live longer than expected, exactly by the amount predicted by relativity.

Fast-moving, fast-living subatomic particles, including muons, can also be found zooming through the Earth's atmosphere. Cosmic rays showering the Earth from space collide with atoms in the upper atmosphere, producing secondary particles that *should* flash out of existence before they reach the ground. But because of time dilation, the particles that are traveling near light-speed manage to make it all the way to Earth's surface, where they are routinely detected by cosmic-ray monitors.

A Universe in Your Back Yard ("Playing God"; *DS9*)

Deep Space 9 Science Log, Stardate 47626.9. Science Officer Jadzia Dax recording.

We have a new baby on board! Possibly the biggest baby I've ever seen in all my lifetimes.

During a scientific survey mission in the Gamma Quadrant, my runabout encountered a subspace interphase pocket. We

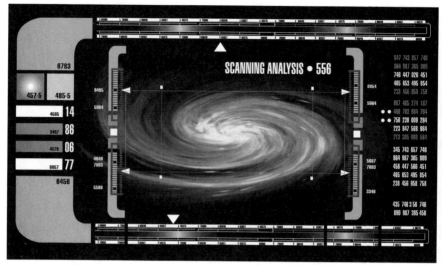

DOUG DREXLER

successfully regained control of the shuttle, but later discov-
ered an energy mass adhering to the starboard warp nacelle.
Subsequent analysis revealed that the energy mass was a
protouniverse in the early stages of development.

This episode is based on yet another mind-bending idea from modern cosmology. Some scientists investigating a variation on the Big Bang theory (called *inflation theory*) believe that it might be possible, under certain conditions, for a small patch of space to expand into another universe. The expanding region of space would mimic the birth of our own universe in the Big Bang. It's also possible that the rate of expansion could increase suddenly and exponentially, inflating the "baby" universe into an "adult" universe every bit as big as our own.

According to inflation theory, the creation of a protouni-verse would require a tiny patch of space in a state known as a *false vacuum*. A false vacuum impersonates a real vacuum in the sense that it appears to possess the lowest possible density of energy (one of the requirements for a true vacuum). The *matter* density of a small patch of false vacuum, however, is extraordinarily large, perhaps as great as 10^{80} grams per cubic centimeter.

It is conceivable that if a minuscule volume of false vacuum, smaller than a proton, could somehow be triggered to expand, it would create a new universe. Inflation theory suggests that an entire universe can evolve from something that has a mass of about an ounce. Once the expansion of the false vacuum is set into motion, the fledgling universe could disconnect itself from our universe through the process of *quantum tunneling*. The new universe would continue to expand in its own spatial domain.

Some scientists speculate that such baby universes are constantly being created, expanding into other dimensions, forming a sort of "froth" of universes in a sea of creation that has always existed and will always continue to exist. Our universe would simply be one bubble in this vast ocean of universes, expanding for hundreds of billions of years, then perhaps contracting once again into the patch of false vacuum from which it came.

Duplication ("The Enemy Within "; *TOS.* "Second Chances"; *TNG)*

***Starship Enterprise* Science Log, Stardate 1674.5. Science Officer Spock recording.**

The presence of an unusual form of magnetic dust has led to an unprecedented transporter malfunction. Beaming up from the surface of Alfa 177, Captain Kirk was, in effect, replicated. His

Lieutenant Riker (Jonathan Frakes) is shocked to find that a different version of himself is commanding the away team. ROBBIE ROBINSON.

personality traits, however, were somehow split between his two incarnations.

Starship Enterprise Science Log, Stardate 46921.8. Second Officer Data recording.

On a routine mission to recover scientific data from the abandoned research station on Nervala IV, the Enterprise has made a striking discovery: another Will Riker.

This "twin" of Will Riker, who chooses to go by the name Thomas (Commander Riker's middle name) was apparently created some eight years ago when then-Lieutenant Riker was sta-

tioned on Nervala IV. The station was abandoned when ion storms raised radiation levels on the surface to an intolerable level. During beam-up Lieutenant Riker's transporter signal was momentarily reflected off the station's shields. The resulting interference pattern replicated Mister Riker, while the "original" successfully beamed aboard the Starship Potemkin. *Neither Riker was aware of the other's existence until the* Enterprise *returned to the Nervala system.*

Thomas Riker is genetically identical to William Riker. Thomas Riker's personality, however, has evolved along very different lines, shaped largely by his eight-year isolation on Nervala IV.

One of the questions raised by the duplication of persons by transporter malfunctions is, Wouldn't the two new people each weigh half as much as the original?

Not necessarily. Einstein demonstrated, in his most famous equation, that matter and energy are equivalent: $E = mc^2$. When matter and antimatter meet, for example, all of their mass is converted into energy by precisely the amount indicated by this equation. (Some physicists even suggested that we dispense with the terms matter and energy and just call everything "mattergy," but this term never caught on; probably just as well.)

During a transporter malfunction, an energy surge could have provided the mass necessary to create a duplicate Kirk or Riker; again mass and energy are equivalent, and can be converted into one another under certain circumstances.

It's easy to calculate how much energy would be required. Let's say Captain Kirk weighed in at around 65 kilos (143 pounds—remember, this episode took place early in the show's first season). When you evaluate an equation in physics, you must be careful to use consistent units. With the mass given in kilos, the speed of light must be expressed in meters per second squared. The resulting energy will then be given in joules. So:

$$E = mc^2$$
$$E = (65 \text{ kilos}) \cdot (3.00 \cdot 10^8 \text{ m/s})^2$$
$$E = 5.85 \cdot 10^{18} \text{ joules.}$$

That's a lot of joules! A one-thousand megawatt nuclear power plant (a facility capable of providing power for all of a small city) would have to run for 185 *years* to produce this much energy.

"The Enemy Within" also raises the age-old nature-versus-nurture debate. How much of human personality is determined by genetics, and how much is shaped by the environment? Studies of identical twins (who share the same genes) who have been separated at or shortly after birth, seem to indicate that many behavioral traits are inherited through our genes. But recent neurological studies have convincingly demonstrated that the environment in which a child grows up has a profound influence on the development of his or her brain, which in turn influences intelligence, emotional development, and creative abilities. This can have substantial effects on personality. I suspect the line between nature and nurture is, to borrow a term from chaos theory, highly fractal. That is to say, the line is extremely crooked, and the closer we look at it, the more kinks and curves we see, ad infinitum.

Merger ("Tuvix"; *VGR*)

Starship *Voyager* Medical Log, Stardate 49672.2. Chief Medical Officer recording.

An unprecedented transporter accident has merged two Voyager *crew members into a single entity. Beaming aboard with a sample of highly unusual, orchidlike plants, Lieutenant*

Tuvix (Tom Wright) a transporter-created hybrid of Tuvok and Neelix. ROBBIE ROBINSON.

Tuvok and Mister Neelix were merged into a single organism through the action of symbiogenic enzymes contained within the plant specimens.

Genetic analysis confirms that strands of DNA from both Tuvok and Neelix are present in the joined person, intertwined in a manner that makes it seemingly impossible to distinguish their original genetic components. The joined person, who refers to himself as "Tuvix," retains the memories of both Tuvok and Neelix, and a sort of "mixed" personality combining traits from both men manifests itself more strongly every day.

Starship Voyager Science Log, Stardate 49688.3. Captain Kathryn Janeway recording.

The Doctor has found a way to tag Mister Neelix's original DNA segments using a radioisotope probe with an affinity for

Talaxian genetic markers. It then became possible to use the transporter to separate and reconstruct Tuvok and Neelix. Despite Tuvix's desire to remain a joined entity, I feel that I have no choice but to recover my lost crew members. It is perhaps the most difficult command decision I have ever made.

Symbiogenesis is a fascinating theory in biology, developed by noted biologist Dr. Lynn Margulis. According to Dr. Margulis, cells that developed early in the history of life on Earth may have incorporated other simple cells into their structures by ingesting them: eating them, in effect. Instead of being consumed, however, these cells became part of the larger cell's working machinery. Dr. Margulis believes this may have been how *organelles*, which are to cells pretty much what organs are to beings like you and me, originally evolved.

The symbiogenesis theory has only been applied to microscopic organisms, and has never been observed in larger animals such as mammals. One of the joys of *Star Trek*, however, is taking cutting-edge ideas from the world of science and extrapolating them into a science-fiction scenario that introduces the audience to new science through an engaging story about one of our characters.

Radioactive dyes have been used for many years to trace the outlines of various structures within the body. The dreaded barium enema lines the intestine with trace amounts of barium, which "glow" in X-ray films, making it much easier for doctors to see structural details in this part of the body. Utilizing the techniques of genetic engineering, it is now possible to tag segments of genes in cell nuclei for the purpose of ready identification.

3. Planetology

"The entire Earth is but a point, and the place of our own habitation but a minute corner of it."

—Marcus Aurelius, second-century Roman philosopher and emperor

Parallel Planetary Evolution ("Miri"; TOS. "Bread and Circuses"; TOS)

Starship Enterprise Science Log, Stardate 2719.5. Science Officer Spock recording.

An impossible discovery—some three hundred light-years from Earth, a planet identical to Earth in every respect: mass, elemental and mineral composition, atmosphere, distribution of land masses, ratio of land to ocean surface, and a human population with technology identical to mid-twentieth–century industrial Earth.

The population has been devastated by a genetically engineered virus whose original purpose was to extend the human life span substantially. Ironically, the virus was successful in the youngest members of the population, but became a deadly pathogen for adults and adolescents.

The discovery of this planet seems to be an incredible validation of Hansen's theory of parallel planet development.

Starship Enterprise Science Log, Stardate 4044.6. Science Officer Spock recording.

While investigating wreckage from the U.S.S. Beagle, *lost in space some six years ago, the* Enterprise *has encountered another example of parallel planetary development. A human population on Planet Eight-Ninety-Two-IV (New General Catalog) has developed a culture remarkably similar to Rome on Earth shortly before the birth of Christ. On this planet, however, Rome never fell. The inhabitants have at their disposal technology equivalent to late-twentieth–century Earth, and use it to perpetuate the rather barbaric values of the early Roman government.*

The landing party discovers a world that resembles Earth from both orbital scans and surface conditions.

Our solar system evolved some four-and-a-half billion years ago out of a great cloud of gas and dust orbiting the *protostar* that became our Sun. Disks of gas and dust orbiting nascent stars beyond our solar system have been observed since the early 1980s, when astronomer Dr. Brad Smith and his colleagues at the University of Arizona photographed a band of dusty material surrounding the star Beta Pictoris. Such disks are now called *protoplanetary disks*, and are thought to be the progenitors of planetary systems.

Stars form when vast clouds of gas and dust in space (nebulae) contract under the influence of gravity. As a nebular cloud contracts, it begins to rotate. The spin of the cloud increases as its diameter decreases. This implies that the rate at which the cloud is contracting will be slowest in the plane of the cloud's rotation. Over time, this has the effect of "flattening out" the cloud, and forming a protoplanetary disk.

Given what we know about planetary and biological evolution, the probability of discovering Earth's identical twin somewhere out in the cosmos is virtually nil. On the other hand, given billions of years of time and uncountable trillions of stars, it seems reasonable to assume that somewhere in the vastness of the cosmos there are planets remarkably similar to Earth, with life-forms that more or less resemble human beings.

The possibility of increasing the human life span is discussed in "The Omega Glory" science log, page 123.

Gas Giants ("Starship Down"; *DS9*)

Deep Space 9 Science Log, Stardate 49266.6. Science Officer Jadzia Dax recording.

During a trade mission in the Gamma Quadrant, the Defiant *was forced to take refuge in the atmosphere of a Class-J planet after an attack by two Jem'Hadar warships.*

The Class-J planet was largely unremarkable, fifty-two hundred kilometers in diameter, possessing a mostly methane-and-hydrogen atmosphere and several natural satellites.

Isaac Asimov once described the solar system as consisting of the Sun, four planets, and debris. The four planets he was referring to are the *jovian planets*, also known by the somewhat less flattering term "gas giants." (Of course, to think of Mercury, Venus, Mars, Pluto, and our Earth as "debris" is hardly flattering either.) Class-J in the *Star Trek* lexicon stands for *jovian*.

The jovian planets in our solar system—Jupiter, Saturn, Neptune, and Uranus—are mostly gaseous bodies. Their thick atmospheres are dominated by hydrogen, which is also the main constituent of the Sun, and the most common element in the universe. Jupiter, largest of the giant planets, contains more than twice the mass of all of the other planets in the solar system combined. A thousand planets the size of Earth could easily fit within Jupiter's immense volume. Jupiter is primarily composed of hydrogen and helium gas, and may or may not possess a solid core, although pressures near the center of this giant world compress the gases there to densities far greater than the density of lead.

Jupiter is sometimes thought of as a "failed" star. If Jupiter had started out with more mass, temperatures and pressures at its core might have become high enough to trigger *nuclear fusion,* the process that powers the stars. As it is, hydrogen at the center of Jupiter is so compressed that it may be in a metallic state: still gaseous in the sense that the hydrogen atoms move about freely, but electrically conductive like a metal. A metallic hydrogen core would explain Jupiter's intense and voluminous magnetic field. Jupiter's *magnetosphere* is in fact the largest continuous structure in the solar system.

On October 6, 1995, two Swiss astronomers, Michel Mayor and Didier Queloz, discovered evidence for a Jupiter-scale planet in a close orbit around the star 51 Pegasi (in the constellation Pegasus), the first clear indication of a planet orbiting another

Sunlike star.[*] Early in 1996, American astronomers Paul Butler and Geoff Marcy announced that they had discovered evidence for jovian planets orbiting two other Sunlike stars, 70 Virginis and 47 Ursa Majoris. The planet orbiting 70 Virginis lies within what is called the "habitable zone" of this planetary system. The planet is at a distance from its sun such that water could exist in a liquid state there—probably not on the planet itself, given its great mass, but if the planet has a system of large moons, as does Jupiter, one or more of those moons might posses lakes or oceans of water, and possibly life.

These planets were not, however, discovered by astronomers peering through the eyepiece of a telescope or looking at a Hubble Space Telescope image. Trying to detect "extrasolar" planets visually is extremely difficult because the light from an extrasolar planet is overwhelmed by the light from its sun. A planet shines only by reflecting light from its sun; planets do not generate their own light. The luminosity of our Sun is about a billion times greater than the light reflected from Jupiter. Extrasolar planets are simply lost in the glare of their parent stars.

To get around this problem, the astronomers used an indirect method to hunt for planets orbiting other stars. When starlight is passed through a *spectroscope*, the spectral lines that characterize the composition of a star's atmosphere can be analyzed. If a jovian-sized planet is orbiting a star, the star's spectral lines will shift back and forth ever so slightly due to the gravitational pull of the planet.

---

[*] However, they are not the first planets beyond our solar system to be discovered. Radio astronomer Alexander Wolszczan discovered evidence for three terrestrial-size planets orbiting a pulsar called B 1257+12 in 1992. Wolszczan observed that the radio signal from the pulsar beat irregularly, most likely due to gravitational tugs on the pulsar from a family of planets.

Planetology

The table below lists some of the extrasolar planets that have been discovered by this technique to date. A few of the purported planet discoveries are being challenged by several astronomers who believe that the observed spectral shifting may be due to changes in the atmosphere of the star, and not the gravitational influence of orbiting planets.

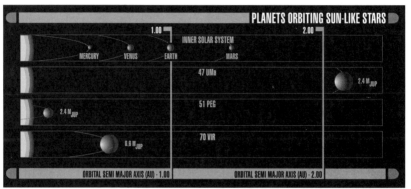

DOUG DREXLER

Rogue Planets
("The Search"; *DS9*)

Deep Space 9 Science Log, Stardate 47222.2. Major Kira Nerys recording.

On route to the Callinon system in the Gamma Quadrant, the Defiant *was attacked by Jem'Hadar warships.*

Constable Odo and I managed to escape in a Defiant *shuttlecraft. Odo felt a strong, primal impulse to proceed to the Omarion Nebula, where we discovered the homeworld of his race: a Class-M rogue planet enshrouded in the nebula.*

Rogue planets may exist in great numbers in the universe. Although our present understanding of planetary formation requires that planets form in orbit around stars, close encounters with other planets within a planetary system—or other nearby stars—could eject a planet from its solar system through a sort of gravitational slingshot effect. Some astronomers think that vagabond jovian planets orbiting the fringes of galaxies might account for some of the universe's *missing mass.*

An internal heat source could conceivably provide a "Class-M" environment for a planet, independent of the need for a nearby star. The core of the Earth is still warm, even after 4.5 billion years, although not warm enough to maintain a comfortable surface temperature should the Sun go cold. The gravitational contraction that created the Earth heated it through friction, and some of that heat is still dissipating. Most of the heat in the Earth's core today, however, comes from the decay of radioactive elements.

Unstable Planets
("Inheritance"; *TNG*)

Starship Enterprise Science Log, Stardate 47414.1. Second Officer Data recording.

The Enterprise was summoned to the Class-M world Atrea IV to prevent a planetary catastrophe. Rapid cooling of the planet's core was triggering massive, planetwide temblors that threatened life on its surface.

Lieutenant Commander La Forge and I, in conjunction with several Atrean scientists, devised a plan for warming the planet's core. The Enterprise used its phaser banks to inject a stream of nadions into Atrea IV's nickel-iron core through vertical conduits drilled through the planet's crust. The nadions initiated a nuclear chain reaction in the core, raising its temperature over the course of five days by twenty-two kelvins. Heating is expected to continue for the next 415 days, with a total change in temperature of 2820 kelvins, sufficient to stabilize the planet's mantle and overlying crust.

The core of the Earth, and presumably other Class-M planets, consists mostly of heavy metals, primarily iron and nickel. These were the densest elements present during the formation of the Earth, and the force of gravity made them sink to the center of our planet, with lighter elements and compounds settling into layers above (a process planetary scientists refer to as *differentiation*).

As noted in the previous log, the core of the Earth is still warm, mostly because of the heat generated by the decay of radioactive elements. In fact, the temperature at the Earth's core is higher than the temperature at the surface of the Sun. If

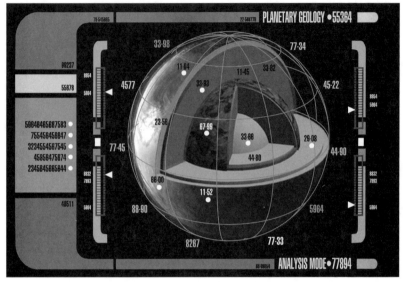

DOUG DREXLER

our planet's core were to suddenly cool, it would shrink, creating dislocations in the mantle and crust (see figure).

Earthquakes occur when segments of *tectonic plates* in the Earth's crust abruptly shift along *fault lines*, which are essentially ruptures in the crust. The energy of an earthquake is measured on the *Richter scale*, developed in 1956 by the geologists B. Gutenberg and C.F. Richter. The Richter scale is a logarithmic scale: a magnitude 4 earthquake is ten times as strong as a magnitude 3 earthquake, and ten times weaker than a magnitude 5 quake. (Shortly after I moved to California, I had the unfortunate experience of being rudely awakened at 4:30 in the morning by a magnitude 6.3 quake. Perhaps the most frightening aspect of the quake was not the shaking but the noise: it sounded like a freight train running at a hundred miles per hour just outside my bedroom window.)

The molten core of the Earth also generates the Earth's magnetic field through a *dynamo effect*. Our magnetic field deflects charged particles streaming out of the Sun in the *solar wind*. Were it not for our magnetic field, a much greater flux of subatomic particles would strike the Earth's surface, with potentially devastating consequences for life. The planet Mars, which is about half the diameter of the Earth and probably has a cold core, possesses at most a very weak magnetic field. Some scientists think that Mars lost much of its original atmosphere because it lacks a substantial magnetic field: over billions of years the solar wind, unimpeded by magnetic deflection, has gradually sloughed away most of the Martian atmosphere.

The core-heating technique in this episode is based on an analogy from nuclear physics. *Nuclear fission* is the term used to describe atoms that are unstable and spontaneously split into two smaller fragments. Nuclear power stations use controlled nuclear fission to create electricity. Certain atoms can be coaxed into fission by neutrons: a neutron striking an unstable atomic nucleus can split the nucleus. In the case of some isotopes of uranium and other elements, several additional neutrons are liberated when the nucleus splits. These neutrons can then go on to split other atoms in a chain reaction. By dropping a handful of neutrons into a mass of uranium in a *nuclear pile* you can start a chain reaction that eventually raises the temperature of the pile several thousand degrees. I thought this would be a useful analogy for reheating the core of the planet, with the phaser bank's fictitious nadions playing the role neutrons play in a nuclear pile.

In reality, the cooling and potential reheating of a planet's core would be a very complex process occurring over millions or billions of years. It seems doubtful that even the *Enterprise* could influence this process in a controllable and beneficial manner.

Planetary Ring Systems
("Emanations"; *VGR*)

Starship *Voyager* Science Log, Stardate 48627.5. Captain Kathryn Janeway recording.

Voyager has made a landmark discovery in the spectacular ring system of a Class-D planet: a new transuranic element, atomic number 247.

Even more remarkably, element 247 appears to be a decay product of deceased humanoid bodies discovered in the larger planetoids that comprise the ring system.

All of the jovian planets in our solar system have rings. The rings of Saturn are the brightest and best known planetary ring system. Saturn was a great puzzle to Galileo, the first person to point a telescope at the planet in the year 1610. In Galileo's relatively crude instrument, Saturn's rings looked like a pair of ears or bumps on either side of a larger disk. A few years later Galileo noted that these "bumps" had disappeared. As telescopes improved, they provided sharper views of the planets. In 1659, Christian Huygens announced that he was able to resolve the "bumps" observed by Galileo into a flat disk structure ringing the entire planet. The occasional disappearance of the rings was explained by the fact that every fifteen years or so the rings are tilted "edge on" toward the Earth, making it impossible to see them even in large telescopes (the most recent "ring plane crossing" occurred in August 1996). This in turn suggests that the rings of Saturn are very thin relative to their diameter; in fact, if you were to build a scale model of Saturn, making the rings only as thick as a piece of typing paper (about 0.1 millimeters), the diameter of the ring system would be about forty meters.

The nineteenth-century physicist James Clerk Maxwell argued that the rings of Saturn are not solid, but consist of uncountable millions of smaller particles orbiting Saturn in much the same way as our Moon orbits the Earth. Maxwell's theory was confirmed in 1895 when spectroscopic analysis revealed that the inner edge of the Saturn ring system revolved faster than the outer edge, which would be impossible if the rings were a single, solid object. The American *Pioneer* and *Voyager* spacecraft have revealed the rings of Saturn to be composed of icy particles ranging in size from a fraction of a millimeter to twenty or thirty meters across.

Jupiter, Uranus, and Neptune also possess thin rings of icy and rocky material. These rings systems are not nearly as extensive as the rings of Saturn and are practically invisible to ground-based telescopes. The rings of Uranus were discovered through a phenomenon called *occultation*. An occultation occurs whenever one astronomical body passes in front of another. Astronomers observing Uranus in 1976 noticed that a bright star passing behind Uranus "flickered" before it was blocked by the disk of the planet. The flickering pattern was repeated exactly as the star emerged on the other side of Uranus's disk, which ruled out the possibility that the flickering was nothing more than twinkling caused by turbulence in Earth's atmosphere. The astronomers concluded that Uranus is encircled by several thin rings.

Planetary rings are probably created when a small moon collides with another moon, or ventures so close to its planet that gravitational *tidal forces* shred it apart. The resulting fragments spread out into concentric orbits, breaking into ever smaller fragments through repeated collisions, eventually forming a set of rings. Ring systems are thought to be a somewhat transient phenomena, lasting perhaps several hundred million years. Rings as magnificent as the rings of Saturn are probably rare. We are truly privileged to live in our solar system at a time when this extraordinary planetary spectacle is readily visible in backyard telescopes. If you've never seen Saturn in a telescope, I urge you to visit a planetarium or local astronomy club and take a look. You'll never forget it.

Comets
("The Deadly Years"; *TOS*)

Starship Enterprise Science Officer's Log, Stardate 3482.2. Science Officer Spock recording.

Scientists at the Gamma Hydra IV research colony have been afflicted by a deadly illness, which has spread to several senior Enterprise *officers, including the captain. The condition is marked by rapid physiological deterioration, in a manner similar to the effects of advanced aging.*

Progeria has been ruled out as the likely disease mechanism. Some form of radiation poisoning is the most probable cause. All members of the recent landing party have been afflicted, with the notable exception of Ensign Chekov.

A comet recently passed through this system. Sensor readings made by Gamma Hydra scientists indicate that the comet's tail extended over 150 million kilometers, and crossed the planet's orbit on Stardate 3461.3. Under normal circumstances, one would expect the planet's atmosphere and magnetosphere to provide adequate shielding against volatile gases and potentially harmful compounds, such as cyanogen, typically encountered in cometary bodies.

Comet Hale-Bopp. ANDRE BORMANIS.

Comets are among the most beautiful of celestial objects. They have engendered feelings of awe and wonder for all of recorded history. At the time of this writing, comet *Hale-Bopp* is gracing Earth's skies, putting on a spectacular show for all to see.

Comets are essentially giant "dirty snowballs" orbiting the Sun in long, elliptical orbits; cometary orbits are so large that it often takes thousands of years for a comet to complete a single circuit. A handful of comets, like Halley's, pass close to the Sun more frequently.

The nucleus of a comet is typically a few kilometers or so in diameter (Hale-Bopp is a relatively large comet, with a nucleus about thirty kilometers across). Comets spend most of their time in the far reaches of the solar system, billions of kilometers or more distant from the Sun. Occasionally a passing molecular cloud, or a nearby star, or a pressure wave crossing the galaxy through the thin interstellar medium, nudges a comet into a path that brings it into the inner solar system. As a comet gets closer and closer to the Sun, its surface is heated. Water vapor and other gases bake off the surface of the nucleus, forming the fuzzy coma and tail that characterizes the look of comets (see photo).

In 1910, Halley's Comet made its regular, every–seventy-six–year visit to our inner solar system. In the United States and other countries, many laypersons were alarmed to learn that the Earth would pass through the tail of Halley's Comet, which was known from spectroscopic observations to contain cyanogen and other noxious gases. However, the atmosphere and magnetic field of the Earth provide more than adequate protection against the rarefied gases found in the tails of comets. Many among the public were nevertheless hoodwinked into buying gas masks and "comet pills" to protect themselves against this alleged threat.

Comets and Prophecies ("Destiny"; *DS9*)

Deep Space 9 Science Log, Stardate 48549.2. Science Officer Jadzia Dax recording.

An unexpected gravitational surge was generated during tests of a subspace relay system designed to provide continuous communication between the Alpha and Gamma Quadrants.

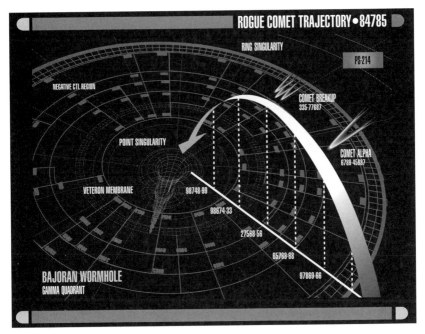

RObGUE COMET TRAJECTORY • 84785

RING SINGULARITY

PS-214

NEGATIVE CTL REGION

COMET BREAKUP
335-77687

POINT SINGULARITY

COMET ALPHA
6789-45887

VETERON MEMBRANE

98748-99

98674-33

27588-56

65768-88

BAJORAN WORMHOLE
GAMMA QUADRANT

97869-66

DOUG DREXLER

*The gravitational surge altered the orbit of a comet, send-
ing it on a collision course with the wormhole. The impending
comet-wormhole collision was interpreted by the more devout-
ly religious Bajorans as the fulfillment of an ancient Bajoran
prophesy. The comet was fragmented by photon-torpedo fire
from the* Defiant *and successfully diverted from the wormhole.*

Historically speaking, comets have been among the most
feared celestial visitors. The comet that graced our skies
in the year 1066 was considered a bad omen for King Harold,
who died later that year in the Battle of Hastings.

Records of comet apparitions dating back thousands of
years have been discovered from civilizations across the globe.
In a wonderful book written in the 1920s, *The Romance of*

Comets, Mary Proctor relates the dread and woe that greeted most comets throughout the centuries. In medieval Europe, comets were portents of disease and pestilence, wars and the deaths of kings. In ancient China, comets were not necessarily bad omens, but they were considered harbingers of future events. Each constellation was a province in a great empire. The planets were the empire's administrators and the stars were its diplomats. In this celestial kingdom, it was decided what would happen to the terrestrial empire of the Chinese, for better or worse. Comets played the role of imperial messengers, shuttling like cosmic couriers among the constellations.

Sadly, comet Hale-Bopp seems to have rekindled some of the superstitions common in ages past. In mid-November 1996, a photograph taken by a Houston amateur astronomer appeared on the Internet seeming to show a "Saturnlike object" in the wake of the comet. The object proved to be nothing more than a misidentified star suffering from optical aberrations in the photographer's telescope. But rumors quickly began to circulate that an alien spaceship was flying in tandem with the comet. In late March, 1997, in an exclusive suburb north of San Diego, California, thirty-nine members of a quasi-religious group, *Heaven's Gate*, took their own lives in the belief that their souls (and perhaps even their physical bodies) would rise into space and fly into eternity aboard the alien ship.

Even though modern science dismisses the notion that comets or other celestial objects dictate the course of human affairs, science has discovered an even more intimate and profound connection between humans and the heavens. Comets brought ices and complex organic molecules to the surface of the Earth in the chaotic years of our planet's youth, coating our world with precious water and, perhaps, spreading the chemical seeds of the multitudinous forms of life that flourish here today.

Asteroid Impacts
("The Paradise Syndrome"; *TOS*)

Starship Enterprise Science Log, Stardate 4888.2. Science Officer Spock recording.

An iron-nickel asteroid on a collision course with a Class-M planet was successfully diverted by a deflector mechanism (apparently constructed by a highly advanced spacefaring civilization) on the planet's surface. The impact, had it not been averted, would have devastated the planet's ecosphere, resulting in massive extinctions of numerous species including, in all probability, the planet's human population.

Meteor Crater in Northern Arizona stands in mute testimony to the tremendous energy—and potentially deadly consequences—of asteroid impacts. A kilometer across the rim and several hundred meters deep, Meteor Crater was blasted out of the high desert some fifty thousand years ago by an asteroid perhaps sixty to seventy meters in diameter.

Asteroids of this size probably strike the Earth once or twice every hundred thousand years, on average. It is impossible to precisely predict when another object of this size might hit the Earth. We do know that there are about two thousand asteroids greater than a few meters in diameter whose orbits cross that of the Earth. The fact that their orbits cross our orbit doesn't guarantee a collision; space is vast, and the Earth and asteroid have to be at the same place at the same time for a collision to occur. Some day, though, another collision like the one that carved out Meteor Crater is inevitable. Over the course of the next several billion years, collisions with asteroids large enough to profoundly alter the Earth's climate are also inevitable.

Since seventy percent of the Earth's surface is covered by water, one would expect that asteroids striking Earth hit water about seventy percent of the time. Cities and towns occupy a little less than one percent of the Earth's surface. A direct asteroid hit on a city is therefore fairly unlikely. However, an asteroid smashing into an ocean would still be far from harmless. Ocean impacts could trigger massive tidal waves and tsunamis, with the potential for wiping out cities all along an ocean coast, as well as blasting debris and water vapor into the atmosphere.

The threat of a major asteroid impact in the not too distant future is small, but some scientists and military planners feel that the potentially disastrous consequences of such an event are worth a little insurance. In principle, it would be possible to divert the path of an asteroid headed toward Earth by exploding nuclear warheads on the asteroid's surface. Recoil from the nuclear explosions would nudge the asteroid onto a course that misses the Earth. Other, less radical, techniques for asteroid deflection have also been considered. In order for such schemes to work, the asteroid would have to be detected many months if not years before a potential impact. Several groups of astronomers routinely search the skies with automated telescopes designed to detect Earth-crossing asteroids and characterize their orbits.

4. Space Medicine

"First, do no harm..."

—Hippocrates

"I'm a doctor, not a bricklayer."

—Dr. Leonard McCoy

Radiation Effects
("The Deadly Years"; *TOS*)

Starship *Enterprise* Medical Log, Stardate 3484.4. Chief Medical Officer Leonard McCoy recording.

On a resupply mission to the science station on Gamma Hydra IV, the Enterprise *landing party discovered that all of the research personnel were suffering from a debilitating physiological condition that resembled extreme aging. Scientists in their late twenties and early thirties were physically similar to humans in their late sixties or seventies.*

The landing party eventually contracted the same malady, with the exception of young Ensign Chekov. Radiation from a comet that recently passed through the Gamma Hydra system was regarded as a possible source of the geriatric condition, but standard hyronoline therapy proved an ineffective treatment. We eventually realized that Chekov was unaffected by the radiation because of high levels of adrenaline in his system, a result of his intense fear reaction to the unexpected sight of a dead scientist in the research station. High levels of adrenaline in Chekov's blood protected him from the harmful effects of the radiation, and adrenaline therapy eventually restored the health of the other members of the landing party.

Radiation sickness is a consequence of exposure to high doses of radiation, typically from naturally radioactive substances, such as radium, or high-energy electromagnetic radiation, such as X rays. We are exposed to naturally occurring radiation all the time; it's only when people are exposed to high doses of radiation in short periods of time, or smaller doses over a longer period of time, that there is a potential danger to health. Exposure to radiation can, in some circumstances, lead

to cancer and other illnesses. Radiation causes cancer by damaging the DNA in a cell's nucleus. If the DNA is damaged beyond
the cell's ability to repair it, a mutation can arise that causes a
cell to reproduce in an out-of-control fashion, forming a malig-
nant growth.

Pierre and Marie Curie were early explorers of the world of
radioactivity. They spent many years investigating the properties of radium, a radioactive element. When radium atoms
decay, they emit *alpha particles*, which consist of two protons
and two neutrons—the nucleus of a helium atom. The kinetic
energy of alpha particles is potentially damaging to human tissue. For many years Pierre Curie carried a piece of radium in his
pocket to investigate how radiation affects human tissue. He
eventually suffered radiation burns, which, ironically, weren't
fatal, as Dr. Curie was killed by a horse and carriage one day as
he was crossing a busy street. Madame Curie, however, ultimately died from radiation poisoning.

Before the manifold dangers of radiation exposure were
fully understood, scientists at Los Alamos National Laboratory
in the 1940s, working to develop the first atomic bomb, handled
radioactive materials in a manner that would probably be considered foolhardy today. After the first atomic-bomb test in the
New Mexico desert, the sand beneath the test stand was fused
by the intense heat of the explosion into a greenish, glassy
material the scientists called *trinitite* (the code name of the
first atom bomb test was "Trinity"). Some of the lab personnel
made necklaces and other souvenirs out of the trinitite, which
was moderately radioactive, and hence potentially health-
threatening.

The reference in Dr. McCoy's report to the comet that
passed through the Gamma Hydra system is somewhat amus-
ing, in that it is based more on superstition than on science.
When the true physical nature of comets started to become

clear in the late nineteenth century, astronomers, using the technique of *spectroscopy*, discovered the presence of various elements and compounds in comets, including toxic substances such as cyanogen. When Earth passed through the tail of Halley's comet in 1910, many people panicked, fearing that our atmosphere would become saturated with poison gases. In truth, the density of gas and dust in the tail of a comet is so low that the probability of a given individual inhaling even one molecule of cyanogen (a harmless amount) was basically zero.

The pioneering work of the Curies earned them one of the ultimate honors in physics: a basic unit of radioactivity is named after them. One *curie* is defined as that quantity of a radioactive substance that produces $3.70 \cdot 10^{10}$ radioactive disintegrations per second (another unit named after a great physicist, the *rutherford* , is defined as 10^6 radioactive disintegrations per second). A radiation *dose* is a measure of how much energy an object will absorb when exposed to radiation; the unit of dosage is *roentgens* (named after yet another physicist). A roentgen is defined as the amount of radiation required to cause $2.08 \cdot 10^9$ *ionizations* in one cubic centimeter of dry air at standard temperature and pressure.

Just one more obscure unit: Since radiation exposure can have profound effects on living tissue, a special unit has been devised to measure radiation doses in humans. A special unit is needed because some radiation will pass right through a human body with no effect, and some weak forms of radiation are completely blocked by skin or clothing. As noted above, the unit known as the *rem* (radiation *e*quivalent *m*an) takes into account how much potentially damaging energy human tissue will absorb upon exposure to various forms of radiation.

Radiation sickness is characterized by nausea, vomiting, loss of appetite, diarrhea, fever, and weakness. In extreme cases, internal hemorrhaging due to tissue damage can also occur.

Radiation sickness is typically treated with basic supportive measures, such as fluid replacement and blood transfusions. Bone
marrow transplants, chemotherapy, and radiation therapy may
also be indicated if leukemia or tumors develop. The "adrenaline
therapy" mentioned in Dr. McCoy's log is not standard medical
practice for radiation sickness, although steroids and other drugs
might be used in some cases to boost a weakened immune system. Radiation can also burn skin and other tissues. Radiation
burns are essentially treated like any other kind of burn.

Gene Therapy
("Masterpiece Society"; TNG)

**Starship Enterprise Medical Log, Stardate 45477.1. Chief Medical Officer
Beverly Crusher recording.**

The Enterprise *has discovered a colony of humans on planet
Moab IV. In the process of helping the colony avert a natural
disaster, we have discovered that the colonists are the result of
a very carefully planned and controlled program of genetic
engineering.*

G*ene therapy* is one of the most promising therapeutic techniques of late-twentieth–century medicine, but it is still in
the early stages of development.

   DNA is the "master molecule" of life. Everything that a cell
does—from basic reproduction to the kinds of chemical compounds it manufactures—is controlled by DNA. *Chromosomes*
are composed of DNA molecules and supporting *histone* molecules. The cells of a human being contain forty-six chromosomes.
Genes are segments of chromosomes (i.e., segments of DNA)
that "code" for the production of various protein molecules,

which in turn form the tissues, organs, and other structures that make up living organisms. Genes therefore determine the physical structures and physiological processes that characterize individuals and species.

Sometimes a person is born with one or more defective genes, or some of his or her genes are damaged, perhaps by exposure to radiation. When this happens, the gene can no longer perform its function in that cell. Genetic defects can also be passed on from parents to children. A great many chronic diseases are a consequence of genetic damage. Cystic Fibrosis (CF), for example, is a genetic illness. In a person who suffers from CF, cells that line the lungs and other tissues exposed to air contain damaged genes that prevent these cells from producing an *enzyme* that is necessary for dissolving mucus. As a consequence, mucus builds up in the lungs, which can make breathing difficult. The excess mucus also promotes the growth of bacteria that can cause respiratory illnesses, such as pneumonia.

CF is treated by various medications and therapies that help break up mucus in the lungs and other tissues. But if it were possible to *repair* the defective gene responsible for CF, the cells could once again produce the needed enzyme. The defective gene responsible for CF was discovered in the 1980s. In principle, a working copy of this gene from healthy cells, inserted into the cell in place of the defective gene, would function normally and produce the required enzyme.

The challenge for medical scientists is to find a way to replace the defective genes in a sufficient number of cells to effect a cure. One possible method under investigation is to genetically engineer a virus, such as a common cold virus, to insert the proper gene into lung cells. Viruses by their nature infect cells and manipulate the genetic machinery of the cell in order to reproduce. A virus could in effect be programmed to insert

Hannah Bates (Dey Young) depends on La Forge (LeVar Burton) to save her world.
ROBBIE ROBINSON.

healthy genes into cells containing defective genes. Such a virus would need to be "hobbled" so that it posed no serious health risk to the patient (this is commonly done to viruses used in vaccines, as discussed in the "Genesis" science log, page 119). A suitably modified virus could be an efficient mechanism for the dissemination of healthy genes. Several more years of research and clinical testing will probably be needed before such techniques are used in standard medical practice.

Spinal Replacement ("Ethics"; *TNG*)

Starship Enterprise **Medical Log, Stardate 45587.4. Chief Medical Officer Beverly Crusher recording.**

Lieutenant Worf has been seriously injured in an accident in cargo bay three. Seven of his vertebrae have been fractured, and his spinal cord has been crushed. Despite my best efforts to stimulate neurological regeneration, my prognosis is permanent paralysis.

Medical Log, Supplemental.

In consultation with neurogeneticist Doctor Toby Russell, I have reluctantly agreed to assist in performing an experimental and highly dangerous genetronic replication technique that could replace Lieutenant Worf's spinal column and restore virtually all musculoskeletal function.

Fractured spinal cords are among the most difficult medical traumas to treat. The spinal cord consists of bundles of nerves leading from various parts of the body to the brain through the *vertebral canal*, which is essentially a column of ring-shaped bones that leads up the center of your back. The individual bones surrounding the vertebral canal are called *vertebrae*.

The vertebrae protect the nerves of the spinal column. Among those nerves are the nerves that carry electrical impulses from the brain to muscles located throughout the body. These are the *motor nerves*, and they make it possible for a person to walk, or pick up and throw a ball, or play the piano. Any physical action that requires the voluntary control of a muscle is mediated by motor nerves. If those nerves are badly damaged or severed due to a spinal-cord injury, motor function is lost.

Dr. Russell (Caroline Kava) gingerly begins the procedure to replace Worf's damaged spinal cord.
ROBBIE ROBINSON.

Unlike most other cells of the body, nerve cells do not regenerate, nor are they easily repaired. When a motor nerve is damaged beyond repair, the result is typically partial or full paralysis of the associated muscles. In a *complete transection* of the spinal cord, the cord is cut all the way through, and all voluntary movement (as well as physical sensations, such as the sense of touch, which are also transmitted to the brain via nerves) below the point of the transection is lost.

Medical science in recent years has made great progress in the treatment of spinal-cord injury. An injection of cortico-steroids immediately following the injury can, in some cases, minimize the complication of paralysis. The public was remind-ed of the serious nature of spinal-cord injury, as well as the great progress that is being made in its treatment, by actor Christopher Reeve's horseback-riding accident in 1996. Considering the extent of his injuries, Reeve is making remark-able progress in regaining muscle function, and is dedicated to someday making a complete recovery through medical advances and his own remarkable determination.

In a new experimental procedure called *functional neuro-muscular stimulation*, an electronic device is used to stimulate electrical impulses in damaged nerves.

Synthetic Organ/Tissue Transplantation ("Life Support"; *DS9*)

Deep Space 9 Medical Log, Stardate 48508.3. Chief Medical Officer Julian Bashir recording.

On Stardate 48498.4, Bajoran Vedek Bareil was killed in a shut-tle accident en route to Deep Space 9. Exposure to an unusual form of radiation during the accident, however, made it possi-ble to revive Bareil approximately one hour later.

Dr. Bashir (Alexander Siddig) wonders if he is helping Vedek Bareil or removing the last vestiges of his personality. ROBBIE ROBINSON.

I recommended he be placed in stasis immediately, pending the development of medical procedures that would ensure his complete recovery. Bareil, however, insisted that I proceed with extraordinary measures to maintain his life so he could continue to assist Kai Winn in critical treaty negotiations with the Cardassians.

In addition to a variety of artificial organ and prosthetic replacements (see my technical paper in the current issue of The Journal of Starfleet Medicine *for details), it was necessary to create and graft several synthetic neural implants into the vedek's brain. The vedek reported some unusual side effects from these implants, including changes in sensory perception. Major Kira became concerned that the essence of the man was somehow slipping away with each new neural graft. The extent of the vedek's injuries eventually proved to be too great to counter with present-day medical science, and Bareil died on stardate 48507.2.*

V edek Bareil's experience in "Life Support" is essentially a retelling of the origin of the Tin Woodsman character in *The Wizard of Oz*. In the L. Frank Baum book (which became the basis for the classic film), the Tin Woodsman was a man who was, shall we say, a bit careless with an axe. One day, while chopping some wood, he accidentally cut off a leg. He managed to replace it with a tin prosthetic. On another occasion, he lopped off an arm, then the other leg, and so on, until eventually every part of him had to be traded out for tin replacements.

Organ transplants are relatively recent developments in medical science. Dr. Christiaan Barnard performed the first successful human heart transplant in 1967. But it is also possible in some cases to transplant organs from other mammals into humans, a process called *xenotransplantation*. In 1984, a baboon heart was transplanted into a young girl with an irreparable heart defect, but her body eventually rejected the heart. Genetically altered pig organs may also someday be transplanted into humans. Valves from pig hearts have been used for many years to replace defective valves in human hearts.

A Scottish sheep named Dolly made headlines in 1997 when she became the first mammal to be successfully cloned. A *clone* is a genetic duplicate of an individual; essentially a delayed identical twin. Before Dolly, most geneticists suspected that every cell of an individual's body, from bone cells to skin cells, contains all of the DNA necessary to make a complete duplicate of that individual. But this wasn't certain until Dolly came along and proved what had been a widely accepted theory, but not a scientific fact.

One of the many ethical issues raised by the advent of cloning is the possibility that someone might create a clone to provide a "backup" supply of compatible blood and organs— just for emergencies. However, the impracticality of cloning, along with the enforcement of strict laws forbidding its practice in humans, should prevent such science-fiction scenarios from ever becoming reality. It is also likely that cloning could some-day be applied to the creation of individual organs suitable for transplant procedures, obviating the need to harvest organs from whole people.

Another prospect is the creation of artificial organs. The creation of artificial blood and organs has been a goal of medical research since at least the 1970s. Dr. Robert Jarvik has created several working artificial hearts that have been used to maintain the lives of people awaiting the availability of donor hearts. The Jarvik heart is a mechanical device, but it may soon be possible to grow living tissues and organs outside the body for later transplant.

By utilizing advanced electronic sensor technology and recent breakthroughs in our understanding of the physiology of vision, medical scientists are close to creating artificial eyes that could be directly linked into the brain's optic nerve. The prospects for replacing damaged brain tissue, however, are still fairly distant. It is nonetheless interesting to speculate on whether such implants would alter our perception of the world, or change our sense of what it means to be human.

Bacteriophages ("Phage"; *VGR*)

Starship Voyager Medical Log, Stardate 48536.1. Chief Medical Officer recording.

On an away mission in an asteroid field, Mister Neelix was assaulted by a race of aliens known as the Vidiians. Using a highly sophisticated transporter device, the Vidiians removed Mister Neelix's lungs for medical purposes. In an inspired stroke of genius, I improvised a set of holographic lungs that were able to support Neelix's respiratory function until a suitable transplant could be obtained.

The Vidiians ruthlessly harvest the organs of many species for transplantation. Their species suffers from an insidious and deadly virus they refer to simply as "the phage." The phage is invariably fatal and cannot be cured. It attacks various organs in the body in an apparently random fashion. The Vidiians have developed an extremely advanced cross-species organ transplantation technology that allows them to extend their lives by replacing phage-infected organs with healthy ones.

With the help of the Vidiians, I was able to transplant a lung from Kes, an Ocampan, into Mister Neelix, a Talaxian, probably the first successful organ transplant between these two species.

The term *phage* is short for *bacteriophage*. The term "phage" itself literally means "to eat." A bacteriophage is a *virus* that reproduces within a bacterium. They live at the expense of the bacteria they inhabit, and in most cases eventually kill their bacterial hosts (essentially by eating them).

Depending on how you look at it, a virus is either the most complex nonliving material known to science, or the simplest

The Doctor (Robert
Picardo) knows that
his superior surgical
skills will assure
Kes's (Jennifer Lien)
recovery.
ROBBIE ROBINSON.

living organism known to science. Viruses occupy a sort of twilight region between living and nonliving matter, requiring the genetic machinery of a host cell in order to reproduce.

A virus consists of fragments of DNA and/or RNA molecules wrapped in a thin skin of protein molecules. The outer protein coating is designed to mimic the shape of large protein molecules that various cells require for their sustenance. Like the Trojan horse, the virus fools a cell into allowing it inside the cell membrane. Once inside the cell, the virus uses the host cell's nutrients, enzymes, ribosomes, and other materials to make copies of itself. A virus is completely incapable of reproducing itself outside a living cell.

Retroviruses, such as the virus that causes AIDS, are particularly aggressive and deadly. Retroviruses contain an enzyme, called *reverse transcriptase*, that can copy the RNA sequences of the virus into the DNA of the host cell, creating a gene within the host cell that is coded to produce the RNA of the retrovirus.

Cross-species transplantation or xenotransplantation has already had some success. The study of bacterial viruses, incidentally, provided some of our earliest insights into the structure and function of DNA.

Mutated T cells
("Genesis"; *TNG*)

Starship Enterprise Medical Log, Stardate 47668.4. Chief Medical Officer Beverly Crusher recording.

A synthetic T cell, created to treat an influenza infection in Lieutenant Reginald Barclay, interacted with an anomaly in Mister Barclay's genetic structure, and mutated into a virulent airborne pathogen.

This pathogen had the incredible facility of activating introns in the crew's DNA, leading to the expression of physical characteristics of distant evolutionary ancestors.

Fortunately, Lieutenant Commander Data was able to engineer a retrovirus that neutralized the pathogen and eventually suppressed the features coded by the introns.

A number of *Star Trek* episodes have pitted the crew against some deadly form of radiation or microbe. The *immune system* is the body's line of defense against viral and bacterial invasion. It also fights the growth of cancerous cells and various natural and artificial toxins.

An *antigen* is any chemical substance that triggers an immune response, causing the body to create antibodies that will attack the antigen. *Antibodies* are protein molecules that are tailored to react with specific chemical groups on the surfaces of antigens. An antibody fits a site on an antigen like a key in a lock, neutralizing the antigen's ability to cause harm to the body. Antibodies are created by special white blood cells, found in the blood and lymphatic tissue, called *B cells*.

T cells, another type of white blood cell, can launch cellular attacks on foreign invaders. They can differentiate into six kinds of cells and each plays a crucial role in the immune system:

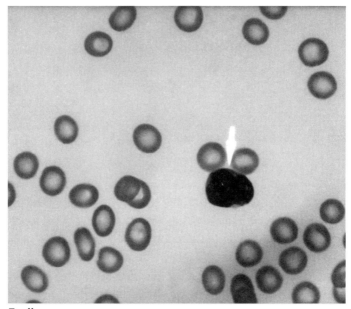

T cells. COURTESY DR. JOHN GLASSCO.

Killer or *cytotoxic T cells* attach themselves to invading cells and secrete various chemical agents (called lymphokines) that attack the foreign cells in a variety of ways.

Helper T cells work with B cells to increase production of antibodies.

Suppressor T cells temper the immune response in the wake of an infection, and prevent *autoimmune responses*, where the body begins to mistakenly attack its own tissues.

Memory T cells remember earlier infections, and maintain a vigilant watch for the recurrence of previously encountered antigens; if the antigen ever enters the system again, the immune system can mount a much swifter counterattack—this is why a person who's had, for example, the measles will probably not show symptoms even if they are infected again.

Amplifier T cells prod suppressor and helper T cells into increased levels of production.

Delayed Hypersensitivity T cells secrete lymphokines that play important roles in allergic reactions; they're also responsible for the "tissue rejection" response that frequently accompanies transplantation procedures.

In addition to these cells, cells called *macrophages* and *plasma cells* also play important roles in the proper functioning of the immune system.

The fight against infectious diseases took a great leap forward in the late eighteenth century when the physician Edward Jenner noticed that a number of women who regularly milked cows rarely contracted smallpox. Cows sometimes suffer from a disease called cowpox, which is often deadly to cows, but causes only a mild reaction in humans. The cowpox virus, however, is biochemically similar to the smallpox virus. Jenner realized that exposure to cowpox was immunizing the milkmaids against smallpox. Some eighty years later Louis Pasteur discovered that injecting animals with a weakened form of a virus protected those animals against that virus.

Vaccines typically consist of chemically crippled segments of viruses and/or bacteria. Injected into the bloodstream, even a dead or disabled virus triggers an immune response. Memory T cells then retain the plan of attack needed to defeat the virus should it ever enter the body. Vaccination programs have eradicated diseases, like smallpox (which has been completely eliminated) and polio, which have killed millions of people in the past.

"Genesis" was basically a horror story, and as such was very difficult to rationalize in purely scientific terms. For one thing, T cells are too heavy to float through the air as an airborne pathogen. Clearly the idea that Commander Riker and other crew members could devolve into primitive human ancestors and then be returned to their normal healthy selves within a few hours is a little hard to believe. In these stories we always try to find a grain of real science that can serve as a springboard for the bizarre events that unfold.

Introns are segments of DNA that seem to serve no obvious, useful purpose in a cell; they don't code for protein production or assist in cell replication. Some (but by no means all) scientists think that a few introns may be segments of DNA left over from earlier stages of human evolution. This idea immediately suggests a wonderful if horrific story: what if some sort of virus activated certain introns that coded for important cell structures in human ancestors millions of years ago?

Immortality
("The Omega Glory"; *TOS*)

Starship Enterprise **Medical Log, Stardate 3484.4. Chief Medical Officer Leonard McCoy recording.**

The Enterprise *has discovered the missing* U.S.S. Excelsior *orbiting the Class-M planet Omega IV. All hands aboard the ship were found dead, victims of an unknown biological agent.*

On the planet's surface, we located the Excelsior*'s captain, Ronald Tracey. Tracey believed he had discovered a fountain of youth on Omega IV, where the life span of the native humanoid population is on the order of one thousand years. Tracey believed that biological weapon researchers on Omega IV many centuries ago had stumbled across a biogenic substance that profoundly reduces the rate of cellular decay. What Captain Tracey failed to recognize is that the current inhabitants of Omega IV are descendents of the survivors of a terrible biological war that only spared individuals with an existing biological predisposition for longevity.*

Human beings in industrialized nations, on average, live around seventy-five years (women generally live a few years longer than men). Is there any way to increase the average life span? Why do people physically deteriorate over time in the first place?

Medical researchers are closing in on an answer to the second question. There appears to be a gene, nicknamed the "suicide" gene, that is activated in order to terminate cell growth. Some cells seemed to be designed to divide and reproduce a certain number of times. The control of cell growth is an important function of every cell; when cell reproduction proceeds in an uncontrolled fashion, cancer is often the result (cancer is in fact defined in terms of uncontrolled cell reproduction). Cells also simply "wear down" over time, like any complex machinery that operates continuously.

Whether it might be possible to control the so-called suicide gene and the other factors that manage the healthy reproduction of cells is still an open question. Some medical researchers believe that no matter how much we learn about genetics and cell reproduction, the human body is only capable of maintaining its health for a bit more than a hundred years, under ideal circumstances. A woman in France recently passed away at the age of 122, but no one has been documented to live longer. Still, medical scientists have made tremendous progress in understanding the factors that can make however many years a person lives healthy and productive.

some remarkable new *composite* materials that may someday be up to the task.

Scientists are often inspired by designs in nature when they attempt to create new materials. Biological evolution has produced a number of remarkably strong but lightweight materials in the plant world. Bamboo is one such material (the people of Korea have a saying that the ideal man is like bamboo: strong but flexible). Bamboo achieves its combination of strength and flexibility with bundles of long, thin organic fibers stretched throughout its length.

Composites are materials made up of two or more separate materials, combined in a way that makes a new material stronger than either of the component materials alone. One of the strongest classes of materials available today is metal-matrix composites. In a metal-matrix composite, thin fibers or "whiskers" of a material such as silicon carbide are embedded in matrices of aluminum and magnesium alloys. The fibers increase the strength and high-temperature stability of the alloys. Metal-matrix composite materials are currently used in missile guidance systems and other applications.

The hardest substance known to materials science is, of course, diamond. It seems likely that someday soon diamond fibers will be synthesized and embedded in metal matrices. Perhaps *Star Trek*'s tritanium could be created by embedding diamond fibers in a matrix comprised of a titanium alloy. Such a composite would almost certainly have exceptionally robust mechanical and thermal properties, and conceivably even meet the demands of twenty-fourth–century spacecraft designers.*

---

*Just to be safe, the *Enterprise* and other starships feature a "structural integrity field" that maintains the hull's rigidity under extreme stress. An inertial damping field protects the crew against the extreme accelerations required to reach warp speeds.

Pergium ("Devil in the Dark"; *TOS*)

Starship Enterprise Engineering Log, Stardate 3199.8. Chief Engineer Montgomery Scott recording.

Operations on the Janus VI mining colony were interrupted by a silicon-based life-form that calls itself a Horta (see the Enterprise *Science Log, Stardate 3196.1, for more information). Damage to the colony's environmental-control system was severe. I was able to improvise a temporary oxygen-pumping mechanism using spares from the* Enterprise *environmental-control system. The colony's carbon dioxide scrubber was damaged but serviceable, and maintained atmospheric carbon dioxide levels within acceptable parameters. The main environmental-control unit was recovered after Science Officer Spock successfully initiated communication with the Horta.*

Janus VI is extraordinarily rich in a wide variety of rare earth elements and exotic minerals, truly a geologist's paradise. It is the principal source of pergium for planets throughout this part of the galaxy.

Problems with environmental-control systems have played a role in several *Star Trek* episodes. Survival in space, or on planets with poisonous atmospheres, will depend on mechanisms that can generate oxygen for astronauts to breathe, remove the carbon dioxide they exhale, and maintain comfortable temperatures.

Manned spacecraft carry tanks of liquid oxygen for breathing air, and use carbon dioxide "scrubbers" to remove exhaled CO_2. On longer-duration space missions, such as a human mission to Mars, it will be necessary to recycle air and water to minimize the mass of consumable materials launched from Earth. NASA and other space organizations are busy developing

Kirk (William Shatner) and Spock (Leonard Nimoy) fire their phasers at the Horta, unaware that they are attacking an intelligent being.

Closed-Environment Life Support Systems (CELSS). CELSS technology mimics the Earth's ecosystem. Carbon dioxide exhaled by astronauts is absorbed by plants, which convert it into oxygen, which the astronauts breathe. The plants can also be used to supplement the astronaut's food supply, further reducing the amount of nonrecyclable supplies needed for the mission. The ultimate goal of CELSS technology is to recycle all the air, food, water, and waste products consumed and generated by astronauts on long-duration space missions.

Transparent Aluminum
(Star Trek IV: The Voyage Home)

Starship Enterprise Engineering Log, Stardate 8399.4. Chief Engineer Montgomery Scott recording.

During our mission to retrieve a pair of humpback whales from twentieth-century Earth, it was imperative that I procure materials with sufficient strength to construct a watertight enclosure within the cargo bay of our borrowed Klingon bird-of-prey. Doctor McCoy and I located a rather charming polymer manufacturing facility in San Francisco that stocked a "plexiglass" material suitable for our purposes. In order to obtain the needed quantity of plexiglass, however, I had to give the facility manager something in return. After an intense discussion with Doctor McCoy, I decided to provide the gentleman with the formulation matrix for transparent aluminum. I haven't had the courage to review the Federation history database to find out if my plexiglass-making friend was ever able to synthesize it.

When light strikes a solid surface, some of that light is reflected, some of it is absorbed, and some of it is transmitted (i.e., passes through). Most of the visible light that strikes a thin sheet of glass is transmitted, and glass is therefore transparent.

Metals of any appreciable thickness are not transparent. Most of the light that strikes a metal surface is reflected, and the rest is absorbed. Interestingly, metals are opaque for the same reason they are good conductors of electricity. The outermost electrons of the atoms in a metal are largely free to move about within the metal. These electrons are the carriers of electric current within metals. When photons of light strike a metal surface, their energy is easily absorbed and re-emitted by the

Conclusive proof that Earth's time line was contaminated by visitors from the future: Dr. Nichols (Alex Henteloff), the inventor of the transparent aluminum matrix, is pictured with Dr. McCoy (DeForest Kelley) and Captain Scott (James Doohan). BRUCE BIRMELIN.

free-roaming electrons. Aluminum makes a particularly good reflecting surface. Most telescope mirrors, in fact, are made from finely polished glass coated with a thin layer of aluminum.

Nevertheless, it's not impossible that a transparent form of aluminum could someday be fabricated. It would be necessary to find a stable configuration of aluminum atoms that would strongly bind the metal's outermost electrons, preventing them from roaming throughout the matrix and knocking back incoming photons. It follows that transparent aluminum would not be a good conductor of electricity.

As our understanding of the physics of solid matter increases, it will one day (perhaps soon) be possible to design materials "atom by atom." Starting with a list of required properties (such as tensile strength, ductility, electrical conductivity, density, and so forth) materials scientists will be able to determine the chemical structure of materials that possess the desired qualities, and then synthesize that substance.

Bioneural Gel Packs
("Caretaker"; *VGR*)

Starship Voyager Personal Log, Stardate 48325.6. B'Elanna Torres recording.

Following Voyager's abduction to the Delta Quadrant by an immensely powerful alien being calling itself the Caretaker, we have begun the task of integrating the Starfleet and Maquis crews and repairing the extensive damage suffered by Voyager.

Despite my absolute opposition to becoming a member of the crew of this ship, I must admit the bioneural gel packs that process navigational data are an intriguing technology. The packs are constructed of artificially generated neural fibers, composed of a variety of complex polymers, with multiple interconnections. Each neural fiber is structured like a humanoid neuron, with a body that fans out into several hundred dendritic subfibers suspended within a biomimetic gel matrix. In a given gel pack, billions of interconnections are possible among the thousands of bioneural fibers, thus creating a massively parallel computing architecture many times more efficient than standard duotronic and multitronic circuitry.

One of the most promising and rapidly advancing areas of computer science research is the field of neural-network computing.

Most computers today are commonly built around a single *central processing unit (cpu)*. The central processor is essentially the "brain" of the computer, performing all of the calculations and logic operations required by the programs the computer is running. The cpu is also a "performance bottleneck" in the sense that the rate at which data or information can flow in and out of the computer is limited by the speed of the cpu. Because of this centralized architecture, computers solve problems and perform calculations in a serial, or linear manner: that is, one single step at a time.

954 || BIONEURAL GEL PACK

DOUG DREXLER

Computer scientists have recognized for a long time that a system designed with a *parallel architecture* could perform many kinds of calculations much more quickly. For example, if a mathematical problem could be divided into a subset of say sixteen separate calculations, each of these separate calculations could be performed by one of many individual processors that combine their results to achieve the final solution to the problem. For some tasks, such as image processing (i.e., enhancing photographic images to improve their appearance or clarify subtle detail), parallel architectures are much more suitable than the traditional central processor approach.

Neural-network computing attempts to emulate the architecture of the human brain with its myriad *neurons* and their complex interconnections. The typical human brain contains some one hundred billion neurons—we have in our heads almost as many neurons as there are stars in the Milky Way. A neuron consists of a bulbous cell from which a long fiber (called an *axon*) extends. The axon branches into several hundred to several thousand *dendrites* that are connected (via *synapses*) to the dendrites of other neurons. This vast and complex array of neurons conducts the electrical signals that underlie all of the activities of the human brain.

Some computer scientists think it may someday soon be possible to create electronic chips that can interface directly with the human brain, potentially providing a user with instant knowledge about any subject and limitless memory.

6. Space Engineering

"The man with a new idea is a crank

—until the idea succeeds."

—Mark Twain

Cloaking Device
("Balance of Terror"; *TOS*)

Starship Enterprise Science Log, Stardate 1711.6. Science Officer Spock recording.

For the first time in nearly a hundred years, a Federation star-ship has encountered a ship from the Romulan Star Empire.

The Romulans are a passionate, sometimes violent culture, steeped in a centuries-old martial tradition. Their warbird-class starships are equipped with a cloaking technology that renders them invisible, presumably through a process involving the selective bending of light—a process which would require a great deal of energy. Sensor readings can establish the general location of a cloaked ship, but a weapons-lock is virtually impossible.

O*ptics* is the science of light. Reflection and refraction are the principal means of focusing light with mirrors and lenses. Optical scientists often consider beams of light as bundles of linear *rays*. Refraction changes the direction of a light ray. A simple, convex glass lens changes the direction of a light ray by virtue of its shape and the fact that the speed of light within glass is different from the speed of light in air or in a vacuum.

The Romulan warbird in "Balance of Terror" presumably used some kind of force field to bend light around the ship in such a way that it was impossible to see the ship itself (see figure). We know today that gravity bends light, but it takes a very strong gravitational field—such as the gravitational field of a black hole—to bend light to a significant degree. Our Sun, the most massive object in our solar system, barely bends a passing beam of light one thousandth of a degree.

A combination of geometry and special materials is used to

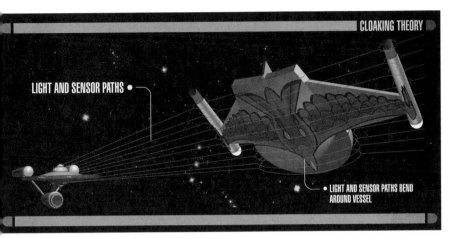

render the U.S. B2 stealth bomber virtually invisible to radar. Composite materials and special coatings in the plane's fuselage and wings absorb much of an incoming radar wave. The unusual shape of the aircraft deflects any residual radar return signal away from the aircraft.

No stealth system is perfect, of course, but the B2 aircraft and its fighter-plane cousin, the F117 Nighthawk, are all but undetectable by present-day radar. The planes are, however, readily visible in daytime; that's why current stealth aircraft are limited to flying night missions. The U.S. Air Force is investigating coatings that might make an aircraft "blend in" with a variety of daytime background scenes. Special "electrochromic" paints change optical properties with the application of electric currents. Like a chameleon, an aircraft with an electrochromic paint job could be programmed to take on the color of the sky, cloud cover, or underlying ground cover (trees, water, sand, etc.), rendering the plane very hard to see in daylight. Combined with current stealth technology, such an aircraft would be extremely difficult to detect visually or by radar.

Thinking Machines
("The Ultimate Computer"; *TOS*)

Starship Enterprise **Science Log, Stardate 4733.1. Science Officer Spock recording.**

Trial runs of Doctor Richard Daystrom's M-5 multitronic computer have ended in tragedy, resulting in the deaths of four hundred seven Starfleet crew members.

The M-5 multitronic unit is, however, an extraordinary if flawed leap forward in computer engineering. By impressing his own neural engrams into the computer circuitry, Doctor Daystrom has devised a means of mimicking the multitudinous interconnections among neurons characteristic of the human brain.

In the first two weeks of May 1997, World Chess Champion Garry Kasparov was challenged to a chess match by the creators of Deep Blue, an IBM chess-playing computer capable of evaluating two hundred million chess moves per second. In the last game of a grueling six-game match, the IBM machine defeated Kasparov (beating him two games to one; the other three games ended in draws), marking the first time a computer has beaten a world chess champion.

Deep Blue is an example of a computer with a *parallel processing* architecture. Unlike a standard home computer, which contains just one microprocessor, Deep Blue contains an array of microprocessors, each with its own memory chip. Each processor is electronically connected to all of the other processors. Deep Blue's chess-playing program was specially designed to take maximum advantage of this state-of-the-art computer architecture, which essentially combines the power of many computers into a single machine.

The M-5 computer represents a major failure for the visionary scientist Dr. Richard Daystrom.

Some people see Deep Blue's victory as a defeat for humans. Many wonder what "uniquely human" capability computers will outdo us at next. But is a computer that beats a world chess champion at his own game really intelligent? Ultimately, it depends on how you define intelligence. The fact that human beings use their intelligence to play a game of chess doesn't mean that a computer that can play chess is intelligent. Humans also use their intelligence to multiply two numbers, but an abacus can do that, more quickly than most people. We don't therefore conclude that the abacus is intelligent.

Deep Blue was programmed by very clever human beings to play chess in a manner that is probably very different from how Garry Kasparov or anybody else plays chess. It is a remarkable achievement of technology, but it does not constitute the demonstration of human intelligence in a machine. Another important distinction is that Deep Blue was *programmed* to play chess; it had no choice about playing Kasparov, and no passion for the game. Unlike humans, computers have no will or volition. They simply do what they are programmed to do.

It should also be noted that there are many different kinds of intelligence. Michael Jordan is perhaps the most extraordinary basketball player who ever lived. His physical prowess on the court is not just a matter of muscles and reflexes; it's also a matter of intelligence. Jordan's brain and mind are actively involved in every move, every decision he makes on the court. His mind coordinates and shapes his athletic skill. This is no less an expression of genius than Kasparov's extraordinary ability at chess, and is not diminished by the fact that we can build machines that are stronger or can move faster than Michael Jordan.

Could we ever prove a computer program is conscious in the same way you and I are? This question leads to another question: What exactly is consciousness? Neuroscientists have made extraordinary progress in the last few years in understanding the functioning of the human brain, but the nature and origin of consciousness remain elusive.

Asteroid Starship ("For the World is Hollow, And I Have Touched the Sky"; *TOS*)

Starship Enterprise **Engineering Log, Stardate 5485.3. Chief Engineer Montgomery Scott recording.**

After successfully deflecting an attack by a barrage of crude thermonuclear missiles, the Enterprise *has discovered a starship constructed out of an S-class asteroid some two hundred kilometers in diameter.*

Traveling under fusion power at sublight speed, the asteroid ship Yonada *was constructed some ten thousand years ago by the Fabrini civilization. It was designed as a multigeneration ship, and is presently occupied by some ten thousand inhabitants who are completely oblivious to the fact that they are living inside a hollow sphere.*

The possible colonization of asteroids has been considered since the dawn of the space age. Unlike planets, asteroids are too small to retain atmospheres; their gravity simply isn't strong enough to keep atmospheric gases close to their surfaces. Some asteroids are, however, rich in minerals and resources that would be extremely useful in building enclosed habitats, perhaps in caves or tunnels beneath the asteroid's surface. There are even a few asteroids that appear to harbor a wealth of precious metals, such as platinum.

A colonized asteroid could in principle be equipped with a propulsion system that would send it on a trajectory out of the solar system. Fuel for propulsion, along with other materials needed to sustain the colony, would be derived from the asteroid itself. A suitably engineered asteroid would be like a small planet, self-contained and self-supporting.

Comets may be better candidates for human colonies than asteroids because they contain, on average, a higher proportion of organic matter and volatile substances that would be useful for maintaining a biosphere.

Unlike the asteroid ship of this episode, asteroid colonies constructed with present-day engineering techniques would not feature surface gravity comparable to Earth. Jenny Craig take note: On the surface of a typical asteroid people would weigh in at just a percent or two of their weights on Earth. Alternatively, an asteroid could be hollowed out to create a large cylindrical cavity. Rotating the asteroid about the long axis of the cavity would provide artificial gravity at any desired level on the inner surface of the cavity.

Suspended Animation ("Space Seed"; *TOS*)

Starship Enterprise Science Log, Stardate 3145.3. Science Officer Spock recording.

The Enterprise *has recovered a remarkable group of people from Earth's distant past.*

Led by Khan Noonien Singh, one of the last despots of Earth's late-twentieth–century Eugenics Wars, the group of ninety-four genetically enhanced men and women were traveling through space in suspended animation in a DY-100-class interplanetary freighter. The fact of their survival over the course of more than two centuries, as well as their audacity in attempting interstellar flight in such a primitive vehicle, speaks of great physical resiliency and perhaps reckless courage.

The landing party is amazed that the *Botany Bay*'s passengers are still alive.

Many animals, such as bears, hibernate during winter months, waiting out the freezing winter weather in underground burrows until the first thaw of spring. During hibernation, the animal's blood pressure, heart and respiration rates, and glandular activity drop to extremely low levels, allowing the animal to survive for months on whatever body fat and fluids they've stored prior to entering the dormant state.

Some animals literally freeze in winter, including certain species of frogs. When the frogs thaw out in early spring, their hearts begin beating to pump blood into their extremities, gradually warming the rest of their bodies until they are completely revived.

These examples of hibernation in nature have led researchers to speculate about whether it might be possible to induce a hibernationlike state in humans, for the purpose of long-duration spaceflight or suspending critical medical conditions that can't receive immediate attention. The question naturally arises, Would we need to freeze humans on long space voyages?

Contrary to what some might think, boredom would probably not be a serious problem on long space missions. Astronauts have plenty of work and research to do aboard a spacecraft. On a nine-month voyage to Mars, for example, hundreds of experiments and observations could be performed en route to the final destination, and at least some fraction of the crew would need to be kept awake to maintain the ship and deal with emergency situations.

On the other hand, placing some of the crew in hibernation would conserve crucial resources, such as air, water, and food. The more supplies a spacecraft needs to carry to sustain its crew, the more massive the spacecraft becomes; hence, more fuel is needed to get the spacecraft wherever it's going. The cost of space missions tends to increase exponentially with the mass of the spacecraft; therefore, astronautical engineers are constantly looking for ways to minimize the mass of spacecraft.

An odd twist to the idea of suspended animation is *cryonic suspension*. A number of people around the world have chosen to have their bodies frozen in liquid nitrogen immediately after death, in the hopes that someday medical science will find a way to revive them and cure them of whatever ailments led to their demises. The big problem with freezing human tissue is that water, unlike virtually all other substances, actually expands by a small amount upon freezing. This has the effect of rupturing cells (which are mostly composed of water) when they freeze, creating massive amounts of cellular damage that we currently have no way of reversing. Frostbite is an example of the kind of damage that cells experience when they are frozen. Frogs that hibernate in a frozen state appear to circulate a natural "antifreeze" agent, consisting of special kinds of proteins that prevents ice crystals from growing to the point that they disrupt cells.

Stratos
("The Cloud Minders"; *TOS*)

Starship Enterprise Engineering Log, Stardate 5822.4. Chief Engineer
Montgomery Scott recording.

*I've just spent the afternoon inspecting the antigraviton emit-
ters that maintain Stratos over two kilometers above the surface of Ardana. I must say they are an impressive piece of work.
The critical balance of the emitter matrix is maintained by a network of active sensors that automatically compensate for
changes in Stratos's mass and thermal density.*

The idea of artificial gravity has been popular in science fiction since H.G.Wells's classic novel *The First Men in the
Moon*. In that novel, a material that repelled gravity, called
cavorite, had been discovered by a scientist working alone in an
isolated laboratory. He soon fashioned a pressurized metal
sphere and coated it with cavorite. Special shutters kept the
cavorite covered, in effect "insulating" it from gravity. When the
shutters were opened the cavorite was exposed, and the antigravity effect hurled the sphere into space.

The notion of a ship with an antigravity coating is intriguing
but unlikely. But is it possible that there is some kind of antigravity force in nature? Dr. Ning Li, a physicist at the University
of Alabama, has recently discovered an interesting effect
involving *superconducting* materials, which are materials that
under some conditions (typically very low temperatures) lose
all resistance to the flow of electrical current. Dr. Li noticed that
when a certain class of superconductors was suspended over a
magnet, an extra repulsive effect would be observed in addition
to the normal magnetic repulsion. She has tentatively concluded that the superconductor might somehow be shielding gravi-

ty to a small degree, essentially an antigravity effect. NASA is currently investigating this phenomenon as part of its Advanced Space Transportation Program, but the research is not expected to produce an antigravity drive in the foreseeable future.

Many years ago the visionary designer and engineer Buckminster Fuller conceived of a floating city he called Cloud Nine. Fuller realized that a geodesic steel sphere about a kilometer and a half in diameter contained a volume of air about one thousand times more massive than the mass of the steel required to construct the sphere. If the air inside the sphere were even one degree warmer than the outside air, the sphere would float. Buildings could be constructed inside the sphere and still not increase the mass of the entire structure beyond the level of buoyancy. According to Fuller's calculations, the warmth generated by people and industrial processes would be sufficient to heat the interior air enough to float the sphere-city like a gigantic balloon. The steel sphere wouldn't need to be solid, either; a properly-fashioned steel frame would float just as well as a solid steel sphere, as long as it could maintain an internal air temperature and pressure higher than its surroundings.

Dyson Sphere ("Relics"; *TNG*)

Starship *Enterprise* Engineering Log, Stardate 46128.4. Chief Engineer Geordi La Forge recording.

I never thought I'd live to see it, but there it is, a Dyson Sphere.

We discovered the sphere when we responded to a distress call from the U.S.S. Jenolen, *an old-style transport vessel that crashed into the sphere in the year 2295. Amazingly, one per-*

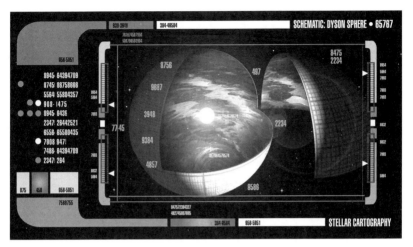

son survived the crash: the legendary Montgomery Scott, who was the chief engineer of the original Federation Starship Enterprise.

The Dyson Sphere is one of the most ambitious space-engineering projects imaginable. Conceived by the visionary twentieth-century physicist Freeman Dyson, a Dyson Sphere would essentially enclose a volume of space perhaps 150 million kilometers in radius with a spherical shell, or alternatively, an open framework. The enclosure would be centered on a star like our Sun and constructed out of materials mined from asteroids, moons, and perhaps even entire planets. Even though the total mass of asteroids, moons, and planets is small compared to the mass of a star, there is more than enough material in our solar system to build a thin shell 150 million kilometers in radius.

The entire structure would rotate, providing artificial gravity through centrifugal force along the inside surface of the sphere. Once the sphere reached the desired rate of rotation, it would, for the most part, keep rotating without the action of an outside force (friction between the outer surface of the sphere and interplanetary gas and dust would tend to reduce the rate of rotation, requiring occasional boosts from thrusters attached to the sphere). Dr. Dyson has suggested that infrared telescopes might be able to detect the unique thermal radiation signature that a Dyson Sphere would radiate. Science-fiction writer Larry Niven has proposed a variation on the Dyson Sphere: a solid ring around a star, 150 million or so kilometers in radius and several thousand kilometers wide, with a wall on each side perhaps 250 kilometers tall to keep the atmosphere from spilling out into space (Niven explores this idea in detail in his *Ringworld* novels).

Dr. Dyson was also a member of a team of scientists at Los Alamos National Laboratory in New Mexico that conceived one of the first nuclear-powered spacecraft designs. Project Orion proposed a rocket that would be propelled by a series of atomic bombs detonated behind it. A "pusher plate" attached to the stern of the spacecraft would recoil with each explosion, pushing the rocket forward. Dyson's group demonstrated that such a scheme could provide a spacecraft with a steady acceleration. A scale model of the Orion rocket—using conventional explosives—was successfully tested in the early 1950s. In the 1960s, NASA built and successfully tested a nuclear rocket engine based on the fission-reactor designs used in nuclear power plants across the world, but no one has yet built and launched into space a rocket powered by nuclear engines.

Solar Sails ("Explorers"; *DS9*)

Deep Space 9 Personal Log, Stardate 48812.1. Commander Benjamin Sisko recording.

I can't fight it any longer. I'm losing too much sleep imagining how they might have done it. The only way to know for sure is to try.

I've ordered the basic materials from a Bajoran supply depot. They will arrive at the station tomorrow morning.

Making use of local resources for transportation has been the key to human exploration of the Earth. Wood-burning locomotives crossing the American West in the nineteenth century were rarely without fuel: When the fuel supply ran out, engineers simply had to stop the train and cut more wood. Sailing ships, of course, utilize the power of trade winds to cross the oceans.

The difficulty and expense of space travel could be greatly reduced if it weren't necessary for spacecraft to carry their own rocket fuel. Spacecraft powered by *solar sails* would take advantage of the largest source of free energy in our solar system: the Sun. The idea of the solar sail is generally credited to Russian engineer Friedrich Tsander, who described the basic concept in 1924. The Sun continuously generates light and heat through the process of *nuclear fusion*. Although it's far too weak to feel, the momentum of photons of light striking a surface imparts a small force, called *radiation pressure*. The Sun also produces the *solar wind*, a stream of charged particles flowing away from the Sun in all directions. Solar sails would consist of ultrathin sheets of aluminum-coated *Mylar* or some other strong but lightweight material, stretching hundreds to thousands of meters across. Radiation pressure from the Sun would push on the sail, in much the same way that wind push-

Sisko proves that his
solar ship can make
it to Cardassia Prime.
ROBBIE ROBINSON.

es on the sail of a boat, providing a gentle but persistent acceleration.

The acceleration produced by a solar sail would be very small: on the order of perhaps a few millimeters per second. But because the Sun constantly radiates energy, the acceleration of the solar sail would be continuous. Over the course of several months, a few millimeters per second's worth of acceleration would impart a velocity of tens of kilometers per second to the sail and its payload—quite respectable for interplanetary travel.

Studies conducted in the early 1980s by the Jet Propulsion Laboratory in Pasadena, California, determined that a square sail eight hundred meters on a side would have been sufficient to propel a fifteen hundred-kilogram spacecraft from Earth orbit to a rendezvous with Halley's Comet during its 1986 visit to the inner solar system. The United States, unfortunately, choose not to launch a spacecraft to Halley's Comet, and a solar sail–powered spacecraft has yet to be built.

The acceleration of a solar sail could be greatly increased by beaming power from Earth's orbit or the Moon directly at the sail. Giant masers or lasers, focused on the sail, could impart significant velocity to a solar sail in a matter of weeks or days.

The pioneering ethnologist Thor Heyerdahl demonstrated how ancient peoples might have sailed the Pacific in extremely simple boats. With five other men, Heyerdahl sailed from Peru to Polynesia in 1947 in a one-sail raft (the *Kon-Tiki*) constructed of balsa wood, demonstrating in a convincing manner that ancient Polynesians could have originated in South America rather than Southeast Asia. He later sailed from Africa to the Americas in a boat made out of papyrus, the plant used by ancient Egyptians to create a paper-like material. The Siskos' expedition is very much in the spirit of Heyerdahl's remarkable voyages.

Space Elevator ("Rise!"; *VGR*)

Starship Voyager **Engineering Log, Stardate 50821.7. Chief Engineer B'Elanna
Torres recording.**

*Mister Neelix has managed to repair an orbital tether system on
Nezu colony, saving the lives of Security Chief Tuvok and several inhabitants of the planet as well as his own.*

    *Rising some eighty thousand kilometers above the planet's
surface, the tether was primarily designed to transport cargo to
synchronous orbit.*

The concept of the "space elevator" was developed in 1960
by the Russian engineer Y.N. Artsutanov. The basic idea is
simple. If a column were to be constructed at the Earth's equator, extending all the way up to *geosynchronous orbit*, any
object that climbs to the top of the column will also be in geosynchronous orbit. A gentle push is all that would be needed to
put that object into its own orbit around the Earth.

    To make the system stable in practice, the column would
need to be twice as tall as the distance from the Earth's surface
to orbit, plus the radius of the Earth, or about eighty thousand
kilometers. The column itself would essentially be a long cable
or tether. An anchor would be placed at the far end of the tether
to maintain tension. The anchor could be a near-Earth asteroid
corralled into orbit by thrusters strategically placed on the asteroid's surface. Once completed, pressurized cabins would be
attached to the column that would rise, like Jack climbing the
beanstalk, to the geosynchronous altitude. Spacecraft rising all
the way to the anchor at the far end of the tether could be
"flung" into other orbits, using the tether as a kind of slingshot.

    A working space elevator would dramatically lower the cost
of getting payloads into Earth's orbit, dropping eventually to

pennies per pound (the cost of getting a pound of payload to low-Earth's orbit on the space shuttle is currently about $10,000). Once the tether and supporting systems are built, the only cost associated with getting into orbit is the cost of the electricity needed to raise the pressurized cabins. Most of that electricity could actually be regenerated when the cabin returns to Earth. The biggest engineering challenge in building a space elevator would be to create a cable that had enough *tensile strength* to support its own weight plus the weight of the cable car. Remember, the cable will be eighty thousand kilometers long. If you've ever tried to lift a big coil of heavy rope, like the rope used to moor a ship to a dock, you know just how heavy a strong rope can be. Until very recently, no one had any idea whether a material strong enough to create a working space elevator could be created.

But the discovery of a unique form of carbon may someday make space elevators possible. In the 1980s, several researchers independently discovered a molecule that consists of sixty carbon atoms arranged in a closed, soccerball-like

DOUG DREXLER

sphere. The carbon 60 molecules are called *Buckminsterfullerenes*, or Bucky Balls, after the inventor of the geodesic dome, Buckminster Fuller. A *carbonaceous asteroid* a couple of kilometers in diameter, brought to Earth to serve as a tether anchor, could probably provide all of the carbon necessary to construct an orbital tether. The tether could be created by automated machines on the asteroid and slowly spun down, like Rapunzel's hair, to the Earth's surface.

Dr. Richard Smalley, a researcher at Rice University, has recently discovered a way to assemble Bucky Balls into tubular structures that have enough tensile strength to support their own weight, and then some, even at lengths reaching thousands of kilometers. So far, these carbon 60 "nanotubes" can only be produced in very small quantities in the laboratory. But if engineers develop a technique to manufacture this material on a large scale, it may only be a matter of time before space elevators become a reality.

Terraforming ("Home Soil"; *TNG*)

Starship Enterprise Science Log, Stardate 41465.2 Second Officer Data recording.

The Enterprise, *responding to a sudden loss of communication with Starfleet engineers on Velara III, has discovered a silicon-based life-form inhabiting that planet.*

Communication with this life-form—which appears to consist of a self-aware network of silicon-based circuitry not unlike late-twentieth–century integrated circuit technology—has revealed that it is indigenous to Velara III. The presence of this life-form strictly forbids any substantial interference in the planet's natural environment and subsequent evolution. Captain Picard has therefore ordered that terraforming operations on Velara III be terminated. Also recommend Starfleet Headquarters immediately dispatch a cargo transport to remove all terraforming equipment for reassignment.

Star Trek has been exploring the concept of *terraforming* other worlds for a number of years. In *Star Trek II: The Wrath of Khan*, Dr. Carol Marcus and her son (by Captain Kirk), David, developed a machine, called the Genesis Device, that could actually transform inorganic matter into organic matter, presumably through some kind of nuclear chain reaction initiated by a fictional substance called "protomatter."

What might surprise some readers is that the technology to terraform other planets already exists, albeit in very crude form, today. A number of scientists and engineers have conceived of several ways that we might transform the planet Mars into an environment more suitable (if not ideal) for human habitation.

Mars in its present condition is a cold, dry place. It is the next planet out from the Sun, and takes just about two Earth years to make one complete orbit. The Martian day is just over twenty-four hours long; Mars has seasons like the Earth, and polar caps consisting of frozen water and carbon dioxide. The Martian atmosphere consists mostly of carbon dioxide, but the atmospheric pressure at the surface of Mars is only about one percent of the atmospheric pressure at sea level on Earth. On a summer day, near the equator, temperatures on Mars might reach a balmy ten or twenty degrees celsius. That same night, however, the temperature can plummet to 150 degrees below zero celsius, because the Martian atmosphere is too thin to retain much heat.

Plans for terraforming Mars involve schemes to thicken the planet's atmosphere. For example, some kind of coarse black dust could be spread across both polar caps. The dust would trap heat, warming the polar caps and causing them to sublimate. The additional carbon dioxide and water vapor would increase the density of the atmosphere and improve its ability to retain heat. This would eventually promote melting of underground permafrost (which seems to be plentiful in the Martian crust) providing even more water vapor for the atmosphere.

Other terraforming plans involve manufacturing *greenhouse gases* on the surface of Mars. Greenhouse gases are gases that are particularly effective at trapping heat. *Chlorofluorocarbons* are a class of greenhouse gases that were commonly used in aerosol sprays until their potentially detrimental effect on the Earth's atmosphere was recognized. Manufacturing vast quantities of chlorofluorocarbons on the surface of Mars could, over the course of many years, increase the temperature of the atmosphere and melt the polar caps, thickening and warming the Martian air. Genetically engineered microorganisms, designed to breathe in carbon dioxide, exhale oxygen, and survive in the harsh Martian climate, are also under study.

Granted that we will probably someday be able to terraform Mars and other planets, is it ethical to try to alter other worlds to suit our needs? Chances are life doesn't exist on the surface of Mars today, but what if there is some form of life beneath the Martian surface? It seems to me that if there is any form of life on Mars, no matter how humble, Mars should be left alone, for purely scientific if not ethical reasons. Even if we can prove that Mars is dead as a rusty doornail, I would hesitate to begin large-scale, uncontrolled experiments on its atmosphere. We really don't know what would happen to Mars if we melted its polar caps and thickened its atmosphere. We would be interfering in the evolution of a planet that has existed for nearly five billion years, a planet that, even if lifeless, is filled with geological wonders and scientific mysteries that could be threatened by terraforming.

On the other hand, life is precious. If Mars is dead, changing it into a world where life can thrive gives life one more chance to flourish in an otherwise cold and lonely universe. Sometime before the end of the twenty-first century, the prospect of terrraforming Mars will probably become a reality.

7. Exobiology

"There may be life in yonder dark, but it will

not wear the shape of man."

—Loren Eiseley, twentieth-century anthropologist

Humanoid Progenitors
("The Chase"; *TNG*)

Starship Enterprise Science Log, Stardate 46736.1. Second Officer Data
recording.

*A long-standing mystery of exobiology has been solved. For
nearly three hundred years, human scientists have wondered
why the Milky Way Galaxy is populated by so many humanoid
life-forms.*

*Considering the dynamics of evolution by natural selec-
tion—which appears to determine the evolution of life
throughout the galaxy—one would expect that bilaterally sym-
metrical life-forms, with two arms and two legs extending from
a central trunk, topped by a head containing the brain and pairs
of eyes and ears, would be relatively rare. And yet nature seems
to have favored this form again and again.*

*It is now clear that this is not a consequence of natural
selection, but the result of a deliberate "seeding" program initiated some four billion years ago by a humanoid species.
These ancient humanoids spread their own genetic material
among Class-M planets throughout the galaxy, in an effort to
guarantee the propagation of their genetic heritage.*

One of the features of the *Star Trek* universe that is particularly difficult to rationalize in terms of present-day
science is the prevalence of humanoid life-forms in our galaxy.
It seems that everywhere our starships turn, another alien,
strikingly similar in appearance to *Homo sapiens*, is poking his
or her nose into our business.

According to our present understanding of evolution, the
fact that humans have two arms and legs, ten fingers and toes,
and so forth is largely a matter of chance. It could have easily

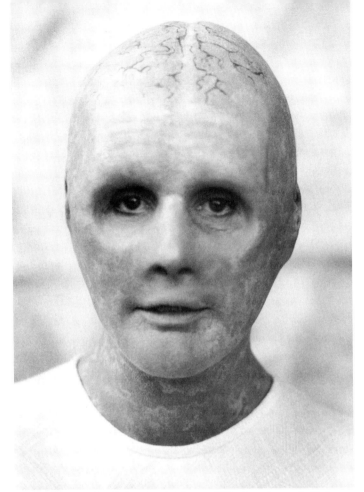

The ancient progenitor (Salome Jens) of humanoid life-forms is revealed to her descendants. ROBBIE ROBINSON.

been otherwise. The incredible diversity of life on Earth suggests that organisms evolving over billions of years in other planetary environments are going to be radically different in appearance and substance from life here.

The reason for so many humanoids on *Star Trek* is not a lack of imagination on the part of our writers, nor ignorance of the basic tenets of evolutionary biology. The simple fact is that human actors have to be hired to play alien roles, and there is only so much that the makeup department can do to make a human look like something else. Creating alien life-forms through special effects is another possibility, but it's extremely expensive and often unconvincing (although within a few years the cost of computer-generated special effects may become low enough to routinely create believable aliens that can be edited into live-action television film). *Star Trek* creator Gene Roddenberry discovered early in the development of the original series that an alien character seemed most "real" when the audience could see the eyes of the actor playing the alien.

The fossil record on Earth dating back a few million years contains a wide variety of forms resembling present day humans. Anthropologists consider the species *Homo habilis* to be the first "true" man, our earliest human ancestor. *Homo habilis* emerged some four million years ago, in an age when forest lands were receding around the world. They were forced to occupy the vast African savannas, filled with all manner of deadly predators as well as potentially nutritious prey. This environment placed a premium on the development of intelligence; given our ancestors' relative lack of natural defenses (sharp teeth and claws, for example), cunning and the ability to reason were crucial to their survival.

Some scientists argue that intelligence has evolved in the universe not by chance but by design. They point to the fact that if the various physical parameters of the stuff of the universe—the masses of the proton and other subatomic particles, the ratio of the strength of the electromagnetic force to the gravitational force, and so on—were even slightly different, atoms would never have been able to combine to form stars and planets and eventually beings with minds capable of wondering about their origins.

Bajorans ("Ensign Ro"; *TNG*)

Starship Enterprise Science Log, Stardate 45082.1. Second Officer Data recording.

On a mission to uncover Bajoran terrorists in the Valo system, the Enterprise *has acquired a Bajoran crew member, Ensign Ro Laren.*

The Bajorans are one of the oldest humanoid races in the galaxy. Their culture is steeped in an artistic tradition that has produced some of the most widely admired sculptures, paintings, and music in the galaxy. The Bajoran home world has recently been devastated by a decades-long occupation by the Cardassians.

In *The Original Series* episode, "The Paradise Syndrome," Kirk, Spock, and McCoy discover a race of Native Americans living on a planet hundreds of light-years from Earth. Spock eventually concludes that a race of aliens transplanted the Native Americans thousands of years earlier, and perhaps spread the human populations throughout the galaxy over the course of several hundreds of thousands of years (foreshadowing the theory developed in the *Star Trek: The Next Generation* episode "The Chase"). Minor physical variations among humanoid races, such as the differences between humans and Bajorans, would then be accounted for by the subsequent evolution of transplanted human groups in their new environments.

What exactly distinguishes humans from other forms of life on Earth? Our intelligence and mastery of technology is an obvious distinction, but there are other fairly intelligent species on Earth (chimpanzees and other primates, whales, and dolphins), and some other animals fashion and use simple tools. The more we learn about life on our planet, the more it seems that our similarities outweigh our differences. In fact, all life on Earth is built on the scaffolding of the same basic molecule: *deoxyribonucleic acid,* or *DNA.* The genes that determine our physical traits are segments of DNA molecules. Only a little more than one percent of human DNA is different from chimpanzee DNA; one could well argue, of course, that that one percent contains some pretty crucial information.

The differences between various subpopulations of humans are virtually insignificant from the perspective of fundamental biology, and yet those minor differences continue to account for much of the world's strife. The science-fiction writer Ray Bradbury once noted that if intelligent aliens were ever to visit Earth, the most important thing they could teach us is that this planet consists of six billion people wrapped in the same skin, and we had better start living that way.

Betazoids
("Encounter at Farpoint"; *TNG*)

Starship *Enterprise* Science Log, Stardate 41156.6. Second Officer Data recording.

The ship's counselor has come on board. Lieutenant Commander Deanna Troi is of mixed human and Betazoid heritage.

This is my first opportunity to study a member of the Betazoid species. Counselor Troi has been quite indulgent of my interest and many questions. I am particularly intrigued by Counselor Troi's empathic ability, as I have no capacity for experiencing emotion. For that reason, the counselor seems to find me to be something of an enigma.

The distinguishing characteristic of Betazoids is their telepathic ability. Counselor Troi, because she is only half Betazoid, has the ability to "read" other people's feelings, but not their thoughts. This is actually true to the origin of the word *telepathy*, which means to sense the feelings of others from a distance, not to read their thoughts.

In an episode of *Star Trek: The Next Generation* I suggested the use of the term *paracortex* to refer to the lobe of the Betazoid brain responsible for their telepathic abilities. It is a common belief that humans use only five or ten percent of their brain capacity. I'm not sure where or when this idea developed, but it has no foundation in fact. Neuroscientists recognize that there is a great deal of redundancy built into the human brain, but little if any of our gray matter goes unused. Virtually all researchers in the field of neurophysiology and cognitive science dismiss the notion that telepathic abilities are latent in some hidden corner of the human mind.

One would think that beings capable of telepathy would have some special structure in their brains, or perhaps some unusual sense organ, that could "tune in" to the electrochemical activity associated with emotions and thoughts—a kind of mental radar, so to speak. Telepathic abilities might evolve in alien species to enable parents to better care for their offspring by sensing their children's mental states and emotional needs.

Bolians ("Conspiracy"; *TNG*)

Starship Enterprise Science Log, Stardate 41785.4. Second Officer Data recording.

During our rendezvous at the planetoid Dytallix B, I had the opportunity to briefly meet Captain Rixx, commander of the U.S.S. Thomas Paine, *and a member of the Bolian species.*

Bolians are blue. Not unhappy, mind you—their skin is dis-tinctly blue in color.

Human beings exhibit a range of skin colors, depending on the level of the biochemical compound *melanin* in the skin. Melanin serves to protect the skin against ultraviolet radiation from the Sun, which can damage DNA in skin cells and lead to skin cancer (still one of the most common forms of cancer today). Humans whose ancestry derives largely from very sunny climes, such as the African continent, have dark skin because people with dark skin were much more likely to survive in those regions than people with lighter skin. People whose ancestors came from Northern Europe, on the other hand, tend to be light-skinned because high melanin content isn't particularly benefi-cial there.

Blue skin might be advantageous on a planet with predom-inantly blue foliage, where blue skin color would serve as a kind of camouflage. Blue pigmentation strongly reflects blue light, which is in the higher energy region of the visible spectrum, and could therefore function as protection against damaging radia-tion from the Bolian sun.

Biologists do not recognize any major biological signifi-cance in minor differences in human skin color. The notion of "race" is not based on biological principles.

The Bolians, incidentally, are named in honor of long-time *Star Trek* director Cliff Bole, who has also been immortalized in the "Cliffs of Bole," a striking geological feature on an unnamed Class-M planet somewhere in the Alpha Quadrant.

The Borg ("Q Who?"; *TNG*)

Starship Enterprise **Science Log, Stardate 42766.4. Captain Jean-Luc Picard recording.**

The entity known as Q has hurled the Enterprise *across seven thousand light-years of space. In this far sector of the Alpha Quadrant we were engaged in a nearly fatal battle with a race known as the Borg.*

The Borg are composed of a variety of humanoid species that have been "assimilated" from numerous worlds across the galaxy. Their biological systems are enmeshed with various cybernetic components that merge each individual into a collective consciousness. Individual will is bent to the will of the Borg collective. The Borg are relentless consumers of material resources and possess no morality or conscience whatsoever. They appropriate any species and technology that will serve the will of the collective, which is simply to grow like a cancer, without purpose, without regard for the lives their assimilation process destroys.

The Borg are perhaps the most chilling villains ever encountered in the *Star Trek* universe. Their name derives from the term cyborg, which is short for *cybernetic organism*. Their relentless determination to assimilate everything in sight is one of their most frightening qualities. They remind me of a comment once made by naturalist and environmental activist Edward Abbey: "Growth for the sake of growth is the ideology of cancer."

People have made use of simple prosthetic devices for centuries. An artificial leg made of wood or plastic can help a person walk, but prosthetics as such cannot be connected to the human nervous system. A person's mind, therefore, cannot

Absorbed into the collective and incorporated into the hive mind, what was human is now Borg. ELLIOTT MARKS.

command a simple prosthetic to move; the prosthetic must be designed in such a way that muscles can manipulate the prosthetic to perform the desired function.

The science of *bionics* seeks to create replacements for lost limbs, organs, and tissues that are fully integrated with connecting tissues and nerves. Researchers have created electrically conducting fibers several microns in diameter that can be grafted into human nerve cells. Bionic devices, such as an artificial hand, will someday be developed that can respond to electrical impulses traveling down the nerve into the artificial component. It's conceivable that sensors in artificial fingers could transmit signals back up the nerve, creating the physical sensation of touch.

Artificial eyes featuring retinas constructed out of light-sensitive *CCD chips* have been developed in medical research laboratories. If the electrical signals from CCDs can be routed into the optic nerve, such devices may someday provide sight to the blind (see the Basic Science Primer for more information on CCD chips and electronic imaging).

Bynars ("11001001"; *TNG*)

Starship Enterprise Science Log, Stardate 41377.3. First Officer William Riker recording.

The Enterprise *computer core has been serviced and upgraded by a unique species known as the Bynars.*

This race has developed an almost symbiotic relationship with basic digital computer technology. They speak and think in a language based on a binary code, which has unfortunately given them a very limited understanding of human behavior and motivation, as evidenced by their inability to conceive of "shades of gray," that is, any response to a question other than yes or no, one or zero.

How humans interact with computers has become a critical question in the late twentieth century. Computers dominate the consumer-electronics market. With the rise of the personal computer beginning in the early 1980s, virtually everyone in today's world uses computers at work, school, or in the home.

Zero Zero (Kelli Ann McNally), one half of a paired set of Bynars, a culture dependent on computers.

When I went to college (not *that* long ago—really) a person typically interacted with a computer by writing computer programs using one of a handful of programming languages available at the time. After you had written your "code," you would sit down at a card-punch machine and type out each line. The card-punch machine would then translate each line of code into a series of holes in IBM cards, a system not too far removed from the "piano rolls" used by player pianos. When you were done typing your code, you handed your stack of cards to a guy sitting in the room that contained the actual computer (typically a machine the size of a small house, replete with vacuum tubes and other electronic oddities). A few hours later the results of the program were printed on big sheets of green and white paper. You'd look it over, realize you misspelled a word in line 329, and begin the process again.

Thankfully, computers are a little less trouble to use today, but they are still far from "easy," to my mind. Punched cards have been replaced by *application programs* that prompt you for the information they need, freeing the end user from the need to write programs. Most people who use computers today in fact have no idea how to even begin to write a computer program. They simply use programs that other people have written, like the word-processing program I'm using to write this book.

But most computer users still interact with their computers by typing. The mouse has taken over part of the typing function, and *voice recognition software* that understands human speech is available for personal computers (although it's still relatively primitive). Text has been replaced in many circumstances by *icons*—pictures—that represent programs or program functions. It will probably be a few years yet before using a computer is as easy as talking to a personal secretary, but that day will eventually come. You'll talk to the computer, and the computer will talk to you. Some people wonder what this will do to literacy. Computers can already check your spelling; if you don't even have to type or read the screen anymore, perhaps literacy becomes of secondary importance.

Cardassians
("The Wounded"; *TNG*)

Starship Enterprise **Science Log, Stardate 44436.3. Second Officer Data recording.**

During our recent encounter with the Cardassian Galor-*class warship* Trager, *I had the opportunity to observe a Cardassian at close range for the first time.*

Bony cranial ridges and an unusually thick neck musculature (compared to typical humanoids) are among the more distinguishing Cardassian features. These structures, coupled with other more common humanoid features, suggest a vicious predatory ancestry. Recent actions by the Cardassians bear out the theory that their evolutionary heritage includes a considerable number of predatory species.

Cardassians are part of a long line of *Star Trek* villains. They are loosely modeled on the Nazi armies of World War II, ruthless and militaristic, bent on conquering the entire galaxy.

Cardassians are probably cold-blooded; in addition to their generally reptilian appearance, we've made several references to their inability to tolerate cold temperatures. Unlike warmblooded animals, which produce their own heat internally through metabolic processes, cold-blooded animals depend on their surroundings to keep themselves warm.

One of the more distinctive Cardassian physical features is their prominent neck musculature. Thick, sinewy cords of muscles extend from the shoulders to the neck, protecting the neck and maintaining the upright posture of the head. This implies that Cardassians have weak spines (but don't tell them I said that).

A product of the militaristic culture that rose on Cardassia, Gul Evek (Richard Poe) reacts as he has been trained. ROBBIE ROBINSON.

Data
("The Measure of a Man"; *TNG*)

Starship Enterprise Personal Log, Stardate 42527.0. Second Officer Data recording.

I have had the very interesting experience of being placed on trial for my very life. Commander Bruce Maddox sought my transfer to the Daystrom Institute for the purpose of conducting experiments on my positronic matrix. These experiments would have required my disassembly, and probably my termination as a sentient entity.

Fortunately, Captain Picard was able to convince a Starfleet hearing that denying my rights as a sentient entity could create a precedent for the production of a class of android slaves, sentient but with no inherent right to self-determination.

The word *robot* became the popular term for human-like machines when the Czech author Karel Capek used it in his play *RUR: Rossum's Universal Robots*. Capek's brother Josef suggested the term for the enslaved automatons described in the play; "robot" derives from a Czech term for indentured servant.

Androids are robots that are crafted to look and act like human beings, presumably to facilitate their use and acceptance among people. As a fully functional android, intelligent and capable of human speech and movement, Data is the ultimate user-friendly computer.

Recent advances in robotics suggest that it may someday be possible to build an artificial device that looks and acts like a human being. The real question is whether such a machine is worth building. The fact they haven't yet been built can largely be attributed to the economic reality that it doesn't make much

Commander Riker
(Jonathan Frakes)
displays a nonorganic
component of Lieutenant
Commander Data.

sense to build such machines. Most robots are built to work on assembly lines. They are designed and optimized to perform specific tasks in manufacturing complexes. Most of these tasks require precise, repetitive motions that human beings are notoriously poor at performing. The shape of an industrial robot is determined by the task it is intended to perform, not by a desire to construct a machine that looks human (even though it may replace a human on the assembly line).

Data's positronic matrix is an homage to the late writer Isaac Asimov, who wrote a series of short stories and novels featuring robots and android characters. Asimov conjectured the development of a "positronic brain" as the breakthrough that led to the creation of intelligent robots. The circuits in a positronic brain would presumably be coursing with positrons, the antimatter counterparts of electrons, although Asimov (to my knowledge) never made clear why positrons were preferable to electrons in robot brains.

Asimov also developed the following three "laws of robotics" that guided the programming of all robots and androids: 1) A robot may never injure a human being, or through inaction allow a human being to come to harm. 2) A robot must obey all orders given it by human beings, unless such orders conflict with the first law. 3) A robot must protect its own existence unless such protection requires violating the first and second laws. Question for discussion: Has Data always obeyed Asimov's three laws of robotics?

Devidians ("Time's Arrow"; *TNG)*

Starship Enterprise Science Log, Stardate 46006.2. Second Officer Data recording.

Starfleet archeologists, investigating a site near the Presidio in San Francisco, Earth, have discovered a startling artifact: my severed head. Geochemical analysis suggests that this artifact originated on the planet Devidia II in the Marrab sector.

At Devidia II the Enterprise *has uncovered evidence that a strange humanoid race, existing in an asynchronous temporal plane, attacked Earth in the distant past. A temporal vortex transported myself, the captain, and several other officers to nineteenth-century Earth. While there, we successfully destroyed a time portal used by the Devidians to attack unsuspecting nineteenth-century humans. The Devidians appear to thrive on the neural energy of human beings.*

Although, the human brain does generate energy through chemical reactions that produce electrical signals transmitted throughout the brain's network of neurons, this electrical energy is no different from the electrical energy in a light-bulb or a car battery. The amount of electrical energy produced in the brain is also very small, and would probably not constitute a particularly nutritious meal for electricity-hungry aliens. Neural energy is a fictional device that's been used in several *Star Trek* episodes.

The "asynchronous temporal plane" referred to in this episode is another fictional device, intended to imply that the aliens live in a sort of parallel universe just out of sync with our own.

Intelligent Saurians
("Distant Origin"; *VGR*)

Starship Voyager Science Log, Stardate 50925.6. First Officer Chakotay
recording.

Some seventy thousand light-years from home, Voyager *has
made contact with an astonishing race of beings whose ancestors evolved on Earth.*

*Intelligent, highly advanced saurians, these creatures are
the descendents of dinosaurs that roamed the Earth some
sixty-five million years ago. Their ancestors were evidently
extremely sophisticated technologically, and developed space-
flight capability in time to flee the Earth before the arrival of the
massive Chixiclub asteroid that wiped out the dinosaurs and
numerous other species at the end of the Cretaceous period.
The asteroid impact also appears to have erased any archaeological evidence of the existence of this race of dinosaurs, as no
fossil record of their existence has been discovered in five hundred years of paleontological research.*

*And yet we must accept that these beings are mankind's
distant cousins. Captain Janeway has determined that we share
a common ancestor: the genus* Eryops, *the last common link
between the dinosaurs and the line of animals that eventually
evolved into mammals and humans.*

Life on Earth began in the oceans, and there it remained for
several billion years. Life did not begin its assault on the
land until some six hundred million years ago, a relatively
recent chapter in the four-billion–year history of life.

Simple forms of plant life were the first to gain a foothold
along the coasts of the barren continent that existed then.
These plants absorbed carbon dioxide and transpired oxygen.

Understanding his own origins is the driving force behind Professor Gegen's (Henry Woronicz) need to know where his species originated.
ROBBIE ROBINSON.

Almost all of the oxygen content of the Earth's atmosphere is the result of plant biology. In a few tens of millions of years, plant life spread across the world's land mass, setting the stage for the arrival of larger organisms. Oxygen-breathing marine life eventually followed the plants, learning to survive first as amphibians in shallow coastal waters, and later evolving into the diverse forms of life that thrive throughout the world's land masses today.

One early description of a dinosaur bone was written in 1677 by Oxford University chemist Robert Plot. Plot, however, didn't realize he was describing a bone from a long-extinct gigantic reptile. Numerous dinosaur bones were discovered in the Sussex region of England in the early 1800s. The British anatomist Sir Richard Owen coined the term dinosaur (a word that literally means "terrible lizard") in 1841. Over the course of the next few decades, the true nature of the massive beasts that had left their bones in the earth became clear.

Eryops lived some 290 million years ago, and was probably the last link between the branches of life that evolved along separate paths into dinosaurs and mammals. About sixty-five million years ago, an asteroid several kilometers in diameter slammed into the ocean just off the Yucatán peninsula. The impact produced a huge explosion that launched massive volumes of debris into the atmosphere, and even into space, triggering a global firestorm that burned for months.

Many paleontologists believe that the dinosaurs were on the road to eternity already; the asteroid was just the last nail in their collective coffin. No plant or animal species is eternal. But if nothing else, the asteroid of sixty-five million years ago hastened the demise of the terrible lizards, clearing the way for the humble tree shrews that eventually evolved into the higher primates, and ultimately us.

Ferengi ("The Last Outpost"; *TNG*)

Starship Enterprise Science Log, Stardate 41390.1. Second Officer Data recording.

The Enterprise *has been attacked by a curious group of humanoids, the Ferengi. The Federation has had limited experience to date with these odd creatures. They possess sophisticated space-flight technology, but appear to be lacking in what the Federation would consider enlightened social development. Like the "Yankee traders" of ancient Earth, they are driven purely by the desire to acquire material goods. Gender bias is rampant in their culture; Ferengi females are prohibited from serving on Ferengi vessels, holding government offices, participating in the workforce, or wearing clothing.*

The most notable Ferengi feature is their enormous ears. Not surprisingly, the Ferengi have extremely acute hearing. Sound is a mechanical wave, which means that sound waves can only propagate through a gaseous, liquid, or solid medium. Generally speaking, the more dense the medium, the faster a sound wave will travel through that medium. For example, sound travels faster through water than through air.

Sound waves cannot propagate through the vacuum of space. In the original *Star Trek* series, Gene Roddenberry, fully aware of this fact, had the *Enterprise* move silently through the galactic void. But in the wake of the *Star Wars* films, the studio became convinced that a loud "whooshing" sound lent drama to the image of a ship zipping through space, and we've been stuck with the sound of the warp drive ever since. (If you really wanted to push it, I suppose you could argue that an astronaut, floating in space as a starship zips by, might hear the low-fre-

As a member of the Ferengi Defense Force, DaiMon Tog (Frank Corsentino), knows that above all else a Ferengi without profit is no Ferengi. ROBBIE ROBINSON.

quency radio emissions of a ship's engines through the com-system speakers in his suit. If you really wanted to push it.)

Ears serve to collect, and to some extent focus, sound waves. Sound vibrations stimulate vibrations in the eardrum, which in turn stimulate electrical signals that match the rising and falling of the sound waves—a process very similar to the way a conventional electronic microphone works.

By virtue of having two ears, and a brain to compare sounds entering each ear, humans and similarly equipped animals can determine the direction of a sound source, an evolutionary advantage in a world filled with potential predators and prey. In some species, ears also serve as cooling mechanisms. The large ears of the desert jackrabbit contain numerous blood vessels that help dissipate body heat.

Gem ("The Empath"; *TOS*)

Starship Enterprise Science Log, Stardate 5125.2. Science Officer Spock recording.

On a mission to rescue research scientists on Minara II before its parent star entered a nova phase, the Enterprise *encountered a unique empathic life-form.*

Called "Gem" by Doctor McCoy, this humanoid female was incapable of speech, despite the presence of vocal cords. Doctor McCoy has speculated that Gem's vocal cords are vestigial organs, evolved in a time before her race developed their empathic skills. Gem's empathic skills are so highly developed that she can essentially merge her nervous system with that of another humanoid to effect healing as well as communication.

Vestigial organs are organs that serve no obvious purpose within an organism. In human beings, the appendix is a vestigial organ. Millions of people have had their appendices surgically removed following an infection, with no ill effect.

Biologists regard vestigial organs as strong evidence supporting the theory of evolution. As a human baby develops in the womb, gill slits briefly appear, presumably a vestigial trace of distant human ancestors that lived in the ocean.

One of the chief problems inherent in the theory of evolution is how to account for structures that need to be fully developed before they can serve a useful purpose. For example, how did structures as complex as wings evolve? Early critics of evo-

The willingness to sacrifice her own life for another will save Gem's (Kathryn Hays) world.

lution, considering the development of wings, asked what good a precursor "prewing" nub would be. This is a good question. A small change in an organism, like the appearance of small appendages on the sides of its body, could be understood in terms of a random mutation. But if wings developed slowly over eons, as the theory of evolution requires, beginning as small nubs on the bodies of insects and evolving over millions of years into wings capable of giving flight, what was the evolutionary advantage of having little prewing nubs in the first place?

An evolutionary biologist in Georgia thinks he's found the answer. A certain species of swamp-dwelling insects uses its wings to help scoot itself across the surface of the water to avoid being captured by predators. As the wings of this insect are clipped back, it moves more slowly over the water, but still significantly faster than if it had no wings at all. When the wings are cut back to nubs, the insect can still use the wing nubs to help propel itself away from predators. Hence, small nubs that conferred an advantage in mobility on water eventually grew to become wings capable of sustaining flight.

The Gorn ("Arena"; *TOS*)

Starship *Enterprise* Science Log, Stardate 3048.3. Science Officer Spock recording.

Investigating the destruction of the Federation outpost on Cestus III, the Enterprise *has encountered a race of intelligent reptilian creatures.*

Calling themselves the Gorn, they claim our outpost was an incursion on their space. Captain Kirk chose to pursue the Gorn back to their home sector, believing that a failure to let their attack on Cestus III go unpunished would be interpreted as a sign of weakness.

Reptiles are among the most primitive animals that still live on the face of the Earth. They are related to the dinosaurs that roamed Earth over sixty-five million years ago. The reptile family includes lizards, turtles, crocodiles, and snakes.

Evolutionary biologists believe that reptiles were the first true *vertebrates* (animals with backbones) to live on the land, emerging during the Carboniferous period some 360 million years ago. They are significantly different from mammals in several important respects. Reptiles do not give birth to live young, but lay eggs (although some reptiles carry their eggs within their bodies until they hatch, giving the appearance that they are birthing live young). They are also cold-blooded, meaning that their body temperature is dependent on the temperature of their environment. For this reason, reptiles tend to live in warm, tropical, or desert climates.

Some of the dinosaurs that flourished during the Jurassic and Cretaceous eras were probably fairly intelligent animals. Intelligence is an advantageous trait for predators, and predatory dinosaurs like the dreaded *velociraptor* may have had fairly large brains relative to their body mass (the relationship between brain to body mass and intelligence is discussed in the "Cat's Paw" science log, page 272).

If the last of the dinosaurs hadn't been wiped out by a global catastrophe some sixty-five million years ago, some dinosaur species might have had the opportunity to evolve to a level of intelligence necessary for tool making, and perhaps the capacity for abstract thought and language.

Jem'Hadar
("The Abandoned"; DS9)

Deep Space 9 Science Log, Stardate 48988.4. Chief Medical Officer Julian Bashir recording.

A race of genetically engineered soldiers, known as the Jem'Hadar, has been developed by the Founders to enforce the rule of the Dominion.

Genetically engineered by the Founders, this young Jem'Hadar (Bumper Robinson) will die without ketracel-white. DANNY FELD.

The Jem'Hadar represent the cruelest possible application of genetic manipulation. Growing from infant to adult at an extraordinary rate, they are effectively programmed to be aggressive and fearless in combat. They require neither sleep nor rest. Their loyalty to the Dominion is insured through a genetic addiction to a chemical substance known simply as "white." It is not clear from our brief encounter with the Jem'Hadar whether any of their genetic programming can be reversed without killing the organism.

The idea of a race of genetically engineered soldiers raises disturbing ethical questions. If we should discover that traits like loyalty and courage have a genetic basis (and I hasten to add that it is by no means clear that they do), does society have a right to instill or enhance those traits in future children? What about attributes like intelligence or physical prowess, or musical or artistic skills? Some researchers even talk about giving parents the ability to choose superficial features in their children, such as eye and hair color.

Few would argue that medical science should be banned from developing *in utero* genetic treatments for potentially life-threatening conditions. Knowing how to treat such conditions, however, will give doctors the power to make other genetic changes to developing fetuses. Whether we use that power will be up to us and those we elect to govern our society.

Kataanians ("The Inner Light"; *TNG*)

Starship Enterprise **Science Log, Stardate 45944.9. Captain Jean-Luc Picard recording.**

While subjected to a low-power nucleonic beam from an alien probe, I have lived a lifetime as another person on another planet.

I was under the influence of the probe for less than half an hour, and yet I feel as if I have lived over seventy years on the planet Kataan. This world was destroyed some one thousand years ago when the Kataanian sun went nova. Desperate that their culture not be erased but incapable of warp travel, the Kataanians decided to launch a rocket-powered spacecraft containing several artifacts and a unique neurological probe. Upon encountering the Enterprise, *the probe transmitted its signal, which essentially "downloaded" into my mind the life history of one of the last generation of men to live on Kataan.*

I can recall his entire life as if I had lived it myself — his passion for learning and music, his love for his wife and children, and all of the small details of daily existence that give life its richness and meaning. It will be some time before I can fully process this remarkable experience, but of one thing I am certain: in experiencing the Kataanian culture in this manner I have been blessed with a great privilege.

One of the most popular episodes of *Star Trek: The Next Generation*, "The Inner Light" raises the question of how a civilization on the verge of extinction might best preserve the essence of its culture.

Anthropologists seek to understand extinct cultures through the society's artifacts and, if they exist, written documents. Based on this limited information, the nature of day-to-day life, religious beliefs, and systems of government can be inferred.

Documents written in languages that are no longer spoken may well be impossible to translate unless a document written in both the extinct language and a known language is discovered. The hieroglyphics that adorn the interiors of Egyptian pyramids were completely unreadable until the discovery of the *Rosetta stone*. The stone, a hard slab of black basaltic rock, was discovered in 1799 by an officer in Napoleon's army. It relates the decree of a priest inscribed in three languages: Greek, Egyptian hieroglyphics, and *demotic writing*, a popular form of Egyptian writing that is a sort of "cursive" form of hieroglyphics. By comparing the Greek text with the hieroglyphics, linguists ultimately deciphered the hieroglyphics.

Klingons ("Errand of Mercy"; *TOS*)

Starship Enterprise **Science Log, Stardate 3205.3. Science Officer Spock recording.**

With the help of the Organians, the Enterprise *has avoided a potentially devastating interstellar war with the Klingons, an aggressive and highly militaristic race bent on the conquest and subjugation of what appeared to be a technologically inferior species.*

The "Errand of Mercy" episode marks the first appearance of Klingons in the *Star Trek* universe. The Soviet Union served as the model for the Klingon Empire, a repressive and brutal regime, ruled by a military elite intolerant of democratic principles, human freedom, and other Federation values. As the

Cold War came to an end, *Star Trek: The Next Generation* on television, and the film *Star Trek VI: The Undiscovered Country*, explored the question of how two former adversaries might learn to trust one another and work together toward common ends (an outcome predicted by the Organians in "Errand of Mercy").

In the original *Star Trek* series, the budget for alien make-up was significantly less than the budget available in *Star Trek: The Next Generation* and the various feature films. Klingons in *The Original Series* featured goatee beards and a swarthy greenish skin tone, but otherwise looked pretty much like ordinary humans. In *Star Trek: The Next Generation* and the film series, Klingons have pronounced forehead ridges and other distinctive facial features. This change largely reflects the fact that the studio is willing to spend more money nowadays on alien makeup.

Some people still want a "scientific" explanation for why today's Klingons look so different from those of *The Original Series*. I would offer genetic engineering as the best theory: the Klingons recognized, sometime in the late twenty-third century, that a genetically engineered warrior class would be more effective in battle, and proceeded to create a physically superior warrior class. In the *Deep Space Nine* episode "Trials and Tribble-ations," our twenty-fourth–century crew traveled back in time to witness key events in the famous "The Trouble With Tribbles" episode of *The Original Series*. The change in the Klingons' physical appearance was brought to Mr. Worf's attention. In his inimitable fashion, Worf gruffly and simply responded, "We do not speak about it."

Lal ("The Offspring"; *TNG*)

Starship Enterprise Science Log, Stardate 43675.2. Second Officer Data
recording.

My efforts to procreate have, regrettably, ended in failure.

*While I was able to create and program a positronic brain
capable of independent learning, the android daughter I constructed to house the positronic brain suffered multiple cascade anomalies which could not be prevented and from which
she could not recover. Prior to her termination, however, I successfully downloaded her life experience into my own positronic matrix.*

One of the most poignant episodes of *Star Trek: The Next
Generation*, the construction of Lal raises the question of
self-replicating machines, discussed more fully in the
"Evolution" science log, page 235.

Many computer scientists believe that an electronic brain
capable of independent thought might someday be created.
The principle challenge in creating such a "thinking machine" is
crafting a computer that somehow rises above its programming. At the present time, computers can only do what they are
programmed to do. "Independent thought" means the ability to
think for oneself.

Computers and programs capable of some degree of learning, a sign of intelligence, have been developed. Critics argue
that such programs are not truly intelligent because they are
simply programmed to explore myraid of alternative approaches
to a problem until they uncover the optimum solution. But this
may well be how humans learn as well. We certainly learn a lot
through trial and error. At the subconscious level, even the most
creative acts of the human mind may be little more than rapid

processing of information accumulated over a lifetime's experi-ence. Some of this kind of information processing certainly goes on at the conscious level when artists, scientists, and inventors seek creative solutions to artistic and technical challenges. As Thomas Edison once said, genius is one percent inspiration and ninety-nine percent perspiration.

Lal was significantly different from her father Data in that she possessed human emotions, which ultimately proved to be fatal. But how would we know if an electronic brain were expe-riencing an emotional response? Crudely stated, emotions in humans and other mammals seem to be associated with cer-tain chemical reactions in the limbic system of the brain. Data presumably created a comparable structure within Lal's positronic brain, and we can only speculate whether her per-ception of what she experienced as anxiety is comparable to that emotional state in people. The name "Lal," incidentally, derives from a Hindi word meaning "beloved."

Native American Progenitors ("Tattoo"; VGR)

Starship Voyager Science Log, Stardate 49245.3. First Officer Chakotay recording.

On a distant world in the Delta Quadrant, I have made contact with a race of beings known to my distant ancestors.

The Sky Spirits are a highly advanced race, with warp tech-nology, but they have chosen to live in a manner that most tech-nological societies would consider primitive. The Sky Spirits' desire to "live lightly on the land" reflects a profound wisdom and a deep respect for the natural environment. Consistent with *their wishes, Captain Janeway has decided not to mine their world for polyferranide minerals needed by* Voyager.

Humans probably came to North America from the Asian continent some ten thousand years ago, near the end of the last Ice Age. At that time, a land bridge existed across what is now the Bering Strait that separates Alaska from Russia. As the Ice Age ended, large ice floes melted, raising the global sea level and inundating the land bridge, effectively isolating the American continent from the rest of the world until the end of the fifteenth century.

Many Native American cultures have a deep respect for the land and its natural beauty, and believe that even inanimate objects, such as mountains and clouds, possess spiritual qualities. This belief is also found in the Japanese religion known as Shintoism.

One of the many unfortunate aspects of the European exploration and colonization of the Americas was the spread of diseases against which the American Indian populations had no immunity. Diseases such as smallpox devastated native populations. The process also worked in reverse: Diseases that existed in North America but were unheard of in Europe were spread across the European continent by returning sailors. The Native Americans also introduced European explorers to tobacco, a plant leaf that American Indians smoked only for ceremonial purposes. Europeans developed pipes, cigars, and cigarettes; the long-term health consequences of smoking became clear in the 1940s and '50s, but the addictive nature of the nicotine in tobacco keeps many people smoking. According to the American Cancer Institute, in the United States alone some four hundred thousand people die prematurely every year as a consequence of smoking; worldwide as many as 3.5 million deaths are attributed to smoking each year.

Mintakans ("Who Watches the Watchers?"; *TNG*)

Starship Enterprise **Science Log, Stardate 43177.9. Second Officer Data recording.**

The sociocultural contamination of the proto-Vulcan humanoid species known as the Mintakans has been minimized through a radical act by Captain Picard.

Initial contamination began when the holographic camouflage used by the anthropological observation team failed, exposing the team to several passing Mintakans. Contamination effects were exacerbated when one of the Mintakans received medical care aboard the Enterprise, *and interpreted the existence of the ship as fulfillment of a religious prophecy, and Captain Picard as a deity.*

The captain proved to a Mintakan tribal leader that he was not a deity when he was pierced by a Mintakan arrow and mortally wounded. Fortunately, Doctor Crusher was able to revive the captain and heal his puncture wound.

Cultural anthropologists sometimes go to great lengths to conceal themselves from the people they study. "Duck blinds," long-range telephoto lenses, and other tools are used to ensure that the culture being studied is not affected by the anthropologists conducting the study. The concern is that people who know they're being watched will behave differently than they would under normal circumstances. Other anthropologists, such as the late Margaret Mead, believe that in order to really understand another culture one must immerse oneself in that culture. By entering the culture and earning the trust of its people, an anthropologist can truly develop an understanding of that culture's norms and values.

The rationale behind the Prime Directive is demonstrated as the Mintakans mistake the captain of the Enterprise for a god.

The idea that a race so similar to the Vulcans in physical appearance and intellectual outlook could evolve on another planet is highly questionable. As I've noted in the science log for "The Chase," we've established on *Star Trek* that all humanoid species derive from the same common ancestor, an advanced space-traveling race that spread its genetic seed across the galaxy. One would expect that these genetic seeds would take root and flourish at different rates and eventually generate different forms, though there might be some convergence of physical forms in similar planetary environments.

Romulans
("Balance of Terror"; *TOS*)

Starship Enterprise Science Log, Stardate 1715.4. Science Officer Spock recording.

Our recent engagement with a Romulan bird-of-prey provided the Federation with the first clear visual signal from the interior of a Romulan vessel, which also relayed the physical appearance of the Romulan species.

They are humanoid in form, with facial features strikingly similar to the Vulcan race. It is my belief that the Romulans are an offshoot of the Vulcan people who left the Vulcan home planet thousands of years in the past, before the development of warp drive.

Centuries of enmity are set aside as the Romulan officer Varel (Susanna Thompson) works with the crew of the Enterprise to save her ship. ROBBIE ROBINSON.

They have seemingly retained and refined the brutal martial philosophy that characterized the culture of my Vulcan ancestors some five thousand years ago. If this is indeed the case, the Romulans could prove to be a dangerous and potentially deadly adversary.

Humans are members of the animal group known as *mammals*. Mammals have large brains, hairy or fur-covered skins, warm blood, and suckle their young. Most mammals give birth to live young, but a subgroup of mammals known as the *monotremes* (of which the duck-billed platypus is an example) lay eggs. Most evolutionary biologists believe that all mammals evolved from a tree-dwelling shrewlike ancestor that lived during the age of the dinosaurs.

Man is a member of a mammal order known as the primates, a group that includes the great apes. All primates have five toes on their feet, as well as collarbones, a feature considered "primitive" in evolutionary terms; most mammals no longer possess a collarbone.

The highest level of primate development is found in the anthropoid group, which includes monkeys, apes, and man. In an evolutionary sense, monkeys and apes are cousins of humans, an idea that doesn't sit well with some people because it seems to demean the human species. But from the point of view of molecular biology it is clear that all life on Earth is related. Every living organism, from the simplest bacterium to man, is a product of the activity of DNA molecules. DNA is the master molecule that controls the growth and function of all living cells. A few biologists even go so far as to argue that humans and other animals are simply hosts for DNA, an idea embodied in the "selfish gene" theory.

About 98.5 percent of the DNA of chimpanzees and humans is exactly the same, atom for atom. One could argue that this means that humans and chimpanzees are (biologically) very much alike, or that the 1.5 percent of the DNA that is different between us is particularly significant. Vulcans and their Romulan cousins are probably even more closely related in the genetic sense, since they have had only a few thousand years to diverge biologically (unless of course the Romulans were already biologically distinct from Vulcans before leaving the Vulcan homeworld).

Shape-Shifters (Star Trek VI: The Undiscovered Country); Odo ("Emissary"; *DS9*)

Starship Enterprise Science Log, Stardate 9538.2. Science Officer Spock recording.

During their internment in the Rura Penthe mining colony, Captain Kirk and Doctor McCoy encountered a remarkable sentient creature named Martia. Martia is a chameloid, or shape-shifter, a being with the ability to mold her physical features into any shape she desires.

Deep Space 9 Science Log, Stardate 46386.4. Science Officer Jadzia Dax recording.

DS9 is blessed to have among its crew Odo, a shape-shifter whose origin is a mystery. Odo can modify his physical form at will, changing into solid and liquid objects as well as other humanoid forms (although he has yet to master a genuinely human face). His shape-shifting ability is facilitated by a number of morphogenic enzymes that form the biochemical foundation of his physiology. Odo's abilities do not come without a price: Every sixteen hours Odo must revert to a gelatinous form in order to regenerate, a process not dissimilar to (and probably every bit as refreshing as) sleeping.

Chameleons, small arboreal lizards commonly found in Africa and Asia, are the inspiration for the various shape-shifters seen on *Star Trek*. Chameleons have the unique ability to change the color of their skin as a means of better blending in with the background, thus avoiding the hungry eyes of potential predators.

The skins of chameleons contain three layers of pigment cells. Each layer corresponds to a primary color: red, green, and

Was Martia (Iman) one of the hundreds of shape-shifter children sent out into space by the Founders? Or was she a chameloid? GREG SCHWARTZ.

blue. Any color in the rainbow can be generated by combining various intensities of red, green, and blue light. By expanding and contracting various cells in these layers, the chameleon can produce any skin color it desires.

Some animals can change their shape in a protective manner, but not nearly to the extent of Odo. Puffer fish can swell their bodies to several times their normal volume, making them look too big to eat to their enemies.

Many other forms of camouflage can be found in nature. A number of insects fade into the woodwork, so to speak, by virtue of the fact that they look like tree branches or leaves. Walking sticks, for example, are almost impossible to distinguish from twigs.

Morphogenic enzyme is the term invented to provide some sense of the biomolecular foundations of Odo's changeling body chemistry. People frequently wonder whether Odo weighs the same when he changes shape into a much smaller object or creature, such as a mouse. Since we've seen other characters pick Odo up without difficulty in these smaller forms, his mass presumably changes along with his shape. This would seem to violate the hallowed physics principle known as the conservation of mass. I suppose we could argue that Odo and other shape-shifters somehow shift some of their mass into energy or another dimension when they reduce their size (a pretty weak explanation, I know, but I do the best I can).

Tamarians ("Darmok"; *TNG)*

Starship Enterprise Science Log, Stardate 45054.3. Second Officer Data recording.

Captain Picard appears to have established a basis for communication with the Tamarians, also known as the Children of Tama, a mysterious humanoid race whose territory includes the El-Adrel system.

Earlier Federation attempts at communication with the Tamarians were completely unsuccessful. Universal translator programs were able to convert their spoken language into English-language components, but the resulting sentences seemed to be composed of endless non sequiturs.

Captain Dathon (Paul Winfield) hopes that a shared risk will prove to be the key to providing common ground with the Federation. ROBBIE ROBINSON.

Captain Picard discovered that the Tamarian spoken language is constructed entirely on metaphorical expressions that reach back centuries into Tamarian history. This fact lies at the heart of previous failures to carry on a dialogue with the Tamarians. For example, if someone familiar with the works of William Shakespeare were to say "Juliet on the balcony," another Shakespeare aficionado would understand this as an expression of longing or romantic desire; to someone unfamiliar with Shakespeare, however, the expression would be meaningless.

> *It is clear that in order to establish meaningful communications with the Tamarians, Starfleet must commit itself to the task of understanding the history and literature of the Tamarian culture*

Language is the totality of sounds and symbols that human beings use to communicate thoughts, facts, and feelings. *Linguistics*, the science of language, recognizes the development of some five thousand different human languages over the course of human history, two or three thousand of which are still spoken today.

Star Trek employs an electronic device called a "universal translator" to instantaneously translate the spoken language of an alien being into equivalent "Federation standard." This device was developed as a means of addressing the improbability of constantly encountering strange alien beings who speak perfect Federation standard. The universal translator is somehow capable of analyzing the brain wave patterns of alien entities and thereby developing a translation matrix that converts their language to ours. It's difficult if not impossible to imagine how such a device might work; in order to function, translation programs that are available for computers today must be programmed with the grammar and vocabulary of the languages they translate.

According to the Old Testament book of Genesis, all people originally spoke the same language. When the people of Babel attempted to construct a tower that would ascend all the way to heaven, God prevented them from completing it by making the workers' languages incomprehensible to one another and scattering the tower builders around the world.

Language and the capacity for abstract thought probably evolved together as our distant *Homo habilis* ancestors evolved into modern humans, but we may never know whether the diversity of languages in the world today evolved from a single common language, or if multiple languages arose independently in different parts of the world. In addition to being one of the most inventive stories ever written about the problem of communicating with alien life-forms, the "Darmok" episode underscores the importance of understanding another person's social and cultural background in order to achieve real communication.

An interesting side note: some human languages, such as Navajo, are spoken but not written languages. Navajo "code talkers" were employed by the allied forces in World War II to relay coded messages. The Axis forces, having no written reference of the Navajo language and no Navajo prisoners to consult, were completely incapable of understanding the Navajo code talkers. Having grown up in Arizona and heard spoken Navajo, I can understand why the Axis powers found this language impossible to translate. To English-trained ears, it is strange and wonderful to listen to, and unlike any other language in the world.

Taurus II Protohumanoids ("The Galileo Seven"; *TOS*)

Starship Enterprise Science Log, Stardate 2828.2. Science Officer Spock recording.

En route to Makus III to deliver critical medical supplies, the Enterprise *encountered a quasi-stellar phenomenon, Murasaki 312. Per standing Starfleet orders,* Shuttlecraft Galileo *was launched to investigate the quasar. I was placed in command of the mission.*

Intense electromagnetic storms forced the shuttlecraft to land on Taurus II, a Class-M planetoid in the heart of the Murasaki system. On the planet we discovered a race of humanoids, large in stature and technologically primitive. At a hunter-gatherer stage of development, the Taurus II humanoids fashioned spears from tree branches fitted with stone arrowheads, comparable to the Folsom point discovered on Earth in North America, circa 1926. Regrettably, two members of the shuttlecraft crew were killed before the shuttle engines could be regenerated to achieve a suborbital trajectory, effecting rescue by the Enterprise.

The Folsom culture was an early North American society of hunter-gatherers that lived some eight thousand years ago. Their spear tips were crafted out of stone and featured a distinctive fluted shape. The first "Folsom point," as the spear tips came to be called, was discovered in 1926 near the city of Folsom, New Mexico (hence the name). It is believed that the Folsom culture hunted a now-extinct species of bison that roamed the Great Plains of North America in large herds that could extend for hundreds of miles.

The Taurus II humanoids featured in "The Galileo Seven" were somewhat similar in appearance to Neanderthal man, a human species that became extinct at least thirty thousand years ago. The experience of the Galileo crew contending with a band of primitive but hostile and dangerous hunters raises an interesting question: if Neanderthal man had survived into the modern era, how would they have been treated by modern humans?

The history of *Homo sapiens* suggests that Neanderthal man's lot among modern humans would not have been a happy one. For thousands of years members of our own species were enslaved purely on the condition of minor differences in skin color or belief systems. Neanderthal man, probably incapable of learning complex language and reasoning skills, might have been readily exploited as slave labor. If the Neanderthals had proven too intractable to train as slaves, they would likely have been exterminated. In a sense, this is after all what did happen to them. Unable to compete for resources with their smarter cousins, the Neanderthals were eventually driven to extinction.

The Traveler ("Where No One Has Gone Before"; TNG)

Starship Enterprise Science Log, Stardate 41266.4. Second Officer Data recording.

On Stardate 41263.1. Starfleet propulsion specialist Kosinski was placed on temporary assignment to the Enterprise *to conduct a series of tests designed to improve warp-drive efficiency.*

The first officer, chief engineer, and I were highly skeptical of Kosinski's theories of warp propulsion, but his predicted gains in warp efficiency were realized in early tests. Further experiments, however, yielded unexpected results as the Enterprise *was propelled several million light-years beyond the Milky Way Galaxy .*

It was eventually discovered that Kosinski had nothing to do with the extraordinary gains in Enterprise *warp power. His assistant, an alien known simply as the Traveler, was amplifying the warp engines through the power of thought.*

The question of whether mind can influence matter has fascinated mankind for centuries. Could it be possible to move an object simply by willing it to move?

Many claims for *telekinesis*—literally moving something

The Traveler (Eric Menyuk), an explorer from a distant galaxy, seeks to study and understand human behavior. DANNY FELD.

just by thinking about moving it—have been made. Various so-called psychics, such as Uri Geller, claim the ability to bend spoons simply by concentrating on the spoon and willing it to bend.

To date, no such claim has held up under scientific scrutiny. The magician James Randi, an ardent debunker of paranormal claims, has demonstrated a number of ways a person can make a spoon appear to bend without touching it. The alleged bending is usually exhibited by holding two identical spoons together to confirm their matching shape. The "test" spoon is then placed on the table where the psychic concentrates intently on it. He then places the "control" spoon against the test spoon, and one is clearly bent more than the other. What the observers of such experiments usually fail to notice is that the psychic spoon bender has been holding the control spoon under the table, bending it to make it look as if the test spoon has somehow changed (try this on your friends sometime). The metal in a spoon can also be made very ductile by repeated flexing, so much so that even the heat from a person's fingers just touching the spoon could cause it to bend. This kind of preparation is done before outside observers are allowed to witness the spoon-bending experiment.

Before any claim about mental powers or other paranatural phenomena can be accepted, it must be demonstrated in repeated, controlled experiments. If something happens only once under unusual circumstances that can never again be repeated, there's simply no way to know whether the occurrence was a fluke or an important new discovery.

Trills ("The Host"; *TNG*)

***Starship Enterprise* Science Log, Stardate 44828.8. Second Officer Data recording.**

On a diplomatic mission to the planet Peliar Zel, Federation Ambassador Odan suffered fatal injuries. While treating Odan, Doctor Crusher discovered that his body hosted another organism, a wormlike creature some thirty centimeters in length.

It was subsequently discovered that this ostensibly parasitic life-form was in fact the intelligent entity known to us as Odan. The ambassador is a member of a joined species known as the Trill. The Trill and its humanoid host live in a mutually beneficial, symbiotic relationship.

Gravely ill, Jadzia
hopes that a visit to
the symbiont pool will
serve to heal her and
the symbiont, Dax.
DANNY FELD.

A ll life on Earth is interdependent. As the nineteenth-century Native American Chief Seattle once said, "Man did not weave the web of life; he is but one strand in it."

Symbiotic relationships are the ultimate expression of the interdependence of living organisms. One of the best examples of a mutually beneficial relationship in nature is found in *lichen*. Lichen are comprised of two radically different organisms, fungus and algae, working together for their mutual benefit. Algae use photosynthesis to produce simple sugars that feed both the algae and the fungus. The fungus in turn protects the algae and provides it with water absorbed from the air.

Not all relationships in nature are so fair and cozy. The predator-prey relationship is definitely a raw deal for the prey (unless the prey is cooked; sorry—couldn't resist). The host-parasite relationship is in some sense a more insidious version of the predator-prey relationship (see the "Operation: Annihilate!" and "Conspiracy" science logs, pages 227 and 229, for more on parasites).

Another interesting interspecies relationship is called *commensalism*. In a commensal relationship, one partner derives a benefit, and the other basically doesn't care; it is neither harmed nor helped by the other partner. The barnacles that live on the backs of whales are an example of a commensal species, although some barnacles are parasitic. Free-swimming barnacle larvae attach themselves headfirst onto the body of a whale. A crusty carapace develops over the larvae as it becomes an adult. The adult barnacle, its head still attached to the whale, feeds itself by using its feet to kick passing food into its mouth. What a way to live.

Vidiians ("Phage"; *VGR*)

Starship Voyager **Science Log, Stardate 48537.6. Captain Kathryn Janeway recording.**

Voyager *has encountered a desperate and dangerous race of humanoids in the Delta Quadrant. The Vidiians are the victims of a devastating infectious agent they call simply "the phage." The phage attacks and consumes various organs and systems in the body, eventually leading to death.*

Despite their highly advanced medical technology, the Vidiians have yet to find a cure for the phage. They have, however, developed a treatment: harvesting and transplanting organs and tissues from other humanoids. The Vidiians use a transporter device to remove and transplant needed organs from unsuspecting individuals. Sophisticated antirejection drugs have been developed by the Vidiians ensure that organs can be harvested from a wide range of humanoid species, including humans, Klingons, and Talaxians.

Skin grafts and organ transplants have become standard medical techniques in the twentieth century. An *organ* is defined as a connected set of two or more different tissues that has a recognizable shape and specific function within the body. The brain, heart, lungs, kidneys, stomach, and liver are some of the organs found within the human body.

Skin grafts are also organ transplants. The skin is in fact the largest organ of the body. Skin grafts are often critical to the survival of fire victims who suffer second- or third-degree burns over large areas of their bodies.

"Stolen-organ" stories have made news in recent years. These stories are frightening, to say the least: A man wakes up in a hotel room with a bad hangover and discovers he's missing

Janeway orders the destruction of her
ship rather than allowing her crew to
become spare body parts for the Vidiians.
ROBBIE ROBINSON.

a kidney. The credibility of most stolen-organ stories is questionable, but there is little doubt that it does happen on rare occasions.

Compatibility is the key issue for organ transplantation. The body's *immune system* is designed to automatically attack any foreign object that enters the body, including a potentially lifesaving organ or skin graft.

Some organs are more amenable to transplantation than others. There is a wider latitude of compatibility for kidney transplants, for example, than for bone-marrow transplants. Matching a transplant candidate's blood type and certain *HLA antigens* (proteins found on the surfaces of white blood cells) to a prospective healthy donor is usually sufficient in the case of a kidney transplant. Bone-marrow transplants, which are used to treat blood disorders, almost always require that the recipient and donor be close relatives (brother and sister, for example).

Prior to a transplant procedure, doctors administer antirejection drugs to suppress the patient's immune response. The risk of this procedure is that the patient's immune system is weakened against infectious diseases as well; recipients who survive the transplant sometimes succumb to viral and bacterial infections that exploit their weakened immunity. Researchers are continually developing new antirejection drugs that prevent the patient's body from rejecting the transplanted organ but preserve the immune response to life-threatening *antigens*. A drug called cyclosporine, which is derived from a fungus, protects against organ rejection in liver, kidney, and heart transplants, but maintains the body's response to various infectious agents.

Vulcans (Star Trek: First Contact)

From the diaries of Zefram Cochrane, April 4, 2063.

My prototype warp-driven starship was successfully launched on schedule.

As extraordinary as the flight itself was, even more extraordinary is the fact that humanity's first flight beyond the speed of light attracted the attention of another intelligent, spacefaring species. These Vulcanoids are human in appearance, with somewhat Satanic ears and pale, almost light green skin. They appear to be a quiet and unemotional people, interested in human culture, but in a detached way.

Since the original *Star Trek* series, the planet Vulcan has been established as a world much warmer than Earth (on average), with a thinner and drier atmosphere. Numerous biological adaptations to extreme heat can be found among the denizens of Earth's deserts. Most desert animals cope with heat in the most obvious way: by staying out of it. Underground burrows and the shade of desert plants are exploited during the day; most desert dwellers do their hunting and feeding at night, when the dry desert air cools down considerably, even after the hottest days. Perspiration is a common heat-coping mechanism among mammals. As the body perspires, sweat evaporates, carrying away heat.

Lungs, the organs of the respiratory system, contain air sacs that are comprised of minute *alveoli*. The alveoli contain networks of fine capillaries that carry blood through the lungs. The blood draws oxygen from the alveoli and releases carbon dioxide; oxygenated blood flows from the lungs, transporting oxygen to cells throughout the body.

The relatively small volume of the lungs disguises the

Earth's historic first contact with aliens was made with the Vulcans (Cully Fredricksen). ELLIOTT MARKS.

incredible surface area of the alveoli. If the internal surface area of the lungs were stretched out flat like a carpet, the total area for an average adult would be about seventy-five square meters, the size of a typical one-bedroom apartment, or some forty times the area of an average human body. Vulcans would presumably require greater lung capacity to survive in the rarefied atmosphere of their home planet. Through nature's clever packing of alveoli, a significantly greater lung surface area could be achieved without greatly increasing the physical dimensions of the lungs.

In the late nineteenth century, astronomers diligently searched for a planet circling the Sun inside the orbit of Mercury, the closest known planet to the Sun. Astronomers suspected that there might be another planet very close to the Sun because of the unusually high rate of *orbital precession* observed in Mercury's orbit. Like all planets, Mercury revolves about the Sun not in a perfect circle, but in an oval-shaped ellipse orbit. Astronomers had noted for some time that the point of Mercury's orbit closest to the Sun, called its *perihelion*, advances through space at a rate that cannot be completely accounted for by Newton's laws of motion. The gravitational influence of another planet inside the orbit of Mercury, however, would neatly account for the observed precession. Before the purported planet was even discovered, it was given the name Vulcan, after a Roman god of fire.

Numerous searches failed to find Vulcan. Einstein's general theory of relativity, which is a theory about the nature of gravity, accurately predicted the precession of Mercury's orbit, and there was no longer any need to invoke the presence of another planet tugging Mercury along. No planetary body has ever been discovered closer to the Sun than Mercury, although some comets, called *sungrazers*, occasionally travel inside Mercury's orbit, and sometimes crash into the Sun, where they are instantly consumed by the solar furnace.

Spock, the most famous of all Vulcans, is the product of a marriage between a Vulcan father and a human mother. The American astronomer Carl Sagan once noted that because of the profound genetic differences likely to be found in alien life-forms, such a mating was about as probable as crossing a human with an artichoke. Through the application of the techniques of genetic engineering, however, cross-species breeding has become possible. Human genes have been successfully introduced into the cells of mice and other organisms, not for the purpose of creating creatures who are half-human and half-something else, but rather to motivate animal cells to manufacture proteins (such as insulin) that are useful in treating people with chronic medical conditions. In the *Star Trek* universe, human-Vulcan and other interspecies offspring are presumably made possible through advanced genetic engineering.

Aliens on Earth
("Little Green Men"; *DS9*)

Deep Space 9 Science Log, Stardate 49211.6. Science Officer Jadzia Dax recording.

My little Ferengi friend has become a little green man.

Quark, Rom, and Nog were on their way to Earth, where Nog will presently enter Starfleet Academy as its first Ferengi cadet. Quark took the opportunity to smuggle a highly unstable compound, kemacite, to some friends in a nearby sector. The kemacite triggered a power fluctuation in the shuttle's warp core, sending the three Ferengi back in time to a crash landing

Retrieved from a classified file marked "Roswell Incident," this photo shows an alien being named Quark (Armin Shimerman) being prepared for interrogation by Army nurse Faith Garland (Megan Gallagher). ROBBIE ROBINSON.

on Earth, near the small town of Roswell, New Mexico, in the Earth year 1947.

The three hapless Ferengi and their shuttle were immediately detained by local military authorities who quickly recognized that they had a genuine group of intelligent alien life-forms on their hands (well, the "intelligent" part might be questionable). Fortunately Constable Odo, acting on a lead that Quark might be smuggling contraband, had hidden himself aboard the shuttle, and managed to effect their escape without significantly affecting the time line.

The most celebrated story in the annals of UFO history is certainly the "Roswell Incident." In the summer of 1947 a strange object crashed into the desert outside of Roswell, New Mexico, a small rural community located near an Air Force base that housed the only atom-bomb–equipped aircraft in existence at the time.

A local rancher discovered the crash debris, which consisted of strange metallic yet flexible fragments and other light-weight but strong materials. He contacted the local authorities, who came to the crash site along with Air Force personnel. They examined and collected the debris for analysis.

The Roswell base press office then issued a report claiming the Air Force had recovered fragments from a crashed "flying disk." The next day, the Air Force retracted the statement, and reported that the alleged disk fragments were in fact pieces of a simple weather balloon.

Years later, stories began to surface that the Air Force was covering up the crash of an alien spacecraft, that alien bodies had been recovered and autopsied, that the material recovered at the crash site was paper thin but stronger than steel and covered with strange hieroglyphic-like markings. These speculations were in part fueled by the fact that the Air Force's insistence that the debris was just a wayward weather balloon was not very convincing.

In 1996 the Air Force finally released previously classified documents revealing that the materials recovered from the crash site came from a set of high-altitude balloons designed to detect shock waves from nuclear explosions. A Navy researcher had discovered that some low-frequency sound waves propagate through the ocean for thousands of miles (this is how whales communicate over great distances). The Air Force was interested in monitoring Soviet research into nuclear weapons, and thought that balloons lofted into the upper atmosphere might detect sound waves created by test explosions virtually anywhere in the world. Balloons made out of a then-new and exotic material similar to Mylar were crafted and launched. When a set of these balloons crashed near Roswell, the Air Force was eager to keep the information about their program secret; if the Soviets learned how we monitor their nuclear tests, they could monitor ours as well, or take countermeasures to conceal their tests.

The culture of military secrecy nurtured by the Cold War has become a fertile breeding ground for conspiracy theories. The Roswell UFO story is perhaps the ultimate expression of this. Despite all of the strange stories and military "disinformation" campaigns, there is no credible evidence to support the contention that an alien spacecraft crashed in New Mexico in 1947.

The American astronomer Carl Sagan noted on many occasions that extraordinary claims demand extraordinary evidence. If someone tells me they saw my friend Brian crossing the street yesterday around five, I'll probably believe them without hesitation. But if they tell me they saw an alien life-form crossing the street, I'm going to need more than just their say-so before I believe it. Many people have seen strange things in the sky, and there are many compelling stories about encounters with alien spacecraft and even alien life-forms. But stories do not constitute evidence.

In cases where groups of credible people have seen or even photographed odd lights in the sky that can't be explained as modern aircraft or natural phenomena, we simply don't know what these lights are. They might be some rare and unknown atmospheric phenomenon, like the "blue sprites" that some-times form over storm systems and rise tens of kilometers into the atmosphere. For decades pilots have reported seeing these strange blue lights, even in perfectly clear weather. But it wasn't until 1994 that a blue sprite was photographed. If they form over storm systems, why are they sometimes visible when there isn't a storm cloud in the sky? Simple: because the blue sprites can rise so high in the atmosphere, the storms that pro-duce them can be beyond the horizon, well below the pilot's field of view.

It's certainly possible that the government is covering up evidence of alien life, but there is no way to determine this until the government or a credible whistle-blower "comes clean" and presents evidence to the public that can be examined and test-ed by a wide array of unbiased experts. I personally would want to see such evidence first hand, eliminating every other viable alternative explanation, before I would be ready to accept the extraordinary claim that life definitely exists beyond Earth.

Keeping an open mind requires maintaining a healthy level of skepticism. This does not mean that every UFO report should be immediately dismissed as nonsense, or that people claiming to have been abducted by aliens should automatically be regarded as "kooks." It simply means there are still many mys-teries in the world, and we just don't know what the truth is behind some UFO reports.

Sporocystian Microbes
("Caretaker"; *VGR*)

Starship *Voyager* Science Log, Stardate 48324.1. Captain Kathryn Janeway recording.

In pursuit of a Maquis raider in the badlands, Voyager *has been swept seventy thousand light-years across the galaxy, into the far reaches of the Delta Quadrant, by a creature that calls itself the "Caretaker."*

We have subsequently discovered that the Caretaker is a sporocystian life-form that has evolved into a highly complex, intelligent entity.

Microbial life is the dominant form of life on our planet. Adding up the mass of all of the living creatures on the planet (the *biomass*), one finds that most of the planet's biomass is found in single-celled, bacterial organisms. When you get right down to it, bacteria rule.

Single-celled organisms have been discovered that thrive in the most unlikely environments. *Chemosynthetic bacteria* live several kilometers deep in the Earth's crust, surviving on sulfur and hydrogen gas. There are bacteria (called *thermophiles*) that live comfortably at temperatures greater than the boiling point of water. Another variety of bacteria lives deep in the ocean near *hydrothermal vents*. These vents, called *black smokers*, continually spew hot sulfur- and mineral-rich water into the ocean. These chemicals are nutrients for the bacteria, which feed other marine organisms, such as several meter-long red tube worms.

Bacteria are often thought of as infectious agents, toxic to human beings and a threat to our health. But there are some bacteria that are essential to human health; we couldn't live without them. They help us digest food and prey on other bacteria that are harmful to us. This is one of the reasons people need to be careful when they take antibiotics. Antibiotics designed to kill dangerous bacteria can sometimes harm the "good" bacteria we need to stay alive.

"Sporocystian" life is a term invented by the writers of "Caretaker," and does not refer to a real class of organisms. Presumably it refers to a life-form that spreads spores as part of its reproductive process.

An interesting bit of bacterial trivia: the dry weight of a human being is about ten percent bacteria.

Symbiotic Spores
("This Side of Paradise"; *TOS*)

Starship Enterprise **Science Log, Stardate 3420.9. Science Officer Spock recording.**

An unusual, space-borne symbiotic spore has been discovered on Omicron Ceti III. When the spore infests a host, it provides protection against deadly berthold rays, as well as a near-euphoric state of mind.

Spores are minute biological structures produced by plant organisms for the purpose of reproduction. Each spore is capable of growing into a mature adult. The dissemination of spores is typically a form of asexual reproduction, meaning that the organism does not require a mate in order to reproduce.

Symbiosis is a biological term that defines a mutually beneficial relationship between organisms from different species.

The plant forms of the space-borne spores discovered on Omicron Ceti III.

Many examples of symbiotic relationships can be found in nature, including inside the human body.

Some biologists think that the structures called *mitochon-dria*, which produce energy in our cells, were once bacteria that took up symbiotic residence in cells billions of years ago, in a process called *symbiogenesis* (described on page 80 in the "Tuvix" science log). Mitochondria possess their own segments of RNA, a molecule closely related to DNA, which supports the theory that mitochondria were once independent organisms.

A number of hallucinogenic plants exist in nature, including peyote and certain varieties of mushrooms. A large fraction of the pharmaceuticals used in modern medicine are also derived from plants.

Tribbles ("The Trouble with Tribbles;" *TOS*)

Starship Enterprise Science Log, Stardate 4526.6. Science Officer Spock recording.

The Enterprise *has successfully interceded in a plot to undermine Federation participation in the Sherman's Planet project.*

Federation agricultural scientists have developed a hardy hybrid grain, quadrotriticale, ideally suited for the mid-northern latitude growing environment on Sherman's Planet. A shipment of quadrotriticale being stored at the station prior to delivery to Sherman's Planet was poisoned by Klingon operatives. The poisoning was discovered when a number of tribbles—small, fur-coated organisms with no obvious purpose except to reproduce, which they do at an alarming rate—died upon eating the grain.

The proliferation of spores is one mechanism of asexual reproduction. Another method is the formation of a new individual from a part of the original that has become detached. For example, a single leaf from a begonia can give rise to an entire new begonia plant, complete with leaves, flowers, stems, and roots. Even some animals can split into parts and form new individuals from the splinters. A flatworm can pinch off a segment from the lower part of its body, which eventually grows into a new flatworm (the tail end of the original flatworm also regenerates). In "The Trouble With Tribbles" Dr. McCoy, however, states that tribbles seem to be "born pregnant," which implies, to say the least, a unique form of reproduction.

The environment generally places brakes on out-of-control population growth through the predator-prey relationship.

Removed from their natural predator-filled environment, tribbles breed at an alarming rate. ROBBIE ROBINSON.

Removed from their natural environment, with no predators to hunt them and keep their numbers in check, the tribbles were able to proliferate profusely. A similar problem exists in Australia, where rabbits, brought to the Australian continent from Europe many years ago, have no natural enemies. The population of rabbits in some parts of Australia has become so large that drastic measures (comparable to beaming batches of tribbles onto a Klingon warship) have been taken to reduce their numbers.

Voles ("Playing God"; *DS9*)

Deep Space 9 Science Log, Stardate 47633.9. Science Officer Jadzia Dax recording.

Chief O'Brien has had little success in dealing with the station's Cardassian vole infestation.

The voles appear to be attracted to the electromagnetic fields propagated within the electroplasma system conduits. They feed on just about anything that contains a trace of organic material, including insulation on power cables, which has been wreaking havoc with station power systems.

Voles are rodents, members of the genus *Microtus*. They're basically mice, and are commonly referred to as field mice or meadow mice. Cardassian voles are presumably a particularly nasty kind of mouse, although even the common household variety mouse is capable of chewing through wiring insulation (which typically results in a fried mouse).

There is a long history of rodent infestations aboard sea- and oceangoing ships. Since rodents can carry diseases harmful or fatal to humans, they can pose a serious threat to the health of a crew on a long voyage. The ease with which rodents find their way into just about any structure suggests that someday we may find them stowing away aboard spacecraft (as opposed to being carried aloft intentionally for experimental purposes).

In *The Wrath of Khan*, Dr. McCoy noticed a mouse skittering along the floor of the Regula I Space Laboratory. This animal was probably a lab animal, and not a hirsute hitchhiker.

Denevan Neural Parasite ("Operation: Annihilate!"; *TOS)*

Starship Enterprise Science Log, Stardate 3291.6. Science Officer Spock recording.

I have survived an attack by the neural parasite that annihilated the human colony on the planet Deneva.

The captain, Doctor McCoy, and I have determined that the parasites are extremely sensitive to energy in the visible portion of the electromagnetic spectrum. Direct exposure to visible light destroys the parasites in short order. By deploying a series of 210 visible-to-ultraviolet-light–emitting satellites in a series of overlapping orbits, we were able to eradicate the planetwide infestation.

A *parasite* is an animal or plant that lives in close proximity to another organism (known as the *host*), deriving benefits from the host, but offering nothing to the host in return. This relationship is very different from a *symbiotic relationship*, where organisms interact in a manner that is mutually beneficial (as in *Star Trek's* Trill species).

Aphids are common plant parasites. They derive nourishment from the sap of certain trees. An aphid extends its *proboscis* (a long, narrow tube, something like a straw) into special cells in the tree that carry sap, or *phloem*. The pressure gradient in the tree cells forces the phloem into the digestive tract of the aphid.

Bacteria that infect other living organisms are also parasites, thriving at the expense of their hosts, and sometimes killing their hosts. The mistletoe plant is also a parasite, which extends rootlike structures into the branches of trees in order

With the rest of the sector threatened, the *Enterprise* must stop a dangerous parasite.

to steal water collected through the tree's roots (think about that next time you kiss someone under a clump of the stuff).

There are a variety of very nasty-looking tapeworms that infect mammals, including humans, and survive by absorbing nutrients from within the guts of their hosts. Some of the more exotic varieties of these tapeworms can grow to several feet in length *inside* a human body, but this is rare.

Some varieties of tapeworm lay eggs in the brains of their hosts, frequently causing seizures. A number of viral and bacterial infections target brain cells and associated tissues. Encephalitis, a viral infection borne by mosquitoes, infects the brain and can cause serious or life-threatening complications. Spinal meningitis is a bacterial infection that attacks the *meninges*, membranes through which the brain receives its nutrients. A variety of drugs have been developed to treat parasitic infections.

The idea of deploying a large constellation of satellites in low orbit in order to "cover" an entire planet is essentially the concept behind a number of satellite cell-phone and pager communication systems currently in development. In these systems, dozens of satellites are placed along several orbits, each orbit inclined to the others by some fixed degree. As the satellites circle the globe, at least one will be above the horizon of a cell-phone user anywhere on Earth. To transmit a signal to someone on the other side of the world, the satellite above the sender passes the signal from satellite to satellite until it reaches one above the horizon of the intended receiver.

Controlling Parasite ("Conspiracy"; *TNG*)

Starship Enterprise Science Log, Stardate 41781.2. Second Officer Data recording.

An extragalactic parasite of high intelligence has taken control of numerous Starfleet officers, including high-ranking members of Starfleet Command. The parasite is capable of manipulating its host by extending neural tendrils into the host's central nervous system and brain stem. Captain Picard and Commander Riker were able to destroy the parasites by killing the "mother" creature, which had infested Lieutenant Commander Remmick.

The origin and ultimate purpose of this parasite remains a mystery.

Many parasites need to jump among hosts of different species because they are adapted to different hosts in different stages of their life cycles. Some parasites actually have the ability to manipulate the brains of their hosts, making it more likely their hosts will be eaten by predators, and thereby providing an avenue for the parasite to insinuate itself in a new body.

A nasty little worm called *Microphallus papillorobustus* works this way. Early in its life it infects a lagoon-dwelling water snail. Next, it swims its way into a shrimp-like animal called a gamarind. Once in the gamarind, *Microphallus* worms its way into the animal's brain, causing the little shrimp to behave in an erratic and foolhardy manner. Instead of staying in the safety of dark, deep waters, the infected gamarind is driven by the parasite to well-lighted shallow waters, where they are much easier prey for birds. The *Microphallus* even alters its host's behavior to the extent that the gamarind doesn't duck underwater for cover when a hungry bird swoops down on it. By increasing the likelihood that a bird will eat the gamarind, the parasite increases its chances of moving into a bird host, the host it needs to occupy in order to reproduce.

The Horta
("Devil in the Dark"; *TOS*)

Starship Enterprise Science Log, Stardate 3199.3. Science Officer Spock recording.

The life-form attacking the miners on Janus VI is the first silicon-based life-form discovered in our galaxy. It is an extremely intelligent animal that calls itself a Horta. It is the last adult of its kind on the planet. The miners had inadvertently destroyed eggs in a hatchery that the Horta was protecting, the culmination of a fifty thousand-year reproductive life cycle.

Living organisms are composed mostly of *organic molecules.* Organic molecules are built around carbon atoms. Carbon atoms can create multiple bonds with other atoms, and thereby form large molecules in many shapes.

The chemical flexibility of carbon is a consequence of the fact that carbon atoms have four *valence* electrons. Electrons in atoms orbit their atomic nuclei in *energy shells* that surround the atom. The outermost shell is called the valence shell. Each shell can contain at most a fixed number of electrons. The innermost shell can contain no more than two electrons. The next shell out can contain eight. Carbon (in its electrically neutral form) has six electrons, two in the innermost shell and four in its valence shell. This means that there are four "vacancies" in the valence shell that can be occupied by electrons from other atoms chemically bonded to carbon. Four hydrogen atoms, for example, can bond to a single carbon atom to form methane (CH_4). There are literally millions of organic molecules known to science, some containing in excess of one million atoms.

Silicon also has four valence electrons in a shell that can

contain eight, and yet we do not see the same wide variety of silicon-based molecules that we see for carbon. This is probably due to the fact that chemical bonds formed with silicon are weaker than the bonds formed with carbon, and are therefore more easily broken.

Nevertheless, science fiction has been intrigued with the possibility of silicon life-forms for some time. With the advent of silicon chip-based computer technology, putative silicon life-forms have increasingly been conceived in terms of electrified crystal networks.

The Microbrain
("Home Soil"; *TNG*)

Starship Enterprise Science Log, Stardate 41467.1. Second Officer Data recording.

The network of naturally occurring silicon-based circuitry discovered in the electrically conducting layer of minerals in the crust of Velara III has been dubbed the "microbrain." We have successfully communicated with this silicon organism; its sentience can no longer be questioned. The microbrain was rather shocked to discover that humanoid life-forms are based on carbon chemistry. With its new understanding of carbon-based life-forms, the microbrain now refers to humanoids as "ugly bags of mostly water."

An electronic creature bearing some resemblance to the "microbrain" has been growing right under our very noses here on Earth: the Internet.

The Internet was initially developed in the early 1970s by the United States' Advanced Research Projects Agency (ARPA)

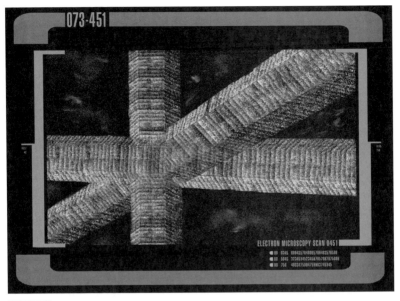

073-451

ELECTRON MICROSCOPY SCAN 0451

DOUG DREXLER

to ensure that Defense Department computers could communicate with one another across the country, even during a nuclear attack. The Internet is essentially a network of computer networks, including a segment now referred to as the World Wide Web. Millions of computers around the world are connected to one another via telephone lines and *modems*. Computers acting as servers for Web sites contain information—in the form of text, pictures, graphics, and so on—that can be called up by any computer linked to the Internet. Computer users can also communicate with one another though electronic mail ("E-mail") programs.

The Internet was not designed from "the top down." It has grown steadily over the years as more and more computers have become part of computer networks, and programs have been designed to simplify the process of communicating with other computers. No one is really in control of the Internet, largely because there is no central computer that runs the Internet.

The idea that a network of electronic connections could develop some form of intelligence was explored in the early 1950s in a short story by Arthur C. Clarke called "Dial 'F' for Frankenstein." In Clarke's story, the electronic circuitry of the international phone system becomes interconnected in a manner not unlike the wiring of neurons in the human brain. A form of intelligence then arises spontaneously in the telephone network.

Many scientists versed in *chaos theory* contend that intelligence is an *emergent property*. Given a brain with sufficient neural complexity, intelligence will eventually emerge as a natural property of the brain. The brains of insects aren't complex enough to give rise to intelligence, but the brains of humans are.

The manner in which computers are connected on the Internet does not resemble the complex structure of the human brain. For this reason (and many others), it seems unlikely that the Internet will ever become a conscious, self-aware entity. On the other hand, when my telephone connection times out just as I'm about to get that last piece of information I've searched the Web over two hours for, I wonder if I should say anything even remotely disparaging about the Internet.

Nanites ("Evolution"; *TNG*)

Starship Enterprise Science Log, Stardate 43129.8. Second Officer Data recording.

Doctor Stubbs's binary star observation project was nearly terminated when Enterprise-D *crew member Wesley Crusher inadvertently created a colony of intelligent nanites that proceeded to occupy the ship's primary computer core. Unaware of their high intelligence, Doctor Stubbs purged a group of the nanites from one of the computer core elements with an intense pulse of gamma radiation.*

The spectacular growth of computer technology in the second half of the twentieth century is largely due to the invention of *integrated circuits* and their subsequent miniaturization. One of the potentially most important developments of the late twentieth century is *nanotechnology*.

What we today call nanotechnology can actually be traced back to an idea developed by the brilliant mathematician Dr. John von Neumann in the 1940s. Von Neumann wondered if it would ever be possible to create a machine he called a Universal Constructor, which could build anything it was programmed to build, and a Universal Computer, which could be programmed to perform any kind of calculation. A combination of these two machines could be instructed to create any desired product. Since it's a fully automated system, the cost of any final product would just be the cost of the materials needed to make it and the energy required by the Universal Constructor.

Furthermore, if the machine could also make copies of itself, its first task could be to make enough copies of itself to serve the material needs of everyone on the Earth. No more

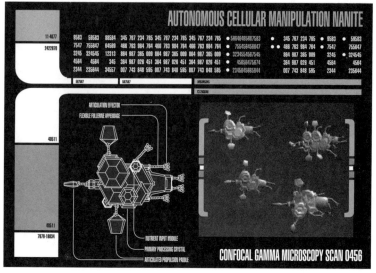

DOUG DREXLER

jobs, nothing but leisure time for everyone. You might recognize the roots of *Star Trek* replicator technology in von Neumann's hypothetical machine. In the 1980s, K. Eric Drexler, then a student at Stanford University in California, realized that it might be possible to make von Neumann machines on a molecular level; after all, the DNA molecule is basically a von Neumann machine. Drexler called these minuscule manufacturing plants *assemblers*.

Technology has progressed to the point where it is possible to manipulate individual atoms using devices called *scanning probe microscopes*. These microscopes use needles whose tips measure only a few atoms in diameter. A sample is placed under the microscope and the needle is passed over its surface, just above but not quite touching it. The electrostatic repulsion between the electrons of the atoms in the needle tip and the electrons belonging to atoms in the sample causes the needle to move. The contours of the surface of the sample can then be measured on an atomic scale. This process can also be used to manipulate atoms, moving them individually to desired locations—potentially the beginnings of a machine that can build structures atom by atom.

More sophisticated techniques for manipulating atoms can be found in various kinds of chemical reactions, especially those involving complex organic compounds. Drexler believes that nanotechnology will eventually make the colonization of space affordable. Assemblers could be dispatched to the Moon or Mars, programmed to build habitats for future colonists. When the habitats are ready, you and your family can move right in.

The Pup ("The Forsaken"; DS9)

Deep Space 9 Science Log, Stardate 46934.8. Science Officer Jadzia Dax recording.

An unoccupied alien probe arrived at the station on Stardate 46925.1. Analysis of the probe indicated the presence of an extremely sophisticated autonomous computer guidance and control system.

Shortly after downloading the software contained within the probe's computer matrix into a DS9 database, we discovered a software life-form inhabiting the station's computer systems. The life-form—nicknamed "Pup" by Chief O'Brien—caused a series of malfunctions until the chief recognized that Pup was simply looking for attention. We eventually managed to remove Pup from our systems and provide it with a good home.

The idea that computer programs might someday become sufficiently complex to develop intelligence or *sentience* has a long history in science fiction. Perhaps the best known intelligent computer in science fiction is the infamous HAL 9000 of *2001: A Space Odyssey*.

Computer intelligence has yet to achieve the level of Hal, but continues to progress. A computer program running on IBM's Deep Blue computer recently defeated Chess Grand Master Garry Kasparov. The idea that intelligence might arise spontaneously when computer circuits reach some critical level of complexity is discussed in the "Home Soil" Science Log, page 232.

Emergent Phenomena ("Emergence"; *TNG*)

Starship Enterprise Science Log, Stardate 47874.1. Second Officer Data recording.

On Stardate 47869.2, the Enterprise *began to experience a series of malfunctions in its primary computer control matrix. Investigation revealed the presence of several anomalous circuit nodes embedded within the control circuitry.*

We suspect these nodes initially formed when the Enterprise *passed through an unusual magnetic storm in the Mekorda sector. Yet they continued to grow and evolve long after the storm had passed. In an emergent process we do not yet fully understand, the nodes transformed the* Enterprise *computer matrix into a spacefaring life-form, which eventually left the ship.*

One of the most exciting developments in late-twenti-eth–century mathematics has surely been *chaos theory*. Simply put, chaos theory asserts that phenomena in nature that appear random may belie an underlying pattern. The American twentieth-century composer George Gershwin once said that he would sometimes hear music in the very heart of noise; in a poetic sort of way, this is the essence of chaos theory.

Another discovery of chaos theory is that a very simple for-mula, repeated again and again, can give rise to very complex patterns. Complex behavior seems to emerge almost sponta-neously in nature, and the concept of the *iterated function* may illuminate this process in a way never before imagined.

Consider the following procedure for generating a picture. Draw a starting point anywhere on a piece of paper. To deter-mine the location of the next point, flip a coin. If the coin comes up heads, draw the next point two-and-a-half centimeters northwest of the first point. If it comes up tails, draw the next point forty percent closer to the center than the first point. If you repeat procedures similar to this several thousand times and graph the points, a recognizable pattern similar to the out-line of a fern emerges.

Contrary to intuition, the intricate structure of a branching fern doesn't need to be represented by a complex equation, but can easily be generated by a very simple formula iterated (repeated) a few thousand times. The other interesting aspect of this process is the coin toss. A procedure based on an act with a random outcome (heads or tails) can produce an orderly structure. Even though you can't guess where the next point on the picture will be until you flip the coin, after a sufficient num-ber of iterations this process will always produce a picture that resembles a fern. The essential simplicity of this scheme may suggest how a simple spore, capable of storing a relatively

small amount of genetic information, can produce a structure as complex as a fern.

The repeated application of a few simple rules can also give rise to phenomena such as flocking behavior. Most people have seen flocks of geese flying in formation like fighter jets in a squadron. But there is no "lead" bird quacking orders to the other geese to keep them in line. The geese simply observe their neighbors and apply a few simple behavioral rules to maintain their relative speed and distance. In this fashion flocking emerges spontaneously, without the need for a leader.

Some cognitive scientists believe that consciousness may also be an emergent phenomenon, arising from the repeated interactions of neurochemicals and electrical signals coursing through the synapses and neurons of the brain.

Space Amoeba
("The Immunity Syndrome"; *TOS*)

Starship Enterprise **Science Log, Stardate 4311.2. Science Officer Spock recording.**

The crew of the U.S.S. Intrepid, *and billions of lives in the Gamma 7A system, have been lost to a form of space life never before encountered by Federation science: a giant, single-cell organism surrounded by a void composed of negative energy.*

Analysis of the interior of the organism indicated that it was about to reproduce through cellular fission. If this organism were to follow a common cellular reproduction cycle, doubling at a constant rate, it would soon pose a grave threat to life across the galaxy. Using a charge of antimatter, the Enterprise *was ultimately able to destroy the organism before it was able to reproduce.*

The science of biology recognizes two basic varieties of living cells. *Eukaryotic* cells enclose their DNA within a *nucleus*, a region within the cell protected by a membrane. They also contain distinct *organelles*, such as *mitochondria*. *Prokaryotic* cells, of which bacteria are the principle example, have no nucleus. The DNA in prokaryotic cells roams around within the cell. Prokaryotic cells were the earliest cells to appear on Earth; eukaryotic cells evolved relatively recently. DNA and RNA work together to build and maintain cell structures.

Every cell in an animal is surrounded by a *cell membrane*; plant cells are surrounded by sturdier *cell walls*. The cell membrane is a kind of gatekeeper, controlling what is allowed to enter or leave the cell. The body of the cell is filled with a fluid material called *cytoplasm* (protoplasm is basically an older word for cytoplasm); the nucleus of a eukaryotic cell contains a

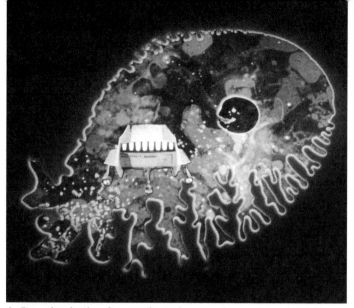
An Enterprise shuttlecraft approaches an immense single-cell space-dwelling organism.

comparable material called *nucleoplasm*. Cytoplasm and nucleoplasm are the packing materials of the cell, holding other cell structures in place, but also providing the medium through which nutrients and other materials travel within the cell.

Organelles are essentially the "organs" of cells. They carry out certain specific tasks within cells, mostly related to obtaining and using energy and proteins. Mitochondria are sausage-shaped organelles that produce energy for cells; think of them as tiny little batteries providing power for the rest of the cell. Mitochondria produce a chemical substance called *adenosine triphosphate (ATP)*, which other organelles can break down for energy. In plants, an organelle called a *chloroplast* acts as the principal site for *photosynthesis*, the chemical process that converts water, carbon dioxide, and sunlight into the simple sugars used by plants for food.

Cells reproduce through an asexual method called *cell division*. Cell division begins when chromosomes in the nucleus split apart and duplicate, a process known as *mitosis*. The strands of the DNA double helix unravel, and then draw up the molecular components needed to form two complete new strands from a surrounding pool of amino acids within the cell. A human cell, containing some one hundred thousand genes, can duplicate its entire ensemble of genes in about seven hours.

The term "negative energy" is not as exotic as it sounds. In fact, it typically refers to a simple mathematical convention. Physicists and chemists sometimes find it convenient to assign negative numbers to the energy of particles, such as an electron orbiting an atomic nucleus. The negative energy value in this case would indicate how much energy is required to separate the electron from the atomic nucleus.

Crystalline Entity
("Datalore"; *TNG*)

Starship Enterprise Science Log, Stardate 41251.9. Second Officer Data recording.

The Enterprise, *returning to my home planet in the Omicron Theta system, has made two disturbing discoveries: The colony has been destroyed by a spacefaring creature known as the Crystalline Entity, and Doctor Noonien Soong, my creator, fabricated parts for another android.*

Lieutenant Commander La Forge and I were able to successfully assemble the second android, who calls himself Lore. According to Lore, I was his prototype. Lore claimed to be a superior being, but demonstrated aberrant and ultimately threatening behavior. We eventually transported him into space, where he is presumed destroyed.

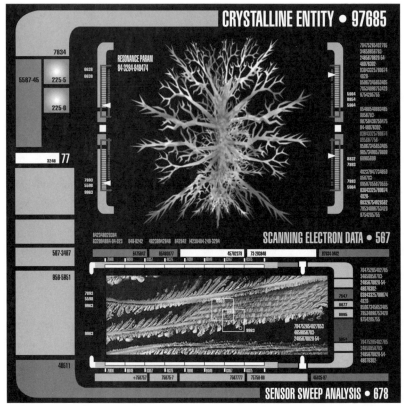

DOUG DREXLER

Crystals are among the most interesting and complex forms of inorganic matter, often treasured for their beauty. Crystals are solids characterized by repeating structures that are typically arranged in lattice patterns.

Most familiar solid substances are crystalline in form, although common glass has an amorphous structure; glass, in fact, is rightly considered an extremely viscous liquid, not a solid. Glass panes flow very slowly over time, as can be seen by examining very old windows in historic houses and churches. Quartz, on the other hand, which can look like glass and is sometimes used in place of glass, is a true crystal.

There are hundreds of different crystal structures that scientists have grouped into seven different "crystal systems." In a given crystal, the arrangement of crystal planes and the angles between them are constant, no matter how big the crystal is or how many times the crystal is broken, a fact discovered by the seventeenth-century Danish scientist Nicolaus Steno.

Crystal structures can be studied by the technique of *X-ray diffraction*. When coherent waves of X rays travel through a crystal, they are diffracted. Depending on the crystal structure, in some places the waves will reinforce one another, and in others the waves will interfere with one another. The resulting patterns of reinforcement and interference can be used to infer the structure of the crystal.

X-ray diffraction has proven to be enormously important in the study of protein molecules. Proteins are very big molecules, sometimes containing as many as a million atoms, and their structures largely determine the kinds of biochemical reactions they will participate in. Protein crystals are grown in laboratories to make it possible for scientists to use the X-ray diffraction technique to determine the structure of biologically important protein molecules. In the near-weightless environment of Earth orbit, very large protein crystals can be grown that aren't distorted by the influence of Earth's gravity. Large-scale protein crystals are frequently grown aboard the U.S. space shuttle.

Various crystals have been discovered in *meteorites*, pieces of asteroids that have fallen to Earth from space.

Junior ("Galaxy's Child"; *TNG*)

Starship Enterprise Science Log, Stardate 44622.1. Second Officer Data recording.

Investigating unusual energy readings in the Alpha Omicron system, the Enterprise *discovered a curious object orbiting the seventh planet in that system. Closer examination revealed that the object was a space-dwelling life-form.*

The creature was inadvertently killed when we attempted to disperse a radiation field with a low-level phaser burst. It was subsequently discovered that the creature was carrying an unborn offspring, which was successfully delivered with the help of Doctor Crusher and Chief Engineer La Forge. The infant proceeded to attach itself to the hull of the ship, drawing sustenance from the energy emissions of the Enterprise *engines. The creature also "imprinted" on the ship, until we were able to guide it to a school of its fellow creatures.*

The twentieth-century Austrian zoologist Konrad Lorenz, a specialist in animal behavior, conducted a famous experiment involving young ducklings. Immediately after the ducklings hatched, Lorenz ensured that he would be the first thing the baby ducks would see. He proceeded to waddle and quack in front of the little ducks, who soon began to follow him around the room, apparently convinced that Lorenz was their mother. Days later, after the ducklings were introduced to their real mother, they still continued to follow Lorenz. Further experiments showed that ducklings will bond with feather-shrouded puppets and other inanimate objects that bear only a superficial resemblance to a real duck.

This kind of response is called *imprinting*. It is a learned

Dr. Crusher (Gates McFadden) knows that her duty is to heal the living; the nature of the life-form does not matter. ROBBIE ROBINSON.

response that can take place only for a few days after the birth of the hatchling. Lorenz's experiment proved that ducklings do not instinctively recognize their mothers, but learn to identify as "mother" the first moving object they see.

Living Nebula ("The Cloud"; VGR)

Starship Voyager **Science Log, Stardate 48526.1. Captain Kathryn Janeway recording.**

Investigating a nebular region rich in omicron particles, Voyager *has discovered an immense space-dwelling life-form.*

The interior of the nebula showed a complex structure never before seen in clouds of interstellar gas and dust. We soon discovered that the "nebula" was responding to Voyager's *presence, and was in fact a living entity.*

Our entry into this space-dwelling life-form damaged a large hollow structure that appeared to be analogous to a humanoid artery or heart chamber. In consultation with the Emergency Medical Hologram, we decided to try to seal the breach we had created in this structure with a narrowly focused nucleonic beam. The operation was a success.

The idea that clouds of matter in space, and perhaps even stars themselves, could be alive has been a science fiction staple for many years. In 1957 the English astronomer Sir Fred Hoyle published *The Black Cloud*, a science-fiction novel that suggested the existence of a living nebula.

Hoyle also believes that the evolution of life on Earth has been driven to a significant degree by actual genetic material that arrived from space. It has been known for some time that comets contain complex organic molecules. Comets bombarding Earth early in its history deposited water and organic molecules on our planet's surface, which many scientists believe was at least a small step toward helping life develop here. Hoyle takes this idea a giant leap forward. He believes that viruses and other genetic material have been arriving on Earth from space throughout our planet's history, not only seeding life but guiding its evolution well beyond the stage of simple, single-cell organisms. No one has yet found a virus or fragments of DNA or RNA in meteorites, or comet dust, and most scientists are skeptical of Hoyle's theory. Within the next few years, however, Japan and the United States plan to launch a comet-sample return mission that will bring pieces of a comet back to Earth for analysis.

Gomtuu ("Tin Man"; *TNG*)

Starship Enterprise Science Log, Stardate 43787.7. Second Officer Data recording.

The Enterprise *has encountered a truly unusual life-form in the Beta Stromgren system, a kind of living spacecraft, constructed by an unknown alien intelligence.*

Federation envoy Tam Elbrun, a Betazoid with formidable telepathic skills, was able to create a symbiotic rapport with the living vessel, which refers to itself as "Gomtuu." Tam Elbrun decided to remain aboard the vessel to explore the galaxy after Gomtuu successfully hurled the Enterprise *and a Romulan warbird clear of Beta Stromgren prior to its explosion.*

B*iotechnology* is one of the most interesting and potentially most important technological developments of the twentieth century. Using organic compounds, scientists and engineers are improving agriculture and animal husbandry, as well as creating materials and devices that mimic the behavior of living tissues and organisms.

Advances in biotechnology have led to substantial improvements in crop yields. Plant-breeding and genetic-engineering techniques have produced crops that have greater resistance to disease, and are better able to survive periods of drought. By manipulating the genes that control cell division, faster rates of crop growth can be achieved. An early example of a vegetable improved by genetic engineering is a variety of tomato that tends to large sizes and maintains its ripeness for longer than average. These advances have also produced some controversy. Many people are concerned over the safety of genetically engineered grains and vegetables. So far, no deleterious effects associated with consuming genetically engineered foods have been observed. Much of what is currently referred to as "genetic engineering" is not very different from the techniques that have been used for centuries to produce hybrid plants.

Genetically engineered bacteria have recently been designed to kill mosquitoes. Mosquitoes can carry potentially deadly diseases, such as malaria and meningitis. Common insecticides such as DDT and malathion are often harmful to wildlife, and insects that are beneficial to plants. Bacteria that are harmless to most organisms but artificially tailored to kill mosquitoes may someday be viable alternatives to more destructive chemical insecticides.

Some scientists are exploring the possibility of using DNA molecules as computers. By their nature, DNA molecules store and process biochemical information. The amino acid components of the DNA molecule in some sense function like the binary codes and operations of computer programs. Using the techniques of genetic engineering, DNA could be manipulated to act like processors in an organic computer. However, scientists have yet to discover a computing application that could be conducted more effectively by DNA-based computers, as opposed to standard microprocessor-based machines.

Aboard the living ship Gomtuu, Tam Elbrun (Harry Groener) finds the peace that has escaped him for so long. ROBBIE ROBINSON.

Vampire Cloud
("Obsession"; *TOS*)

Starship Enterprise Science Log, Stardate 3626.4. Science Officer Spock recording.

An Enterprise *landing party has been attacked and killed by a nebulous space-dwelling creature. Captain Kirk, believing the entity responsible for the deaths of several crew members aboard the* U.S.S. Farragut *eleven years ago, ordered the* Enterprise *to pursue the creature.*

Like the vampire bat of Earth, the creature feeds on fresh blood rich in hemoglobin. I survived an attack by virtue of the fact that Vulcan blood chemistry is based on copper compounds.

The creature is capable of traveling at warp, the only biological organism known to possess this ability. The cloud was pursued to its homeworld, the Class-M planet Tycho IV. Using a bottle of human blood and plasma as bait, the creature was lured to a small antimatter charge and destroyed.

Vampire bats typically live in the tropical and subtropical forest and jungles of Central and South America. Most bats feed on flying insects, but the vampire, a small, brown bat, feeds on fresh blood that it sucks out of the veins of resting animals.

Bats are the only mammals capable of flight. They are nocturnal creatures, and most bats use the rather amazing technique of *echolocation* to navigate and seek prey. Echolocation works like this: the bat emits a series of short, high-pitched squeaks, some fifty per second. The sound waves generated by the squeaks bounce off of anything in their path, even objects as small as insects. Using its supersensitive ears to listen to the echoes of its squeaks, a bat can judge the distance and location of anything in its path, and even identify potential prey. Bat echolocation inspired the *sonar* systems that submarines use to navigate underwater and search for enemy vessels. The "pings" generated by sonar systems work in the same fashion as a bat's squeaks.

Sonar eventually inspired *radar* (one of the most crucial technical developments of World War II), which uses echoes from high-frequency radio waves to locate and identify distant targets. Since radio waves, unlike sound waves, can propagate through space, radar can be used to study surface features on other planets in our solar system. The *Magellan* spacecraft constructed a high-resolution map of the surface of the planet Venus using an orbiting radar system in the early 1990s. Venus is perpetually shrouded in thick, sulfurous clouds, making visual observations of the planet's surface from space impossible.

Also in this episode, Captain Kirk noted that no natural object is capable of traveling faster than the speed of light. Sometimes a trick of perspective can make a natural phenomenon appear to travel faster than light. So-called *superluminal jets* have been discovered emanating from several unstable stars in our galaxy. These jets of subatomic particles and plasma only *appear* to move faster than the speed of light, due to the angle at which we are viewing them and the techniques we use to calculate their velocity.

It is, however, possible for an object to travel faster than the speed of light in the Earth's atmosphere or some medium other than a vacuum. Light doesn't travel as quickly in air or water as it does in a vacuum. *Cosmic rays*, trains of extremely energetic subatomic particles flying through space, often enter the Earth's atmosphere at speeds greater than the speed of light in air. As these cosmic rays crash into air molecules, they emit *Cherenkov radiation*, a kind of radiation emitted by particles traveling faster than the speed of light in a given medium.

Armus ("Skin of Evil"; *TNG*)

Starship Enterprise **Science Log, Stardate 41606.4. Second Officer Data recording.**

A unique and unequivocally malevolent life-form has been discovered on Vagra II. Forced to make an emergency landing there, Counselor Troi and shuttlecraft pilot Lieutenant Ben Prieto were held hostage by this entity, which calls itself Armus.

Armus claims he is a manifestation of pure evil, shed like the skin of a snake by a race of super beings seeking to purge themselves of all hateful emotions. His physical appearance resembles a pool of hydrocarbon residues, highly viscous and opaque. Sensor readings of the entity were inconclusive.

Captain Picard eventually effected the rescue of Troi and Prieto, but not before Armus took the life of the chief security officer, Lieutenant Tasha Yar. The loss of Tasha has been deeply felt by the entire crew. The captain has recommended a complete quarantine of the Vagra II system.

The premise of "Skin of Evil" has a very literary quality; the desire to purge evil influences and "negative" emotions is a theme found throughout Western literature, and many religious teachings and practices as well.

Scientifically, it would be difficult at best to explain how a race of beings could eliminate their darker impulses and in so doing create a living and intelligent creature. The notion of "shedding" these qualities, however, is inspired by the manner in which snakes periodically shed their skin (a process called *molting*). When a snake begins to shed its skin, the old skin undergoes certain chemical changes as new layers of skin cells are prepared below. The old skin becomes dry and brittle, and eventually splits, usually beginning in the facial area surround-

Moments before Tasha Yar's (Denise Crosby) senseless death, Armus reveals himself to the away team.

ing the snake's lips. Once the old skin has split open, the snake wiggles its way out, revealing its new skin, which is often very colorful and iridescent.

Representing Armus as an oil slick is also an interesting touch in the sense that petroleum, which consists of hydrocarbon molecules, is the organic residue from dinosaurs and other living organisms that died and decayed over sixty-five million years ago. Whenever you fill your car with gasoline, you're filling up on dead dinosaurs.

Ian Andrew Troi
("The Child"; *TNG*)

Starship Enterprise Medical Log, Stardate 42083.2. Chief Medical Officer Katherine Pulaski recording.

Ship's counselor Deanna Troi was impregnated by an unknown alien life-form, and in a matter of days gave birth to a male humanoid child who grew at an unprecedented rate.

Named Ian Andrew by his mother, the child grew at a rate four hundred times the human-Betazoid norm. Aside from the rapid developmental cycle, physical and mental development appeared to be quite normal, with the exception that Ian Andrew proved to be a source of eichner radiation, a rare form of particle radiation. Harmless to humanoids at low levels, the eichner radiation did, however, pose a threat to a supply of medical plasma the Enterprise *was transporting to plague victims on the planet Rachelis.*

As Ian Andrew began to mature into adulthood, his origins and purpose became clear: he was a spacefaring entity who took humanoid form to learn about human life firsthand. To avoid harm to the Enterprise *crew and its supply of medical plasma, the entity departed the ship.*

In just nine months a human being grows from a single cell to a fully formed infant. This remarkable rate of growth is reduced substantially after birth. Most children, as they continue to grow, however, experience "growth spurts," gaining a centimeter or two in height in just a few months.

The rate of growth of Ian Troi is unprecedented in the human species, but there is an extremely rare medical condition, called *progeria*, that mimics the physical symptoms of old age in children. Children who suffer from this condition are physically weak and have weakened immune systems and a range of chronic illnesses common to people in their seventies or eighties. Progeria victims typically die in their teens, although they appear to be much older, with wrinkled skin and hair loss commonly seen in elderly people.

The other side of this unusual medical coin is the possibility that the human aging process could be decelerated or reversed, not during gestation or childhood, but after adulthood has been reached.

Moriarty
("Elementary, Dear Data"; *TNG*)

Starship Enterprise **Science Log, Stardate 42291.1. Second Officer Data recording.**

In an attempt to create a holodeck adversary worthy of myself in the role of Sherlock Holmes, Lieutenant Commander La Forge has inadvertently produced a sentient and highly sophisticated intelligent entity within the Sherlock Holmes simulation.

The entity is based on the recurring character of Doctor James Moriarty featured in a number of Sherlock Holmes stories. In his holodeck incarnation, Moriarty was conscious of his own existence, and able to take control of various Enterprise *systems through the holodeck-computer interface. Moriarty also held Chief Medical Officer Katherine Pulaski hostage and demanded to be freed from the holomatrix. Captain Picard explained to him that this was impossible, but promised to save his program until a method could be devised to provide this strange new computer-generated life-form with the ability to leave the holodeck.*

Moriarty is what some computer buffs would call an "intelligent agent," a piece of software smart enough to find its way around a larger computer system. The Internet, which includes the World Wide Web, is a network of computer networks that has been growing at an exponential rate since the early 1990s. As a consequence of this extraordinary growth, it's becoming more and more difficult to find specific information on the Web. Intelligent agents may soon change that.

Various "search engines" have been created to help end users find specific information on the Web. Suppose, for example, you wanted to find out about John F. Kennedy, the thirty-fifth President of the United States. You would type "John F. Kennedy" into the Web-searching program, and it would generate a list of all documents on the Web that include references to John F. Kennedy. There would be thousands of documents on this list, including a few documents referring to John F. Kennedys who weren't the thirty-fifth President, but just happen to have the same name. The search criteria can be made more specific, but with today's search engines you're basically limited to just typing sequences of words, hoping that they will match documents that contain the information you're looking for.

An intelligent agent would be a much more sophisticated piece of software, capable of understanding, to some degree, the *intent* behind a user's request. The intelligent agent would travel the Web, searching for the kinds of information requested by the user, interacting with database software and other intelligent agents as necessary. Intelligent agents would also be capable of learning and better understanding the needs of their end users as time goes on.

Professor James Moriarty
(Daniel Davis): a sentient
being or a sentient subroutine?
ROBBIE ROBINSON.

Ronin ("Sub Rosa"; *TNG*)

***Starship Enterprise* Medical Log, Stardate 47427.9. Chief Medical Officer Beverly Crusher recording.**

Attending the funeral of my grandmother at the Caldos colony, I encountered a man who called himself Ronin. I was strangely drawn to this man, and later discovered that, despite his youthful appearance, he had been romantically involved with my grandmother.

I too fell under Ronin's spell, and was ready to resign my Starfleet commission when I discovered that "Ronin" was an anaphasic life-form, an entity composed of energetic plasma in a subspace field, who used human females to maintain his form.

Possession, or the control of a person's mind by an alien entity, has been featured on *Star Trek* several times. There is a long history of human possession by demons and other unseemly creatures in the folklore of many cultures.

The modern incarnation of this phenomenon is the rash of alien abduction reports that have been in the news in recent years. According to some surveys, hundreds of thousands of Americans claim to have had some kind of abduction experience. The typical abduction report is recalled through hypnosis. The victim usually recalls being forced aboard an alien spacecraft and subjected to various kinds of probes and medical experimentation.

Despite the many alleged reports of alien abduction, it seems hard to believe that alien beings capable of interstellar travel would kidnap humans and subject them to extremely crude "medical" procedures. A civilization advanced enough to travel the stars would surely have advanced medical knowl-

Now Beverly (Gates McFadden) comprehends the danger that Ronin represents and can take only one action. ROBBIE ROBINSON.

edge; a single drop of blood is all they would need to determine the entire genetic and biomolecular structure of any individual.

The myriad reports of alien abduction, however, may be the expression of a deeper psychological phenomenon. The alien beings reported by most "abductees" have small bodies with large heads and eyes, essentially the body structure of small children. Perhaps abduction experiences are really subconscious memories of unpleasant events the abductees experienced in the first few years of life, an age before most people can form coherent, conscious memories. This seems to me to be a much more likely explanation for abduction reports than encounters with aliens behaving badly. Alternatively, the twentieth-century psychoanalyst Carl Jung believed that there is a "collective unconscious," a set of common images and memories that all humans share at the subconscious level. Perhaps the alien figures reported by abductees are a manifestation of this collective unconscious.

More importantly, if we were ready to accept stories of alien abduction as conclusive proof of a genuine alien presence on Earth, then wouldn't we also be forced to accept the reality of elves, and fairies, and unicorns, and the hundreds of other strange beings that millions of people have claimed to encounter over the centuries? The accounts of eyewitnesses, no matter how compelling or how similar their stories, do not constitute sufficient evidence for the assertion that alien life-forms are abducting human beings. Extraordinary claims demand extraordinary evidence. Accepting verbal accounts of abduction as credible evidence is very much in the spirit (pardon the pun) of the mentality that gave rise to the "witch trials" that unleashed horrific suffering and death on thousands of innocent men, women, and children in the fifteenth through seventeenth centuries.

Two-Dimensional Life-Forms ("The Loss"; *TNG*)

Starship Enterprise Science Log, Stardate 44362.1 Second Officer Data recording.

En route to T'lli Beta, the Enterprise *encountered highly unusual readings on main sensors, followed by a malfunction of the warp drive.*

It was eventually discovered that the drive malfunction was caused by a unique space-dwelling life-form that exists in a two-dimensional plane. These life-forms derive the energy they need to survive from cosmic string fragments. Using the main deflector dish, the Enterprise *was able to generate a graviton pulse that harmonically stimulated a nearby string fragment, guiding the life-forms to the fragment, which may in fact be their natural home.*

For many years mathematicians have contemplated the existence of "higher dimensions," that is, dimensions beyond the familiar height, width, and depth accessible to human vision. Until the current century, however, most mathematicians and scientists considered the world of higher dimensions to be a purely abstract domain—something that could be imagined and manipulated in mathematical formulae, but lacking an independent existence in the "real" world.

Around the year 1900 the English mathematician Charles Howard Hinton developed a technique for "visualizing" higher dimensions. Specifically, he created a method whereby a four-dimensional cube—called a *hypercube*—could be imagined. First, consider a three-dimensional analogy. A three-dimensional cube can be unfolded to create a flat, two-dimensional shape: a cross. The basic geometric properties of a cube can be deduced

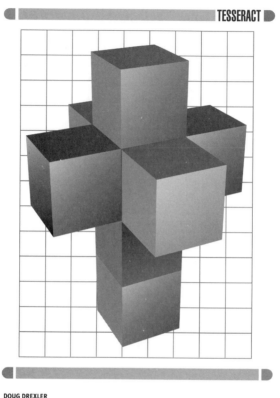

DOUG DREXLER

by examining its two-dimensional projection. In the same fashion, a hypercube unfolded into three-dimensional space would produce a series of cubes stacked into a cruciform configuration with two crossbars. This object is called a *tesseract* (see figure). Hinton eventually concluded that this three-dimensional projection of a hypercube is as close as human beings can ever come to visualizing a four-dimensional object. Nevertheless, the geometric properties of a four-dimensional hypercube can be inferred by studying the tesseract.

Zalkonian "John Doe"
("Transfigurations"; *TNG*)

Starship Enterprise **Science Log, Stardate 43965.2. Second Officer Data recording.**

The Enterprise *recovered a humanoid in critical condition from the wreckage of a space vehicle in the Zeta Gelis star cluster. Chief Medical Officer Beverly Crusher was able to stabilize the patient using neural elements from Chief Engineer Geordi La Forge's VISOR device.*

Upon regaining consciousness, the patient claimed to have no memory of his accident or identity. "John Doe," as he came to be called, demonstrated extraordinary recuperative powers, but also displayed a significant rate of cell mutation. Shortly thereafter, a representative of a race known as the Zalkonians rendezvoused with the Enterprise *and claimed that John Doe had committed serious crimes against his people. It was subsequently revealed that John Doe was undergoing a profound physical transformation that was considered threatening to the prevailing social order established by the Zalkonian government. Upon completing his transformation, John Doe became a creature of free space and departed the* Enterprise, *thankful for our assistance.*

The transformation of John Doe raises the interesting question of the future of human evolution. Speculations about our biological future often include complete baldness (based on the fact that our early ancestors were much hairier than we are), fewer teeth, and additional fingers. Such predictions, however, ignore two important facts.

Firstly, the evolution of any species is a consequence of the interaction of that species with its environment. Unless we can

John Doe's (Mark LaMura) solid form is actually just a step toward his final meta-morphosis. ROBBIE ROBINSON.

predict the future condition of the human environment, there is no way to predict the future evolution of human beings. Furthermore, humans, more than any other animal, are capable of modifying their environment to suit their needs. If we successfully maintain the environment in which we currently live, the only mechanism that would motivate change in the human species would be random mutations that confer some kind of biological advantage that could be inherited by offspring, or intentional manipulation of human genetics through genetic engineering.

Our knowledge of the fundamental mechanisms of evolution will soon place us in control of our biological destiny. Comprehensive knowledge of the workings of the DNA molecule opens the possibility that we may someday manipulate our own genes to create specific physical traits in our offspring. This is, to say the least, an awesome and potentially frightening prospect.

Apollo ("Who Mourns for Adonais?"; *TOS*)

Starship Enterprise **Science Log, Stardate 3470.4. Science Officer Spock recording.**

A routine survey mission to the planet Pollux IV revealed the presence of an extraordinary being who claimed to be Apollo, one of the gods found in the mythology of the ancient Greek people of Earth.

The Apollo being was able to channel energy through a unique, electrically conductive organ in his chest cavity. The energy source was an artificial structure, shaped in the form of an ancient Greek temple.

Apollo constrained the Enterprise *in an unusual force field that superficially resembled a human hand, and held a landing party, including Captain Kirk, hostage. Focused, resonant pulses from the ship's deflector shields were able to negate sections of the force field, creating windows for communication and phaser beam transmissions.* Enterprise *phasers were able to destroy the temple structure, neutralizing the force field and robbing Apollo of his energy source.*

Unfortunately, in the wake of his defeat, Apollo choose to terminate his existence in our realm. It is not clear whether Apollo

Claiming to be the Greek god of music and light, Apollo (Michael Forest) demands the worship of the *Enterprise* crew.

died in the sense that humanoids understand death, or trans-formed his life into a plane of existence alluded to by Apollo in dis-cussions with archaeology and anthropology officer Lieutenant Carolyn Palamas. The question of whether the being who claimed to be Apollo was in fact a long-lived space traveler, who, along with a number of compatriots, visited Earth nearly ten thousand years ago and formed the basis of Greek mythology, may never be resolved. Further investigation of relevant archaeological evidence on Earth and other nearby Class-M planets is recommended.

The ancient Greek myths, which form the foundation of western literature and art, were first committed to papyrus by the poet Ovid in his work *The Metamorphosis*. The stories of the Titans and the Gods of Olympus were undoubtedly passed down orally through countless generations seeking to understand the natural environment and the perils and puzzles of human life.

According to the ancient myths, Apollo was the Greek Sun god, the son of Zeus (leader of the gods of Olympus) and Leto, a mortal; Apollo was also the twin brother of Artemis. He was an accomplished archer, and a patron of physicians, poets, and farmers. During the Trojan War, Apollo sided with Troy, bringing a devastating plague on the Greeks.

Chariots of the Gods, a book written by Erich von Daniken in the 1960s, popularized the notion that the gods of Greek mythology were in fact astronauts from some far civilization whose technology inspired fear and awe in the simple herdsman of the Mediterranean five thousand or more years ago. Although intriguing, there is no evidence to substantiate the idea that alien astronauts visited Earth in the distant past or inspired the mythical stories recounted by Ovid and others.

The idea that Apollo could channel electrical energy through an organ in his body is based on real animals—such as the electric eel of the Amazon river—that have this ability. Four families of bony fish and several torpedoes and rays possess *electric organs*. Electric organs are probably derived from muscle tissues, which conduct electrical signals to and from the brain. The organs are typically arranged into plates that form organic electrical storage batteries. The electric eel can generate shocks as strong as 550 volts, killing or paralyzing prey and protecting the eel against predators.

Douwd ("Survivors"; *TNG*)

Starship Enterprise **Science Log, Stardate 43156.1. Second Officer Data recording.**

Responding to a distress call from the human colony on Delta Rana IV, the Enterprise *has discovered that the entire colony has been destroyed, apparently by a hostile alien force known as the Husnock. Miraculously, two colonists survived the devastating alien onslaught: Kevin and Rishon Uxbridge, an elderly couple from Earth. The* Enterprise *subsequently engaged and repelled a Husnock warship returning to Delta Rana IV.*

Starship Enterprise **Science Log, Supplemental.**

We have determined that the Husnock warship that fired on the Enterprise *was an elaborate illusion created by Kevin Uxbridge, who is not human but an ancient and immensely powerful being known as a Douwd. He explained that the destruction of the colony and his mate at the hands of the Husnock occurred several years ago; the Douwd had been maintaining the illusion of the colony as a self-imposed punishment. When the colony was destroyed, the Douwd exterminated the entire Husnock species through his incalculable mental power.*

All of the members of a population of living organisms that can interbreed and produce fertile offspring under natural conditions are members of the same *species*. Most species on Earth contain millions or billions of members; the human species is currently close to a population of six billion. Animals whose populations are so small that even a minor change in their environment could lead to extinction are considered *endangered species*.

The destruction of entire species happens on Earth on a

regular basis. No species lasts forever, but some manage to survive longer than others; the various species of shark have been around for over 350 million years. In order to survive, a species must frequently adapt to its environment. The process of adaptation often produces physiological changes that lead to new species.

Mass extinctions periodically occur on Earth. During a mass extinction, a substantial fraction of all species dies out, typically due to a radical change in the environment. The last mass extinction happened about sixty-five million years ago, when some seventy percent of all species—including the dinosaurs—disappeared from the face of the Earth. The leading theory of the cause of this mass extinction is an asteroid collision. The *geological record* clearly indicates that an asteroid or comet several kilometers in diameter smashed into the Earth in the vicinity of what is now the Yucatán peninsula. The impact blasted billions of tons of dust and debris into the upper atmosphere, and triggered fires around the globe. The smoke from these fires, combined with the dust released by the initial impact, blotted out sunlight for months and possibly years. Most of the plant life dependent on sunlight soon died, followed by the animals that ate those plants, and the animals that ate *those* animals, and so on.

Some biologists argue that Earth is currently in a period of "mass" extinction as a consequence of the impact of human activity on the environment. Part of the problem of judging this assertion is that it's very hard to determine how many species currently exist. Estimates of the total number of species range from a few million to ten million.

As the human population of the Earth continues to swell exponentially, the danger to the ecosystem is likely to grow. Human encroachment on formerly pristine wilderness and increasing levels of atmospheric carbon dioxide due to industrial activity are only two of the myriad and complex factors affecting the ecosystem today. It isn't clear what the ultimate impact of human activity on the environment will be; no one knows, for example, whether natural processes might compensate for increases in atmospheric carbon dioxide. It is clear, however, that humans are capable of altering the environment on a global scale. We are unwittingly conducting a massive, uncontrolled experiment on the Earth's environment, the only place in the universe we know is capable of supporting human life.

Korob & Sylvia ("Cat's Paw"; *TOS*)

Starship *Enterprise* Science Log, Stardate 3021.1. Science Officer Spock recording.

On the planet Pyris VII, the Enterprise *has encountered beings from another galaxy with intentions of conquering our galaxy.*

Assuming human form and calling themselves Korob and Sylvia, these aliens possessed a device capable of instantaneously transmuting energy into matter. The transmuter was controlled by the thoughts of its user, making it an extremely powerful and potentially deadly tool.

When Captain Kirk destroyed the transmuter, the true nature of Korob and Sylvia was revealed: physically diminutive, possibly avian creatures incapable of surviving for more than a moment in the Class-M environment of Pyris VII.

Chances are we won't need to leave the galaxy to discover exotic alien life-forms. As noted in earlier logs, the diversity of life on Earth suggests that life on other worlds, evolving under different circumstance and perhaps based on different sets of organic molecules, is likely to be far stranger than anything we're familiar with on Earth.

Korob and Sylvia, alien life-forms from beyond our galaxy.

"Cat's Paw" does raise an interesting question: How small can an organism be and still be intelligent? In Earth life, intelligence seems to be strongly correlated with a high brain-to-body-mass ratio. A typical human brain weighs about 1.3 kilos (three pounds). *T. rex*, who weighed about 190 tons, had a brain about the size and mass of a walnut.

Another aspect of this question involves the size of brain cells. Human brain cells average about twenty microns in length (not including the axons and dendrites), and there are some one hundred billion such cells in the typical human head. But it's conceivable that brain cells evolving on another planet could be much smaller than human brain cells, or that an entirely different and more compact neural architecture could give rise to intelligence.

The relationship between science and magic explored in "Cat's Paw" is also (to quote a certain Vulcan) fascinating. *Star*

Trek has featured several episodes where science triumphs over superstition. And yet an intelligent, enlightened person from the nineteenth century would certainly find the marvels of late twentieth-century technology to be "magical" in their power. As science fiction writer Arthur C. Clarke once pointed out, any sufficiently advanced technology is indistinguishable from magic.

Trelane ("The Squire of Gothos"; *TOS*); Q ("Encounter at Farpoint"; *TNG*)

Starship Enterprise Science Log, Stardate 2128.5. Science Officer Spock recording.

Several Enterprise *bridge officers have been abducted by a super being of extraordinary power. Calling itself Trelane, the entity was capable of creating breathable planetary atmospheres and even moving planets through space, through the action of an extremely sophisticated device controlled by his thoughts. Trelane was eventually restrained by his parents (if that is even the appropriate term) before he could seriously harm the crew.*

Starship Enterprise Science Log, Stardate 41156.2. Second Officer Data recording.

The Enterprise *and her crew have been tested by a being of great power and intelligence. Calling itself Q, this entity is capable of manipulating matter and energy at galactic scales, and even altering fundamental physical constants.*

Trelane and Q represent essentially omnipotent beings who, like the gods of ancient Greece, frequently interfered in human affairs for the sake of amusement, and sometimes

Making use of an image that Janeway and Tuvok can understand, Q (Graham Gerrit) and Q (John DeLancie) create a symbolic version of the Q continuum.
ROBBIE ROBINSON.

less benign motives. They are also tricksters, taking great delight in deceiving and manipulating our very serious Starfleet officers.

Trelane is, in a sense, the inspiration for Q. Both characters live on another "plane of existence," and both have apparently evolved from humanoid ancestors more or less comparable to us in terms of physical attributes and technological capabilities. There has been some fan speculation that Trelane and Q are related (like father, like son...), but this has never been explicitly established in any of the television episodes or films.

The idea that there may be other dimensions or planes of existence beyond human perception dates back at least to ancient Greece. The ancient Greek philosopher Plato believed that there are four planes of existence arranged in a hierarchy. The highest plane is the plane of ideas and knowledge. Below this is the plane of pure mathematics, followed by the everyday world, and at the bottom, the world of shadows. The things we see and touch in the everyday world are in a state of flux; reality, according to Plato, is composed of constant universal forms.

Flowers wither and die but the form and idea of *flower* never changes.

Q and Trelane hardly behave like devotees of Plato, but it is interesting to speculate on the nature of reality and the possibility that the world we perceive with our senses is merely a projection of some deeper reality. The domain of science, unfortunately, is restricted to the world we can perceive with our senses, and has nothing to contribute to the debate over the ultimate nature of reality. The science of *quantum mechanics*, however, at least suggests that the world of the senses may not be up to the task of understanding the fundamental nature of reality. Scientists probing the structure of atoms and subatomic particles have discovered that commonsense notions of things like particles and waves fail to have meaning in the world of the very small. Protons and electrons don't look or behave like tiny pellets, but more like careening packets of energy, sometimes interacting like billiard balls, sometimes storming through space like ocean waves.

Science is essentially descriptive. We can measure the charge and mass and some other physical properties of an electron, but we may never understand the fundamental essence of an electron. What, after all, is "charge," except a label for a property that we understand only in descriptive terms?

Organians
("Errand of Mercy"; *TOS*)

***Starship Enterprise* Science Log, Stardate 3202.4. Science Officer Spock recording.**

Captain Kirk and I have encountered an immense alien intelligence, billions of years old, possessing an intellect far beyond human comprehension.

For uncounted millennia the Organians have maintained the appearance of simple humanoids living in a preindustrial society. This façade was created to provide the Organians with a means of interacting with less evolved life-forms.

The Organians represent beings of "pure energy," meaning they do not possess physical bodies, i.e., they are *noncorporeal*. The chief question raised by the idea of noncorporeal beings is, Could a field of energy remain organized at such a level of complexity?

In his special theory of relativity, Einstein showed that energy and matter are basically opposite sides of the same coin. It is possible to convert matter into energy through nuclear reactions, and it is also possible, under some circumstances, to turn energy into matter. As far as we know today, energy fields are invariably generated by some kind of physical process. No one has yet discovered a process in nature that matches the level of complexity of the electrical activity in the human brain.

Some philosophers have argued that consciousness does not arise in the brain, but that the brain serves as a kind of receiver for a universal intelligence that created and permeates the cosmos. After death our minds return to that infinite consciousness that runs the universe as it contemplates its own being and purpose. This is certainly an interesting speculation, but is not based on established scientific findings.

The great riddle, the big question in science and perhaps in life is, What is the nature of the primal "stuff" of the cosmos, the particles and forces that can build stars and planets, brains and minds?

Afterword

"The important thing is not to stop questioning."

—Albert Einstein

It should always be remembered that science is about asking questions. The importance of continuing to ask questions, never automatically taking anything an authority tells you at face value, cannot be overemphasized. Even the most brilliant scientists sometimes make mistakes, or get their facts wrong. Furthermore, what is widely accepted as scientific fact by one generation may be completely discounted by later generations. This is not to say that the findings of modern science can't be trusted; clearly, thousands of technical innovations in medicine, electronics, aviation, and myriad other fields testify to the extraordinary power of the scientific method. When a cherished scientific theory is overturned, it is typically because a new, more powerful theory, incorporating many features of the earlier theory, has provided even greater insight into the workings of nature.

The *Star Trek* view of the future is an essentially optimistic view, a future with few limits, few boundaries. The science-fiction writer Jules Verne once said, "What one person can imagine, another can create." And yet who could have imagined, three hundred years ago, nuclear-powered spacecraft, desktop computers, solar cells, genetic engineering, and a thousand other miracles of modern science and technology that are largely taken for granted today?

The visionary Renaissance artist and inventor Leonardo Da Vinci (a recurring character on *Star Trek: Voyager*) imagined a variety of flying machines, including one based on the principles used to build modern helicopters. Of course, Leonardo's drawings of flying machines bear only marginal similarity to modern aircraft. The same will certainly be true of *Star Trek's* vision of starships and other twenty-fourth–century technologies. Future starships will no doubt look very different from the *Starship Enterprise*, but almost certainly starships will someday be built. There are no fundamental laws of physics that preclude the possibility of interstellar travel (at least at sublight velocities), and we may yet discover some ingenious means to travel faster than light. It is the hope of everyone involved with the creation of the *Star Trek* universe that humanity will rise above the differences that divide us and join together in the great adventures that await us among the stars.

A Basic Science Primer

This section is an *extremely* cursory overview of some of the basic definitions and concepts discussed in the science logs. It is not by any means intended to be a complete review of basic astronomy, physics, chemistry, and biology. For more information, I refer the interested reader to the books noted in the bibliography, as well as introductory high school or college science texts.

Units of Measurement

The following is a brief review of some of the international-system units commonly used in the sciences and throughout the various science logs.

Mass is measured in *kilograms*; a kilogram is about 2.2 pounds. Distances are measured in *meters*. A meter is approximately thirty-nine inches. A *kilometer* is a thousand meters, which is about 0.6 miles. Very small distances are typically measured in *microns*; a micron is a millionth of a meter. Another unit of very small distances, commonly used in optics, is the *angstrom*, which is a ten-millionth of a meter. The wavelength of visible light ranges from about four thousand angstroms (blue) to seven thousand angstroms (red).

Angles are measured in a unit called *radians*, but a more convenient unit for the purposes of this book is *degrees*. A circle contains 360 degrees. A degree is further divided into sixty *minutes of arc*, and a minute of arc contains sixty *seconds of arc*.

Since astronomical distances are typically very large, a special set of units is used in astronomy. The *astronomical unit* is the mean distance from the Earth to the Sun, about 150 million kilometers. A *light-year* is defined as the distance a beam of light, traveling at 186,000 miles per second, travels in one year. The average distance between stars in the spiral arms of our galaxy is four or five light-years. The next closest star to our solar system, Proxima Centauri, is a little more than four light-years away. Four light-years is roughly equal to twenty-four *trillion* miles! A *parsec* is the distance from the Earth that a star or other astronomical object would have to be to shift its apparent position (due to parallax) by one second of arc as the Earth moves from one side of its orbit to the other. A parsec is equal to 3.26 light-years.

Big and small numbers are very common in astronomy and physics. To make it easier to handle such numbers, mathematicians long ago devised *exponential notation*. In exponential notation, the exponent is used to indicate how many zeros follow the number before the exponent. For example, $3 \cdot 10^4$ ("three times ten to the fourth power") represents a three followed by four zeros (30,000), or thirty thousand. Negative exponents are used for very small numbers: $7 \cdot 10^{-3}$ represents 0.007, or seven thousandths.

The basic unit of force in physics is the *newton*, named in honor of Sir Isaac Newton. A newton is the amount of force required to impart an acceleration of one meter per second to a one-kilogram mass. Another unit, the *dyne*, is used for smaller forces; one newton equals 10^5 dynes. Energy is often defined as the ability to do work. The basic unit of energy in physics is the *joule*, which is the amount of work done by a force of one newton applied over a distance of one meter. The basic unit of power is the *watt*. A watt is simply one joule of energy expended (or consumed) per second. In atomic physics, energy is commonly measured in *electron volts (ev)*. One ev is the kinetic energy (energy of motion) imparted to an electron when it is accelerated through a potential difference of one volt. Since Einstein demonstrated that matter and energy are equivalent, the masses of subatomic particles are frequently given in electron volts.

In the United States, newspapers and television news shows typically report local temperature in degrees Fahrenheit. In the metric system, temperatures are measured in degrees *celsius (C)* or *kelvins (K)*. Water freezes at zero degrees C, and boils at one hundred degrees C. *Absolute zero*, the temperature at which all motion would theoretically cease,* is −273 C, and is also defined as zero degrees kelvin, or zero kelvins. A change in temperature of one degree C is equivalent to a change in temperature of one kelvin, hence, the freezing point of water is 273 kelvins.

* In practice, this can never happen, due to quantum mechanical effects.

The Milky Way Galaxy

In the *Star Trek* universe, the United Federation of Planets was chartered to facilitate the peaceful exploration of the *Milky Way Galaxy*, a pinwheel structure of four hundred billion stars stretching one hundred thousand light-years end-to-end. The Earth orbits an average *main sequence* star located in one of the spiral arms, about thirty thousand light-years from the galaxy's center. The Sun and its planets comprise our *solar system* (or planetary system; the terms are interchangeable).

On *Star Trek* we divide the galaxy into four equal-sized quadrants (this is not common practice in real astronomy). Each quadrant contains approximately one hundred billion stars. Earth and the majority of Federation planets are located in the Alpha Quadrant. The DS9 *wormhole* leads from the Alpha Quadrant to the Gamma Quadrant.

Stars

Stars in the Milky Way Galaxy feature a wide variety of masses, diameters, surface temperatures, and luminosities. Every star is essentially a spherical mass of very hot gas, primarily hydrogen, producing energy through the process of *nuclear fusion*. Deep in the cores of most active stars, gas pressures reach thousands of times the atmospheric pressure at the surface of the Earth. Temperatures rise to millions of kelvins or more. The intense pressure and heat in a star's core forces some of the hydrogen atoms there to fuse into helium atoms. This process releases energy in the form of X rays. The X rays generated in a star's core radiate outward toward the star's surface, losing energy along the way as they ricochet among the innumerable atoms comprising the star's bulk. Eventually this radiated energy emerges from the surface of the star, primarily in the form of visible light.

The star most familiar to humankind is the Sun. The Sun is a more or less average star in terms of mass and luminosity. It is classified as a G-type star. Following a convention established in the nineteenth century, stars are classified by letters that roughly correspond to their surface temperatures. The letter sequence of stellar classification, in descending order of temperature, is

O B A F G K M N.

O-type stars are the hottest stars, with surface temperatures sometimes exceeding forty thousand kelvins. G stars, like the Sun, have surface temperatures on the order of six thousand kelvins. N stars, the coolest stars, are a relatively "chilly" three thousand kelvins. (The letter assignations can be remembered by the phrase, Oh Be A Fine Girl [or Guy], Kiss Me Now.)

Stars come in many sizes, from dwarfs to giants. The Sun is an average-size star, perhaps even a bit on the small side at roughly 1.4 million kilometers in diameter. One of the largest stars in our neighborhood, Betelgeuse, a red giant, averages several hundred million kilometers in diameter. Placed at the Sun's location, Betelgeuse would extend beyond all of the planets in the inner solar system, including Earth. The diameter of this red giant is not constant, but changes as the star pulsates; Betelgeuse is an example of a *variable star*. The brightness of Betelgeuse varies in rhythm with its pulsating atmosphere.

Single stars are in the minority in our galaxy. Most stars are gravitationally bound to a stellar partner. *Binary stars* are two stars that orbit around the same point in space, called the *barycenter* of the binary system. For two stars of identical mass, the barycenter is located exactly between them. In most binaries, the two stars have different masses; in these cases, the barycenter is proportionally closer to the more massive member of the pair. *Trinary stars*—systems consisting of three stars orbiting a common point in space—are also fairly common, the closest example being our nearest stellar neighbors Alpha Centauri A and B and their diminutive companion Proxima Centauri.

The ancient Greeks identified patterns among the stars and gave them names. These are the *constellations*, predominantly named after the characters of Greek mythology. From their Mediterranean home, the Greeks could not see most of the stars of the southern hemisphere. Post-Renaissance explorers observed the southern skies and designated constellations there. Many of these constellations were named after the inventions that made world-ocean exploration possible: Sextans (the sextant), Vela (the sails), and so on. Other cultures, such as the Navajo of Arizona and the Mayans of Central America, created their own constellations. Today there are eighty-eight constellations recognized by the International

Astronomical Union (IAU). At about the end of the nineteenth century, the IAU drew formal boundaries around the eighty-eight constellations, and these borders are still used today.

The ancient Greeks rarely bothered to name individual stars; they were mostly interested in star groups. The ancient Persians, on the other hand, were mostly interested in observing individual stars: The stars' rising and setting times were used as a kind of celestial calendar. Most of the star names we use today are therefore Arabic in origin: Antares, Rigel, Zuben el Genubi, and so on.

A star can also be named by its brightness (as seen from Earth) within its home constellation. The letters of the Greek alphabet are used to designate relative brightness. The brightest star in the constellation Orion, for example, is Alpha Orionis, which is also known as Betelgeuse. The second brightest star in that constellation is Beta Orionis, etc. Note that the genitive form of the constellation name is used in this naming scheme.

Planets and Planetary Systems

Planets are spherical cosmic bodies substantially smaller than stars, composed of varying combinations of metals, minerals, liquids, ices, and gases. Unlike stars, planets do not generate light and energy through nuclear fusion. Planets appear as points of light in the sky because they reflect sunlight. The two major classes of planets are the *terrestrial planets*, which feature solid surfaces and relatively thin atmospheres or no atmosphere at all; and *jovian planets*, large, mostly gaseous bodies that may or may not include solid cores.

In the *Star Trek* nomenclature, terrestrial planets with breathable atmospheres are called *Class-M* planets. Gas giants like Jupiter are known as *Class-J* planets (*J* stands for *jovian*).

The Fullness of Space

Contrary to popular belief, space is not empty. The mixture of rarefied gases, dust particles, and *electromagnetic fields* that permeate most of the galaxy is called the *interstellar medium (ISM)*. The average density of the interstellar medium is extremely low: roughly one atom of hydrogen per cubic meter. By comparison, a cubic centimeter of air on Earth at sea level contains some fifty billion billion atoms. Hydrogen atoms are the most common constituent in the ISM. (Hydrogen is, in fact, the most common element in the universe.) Heavier elements, as well as molecules, including some simple organic molecules, are also found in the ISM.

Grains of interstellar dust are found throughout the ISM. They are typically comprised of a core of silicate or graphite (carbon) material, surrounded by a mantle of lighter molecules (often ices of methane, carbon dioxide, ammonia, and water). The surfaces of interstellar dust grains can act as catalysts for relatively complex chemical reactions, producing organic molecules that form a coating on the grain. Dust grains, attracted by their mutual gravity, often accumulate in *molecular clouds*, which can span many light-years.

A large interstellar cloud of gas and dust is called a *nebula*. In addition to being extraordinarily beautiful, nebulae are the birthplaces of stars. Drawn together by gravity, clumps of gas and dust collapse within a nebula, growing hotter through friction, drawing in more nebular matter as the knot of gas grows. Eventually a pocket of gas becomes hot and dense enough to cause the hydrogen atoms at its center to collide and fuse into helium atoms. Through this process a star is born.

How long a star will live is largely a function of the star's mass. Very massive stars exhaust their supplies of hydrogen much more quickly than lower-mass stars. The amount of time a star spends on the *main sequence* of stellar evolution can range from a few million to ten or more billion years. Our Sun, a fairly average star, has been converting hydrogen into helium more or less steadily for some five billion years, and will probably continue to do so for another five billion years.

Atoms and Subatomic Particles

The early-nineteenth–century chemist John Dalton established the modern *atomic theory of matter*, which asserts that all the different forms of matter we find in the world are composed of various combinations of a small number of *chemical elements*, or atoms. The *periodic table of the elements* charts the basic properties of the atoms that make up ordinary matter.

An atom itself is made up of subatomic particles. The particles in an atom are organized into a *nucleus*, composed of *protons* and *neutrons*, surrounded by a cloud of *electrons* in orbit around the nucleus. Many subatomic particles carry an electrical charge. Protons have a positive electrical charge, electrons have a negative charge, and neutrons have no charge. The force of attraction between positive and negative charges keeps electrons in orbit around the nucleus.

Some particles are made up of even smaller particles. Protons and neutrons, for example, are composed of particles called *quarks* (not to be confused with a notorious Ferengi bartender). Electrons, on the other hand, are *fundamental particles*; they cannot be further broken down (so far as we know) into smaller constituents. Quarks are also fundamental particles.

Since the English physicist Ernest Rutherford discovered the electron in 1910, hundreds of other subatomic particles have been discovered. Most of them are unstable, short-lived particles,

A Few Subatomic Particles

Name	Mass*	Charge
Proton (consists of three quarks)	1	+1
Neutron (consists of three quarks)	1	0
Electron (fundamental particle)	1/1836	-1
Neutrino†	$<10^{-8}$	0
Quarks:		
Up	1/235	+2/3
Down	1/135	-1/3
Strange	1/6	-1/3
Charm	1.6	+2/3
Bottom	5.2	-1/3
Top	170	+2/3

A proton consits of two up quarks and a down quark; a neutron consists of two down quarks and an up quark. Particles called *gluons* bind quarks together within protons and neutrons. Quarks and electrons are fundamental particles, i.e., they are not composed of still smaller particles (so far as we know).

*In terms of proton mass; the neutron is actually slightly more massive than the proton.
†It is not clear whether the neutrino has mass, but if it does, its mass is very small.

byproducts of *nuclear reactions* or other energetic processes. Some subatomic particles are listed in the table on page 286.

All of the subatomic particles discovered to date have corresponding *antiparticles*. The antiparticle corresponding to the electron, for example, is the *positron*. It has the same mass as an electron, but an opposite electric charge. *Antimatter* is the term given to the family of antiparticles; in the *Star Trek* universe, various forms of antimatter play an important role in starship propulsion and power generation.

Molecular Biology

Living tissues are primarily made up of very complex *organic molecules*. The carbon atom is the defining constituent of an organic molecule. Any molecule that contains carbon (with the exception of a few simple compounds such as carbon monoxide and carbon dioxide) is considered an organic molecule.

A chemical formula is a shorthand way of writing down the name of a chemical compound or molecule. Carbon monoxide consists of one atom of carbon and one atom of oxygen. Its chemical formula is CO. Carbon *dioxide* consists of one atom of carbon and *two* atoms of oxygen. Its chemical formula is CO_2.

Atoms in molecules are held together by *atomic bonds*, which arise from forces due to the interaction of the atom's electrons. There are a number of different kinds of atomic bonds, but the most common are *ionic* and *covalent*. In an ionic bond, one atom gives up an electron to another atom. The atoms are bonded together by their electrical attraction: the atom that lost an electron has a net positive charge, and the atom that gained an electron has

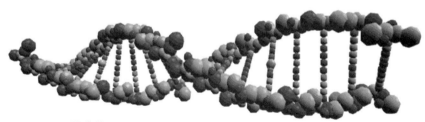

DNA double helix. MIKE OKUDA.

a net negative charge. In a covalent bond, electrons are shared between atoms.

DNA, or *deoxyribonucleic acid*, is an extremely complex organic molecule, and in fact is the "master molecule" of all life on Earth. DNA molecules are made up of two intertwined chains of simpler molecules called *bases*, assembled on rails of sugar and phosphate molecules like rungs on a ladder (see figure). The characteristic double-helix shape of the DNA molecule was discovered by Watson and Crick in 1955. Four different kinds of molecules form the rungs of the DNA ladder: adenine, thymine, guanine, and cytosine, which are typically referred to by their first letters, A, T, G, and C. In the DNA molecule, A always pairs with T, and G always pairs with C.

DNA molecules replicate by "unraveling" their rails. Each rail keeps its associated base. Complementary bases (A for T, G for C) attach to the free bases until two new strands of DNA are created.

Fields and Electromagnetic Radiation

Every subatomic particle is the source of at least one *field*. A field is essentially a mathematical representation of the "sphere of influence" of a charged particle. Particles interact through their fields. A proton at rest, for example, exerts a force on an electron through the action of an *electric* field. Moving electric charges generate *magnetic* fields.

The nineteenth-century English physicist Michael Faraday recognized that a fundamental relationship exists between electricity and magnetism. Another nineteenth-century physicist, James Clerk Maxwell, a Scotsman, determined that ripples in electric and magnetic fields, propagating through space, create *electromagnetic (EM) radiation*. Maxwell discovered that electromagnetic radiation travels through space at the speed of light, and he concluded that light is a form of electromagnetic radiation. We now know that radio waves, infrared radiation, visible and ultraviolet light, X rays, and gamma rays are all forms of electromagnetic radiation.

The Electromagnetic Spectrum and Basic Sensor Technology

Visible light is the most familiar form of EM radiation. The colors of the rainbow, however, comprise only one small segment of the *electromagnetic spectrum*. To make an analogy with sound, if the EM spectrum were the keyboard of a piano, humans would be able to hear only a few notes near middle C (it should be noted that sound waves are *not* EM waves; sound waves are periodic vibrations in the air or some other physical medium, and therefore cannot travel through the vacuum of space).

Waves and Photons

Electromagnetic waves are characterized by two numbers: *wavelength* and *frequency*. The wavelength of an EM wave is the distance between adjacent wave crests or troughs. This distance can be measured in meters or angstroms (10^{-10} meters). Frequency is the number of waves that pass a given point in a given time. The unit of frequency is the *hertz*, or *reciprocal seconds*. One hertz corresponds to the passage of one wave per second.

The wavelength of light perceived by human eyes as "red" is about seven thousand angstroms. Deep blue or violet light corresponds to roughly four thousand angstroms. The rest of the familiar "colors of the rainbow" fall somewhere in between. In order of decreasing wavelength, the colors of the rainbow are Red, Orange, Yellow, Green, Blue, Indigo, Violet (which can be easily remembered through the acronym ROY G. BIV).

Radio waves have the longest wavelength of all EM waves, sometimes stretching many kilometers, but more commonly on the order of a few meters. Their frequencies range from a few hertz to thousands and millions of hertz. Next comes infrared radiation, ranging in wavelength from around one micron (a millionth of a meter) to seven thousand angstroms. As mentioned above, visible light extends from about seven thousand to four thousand angstroms. Ultraviolet light ranges from four thousand angstroms to about ten angstroms. X rays have shorter wavelengths (and thus higher energies) still: about ten angstroms to .1 angstrom. Finally, any EM wave whose wavelength is less than .1 angstrom falls in the gamma-ray portion of the spectrum.

Maxwell discovered that the product of any electromagnetic wave's wavelength (represented by the Greek letter λ, lambda) and frequency (represented by the Greek letter ν, nu) is always equal to the speed of light, i.e., λ•ν = c. Knowing the wavelength of an EM wave, one can easily determine its frequency, and vice versa. It was also discovered around this time that the energy of an EM wave is a function of its frequency: the higher the frequency of an EM wave, the greater will be its energy. The German physicist Max Planck recognized around the beginning of the twentieth century that the energy of an EM wave is equal to its frequency times a constant of proportionality (now called *Planck's constant*) whose value he determined. The energy of a photon in joules, E, equals h•ν, where h, Planck's constant, is $6.63 • 10^{-34}$ joule-sec, and ν is the frequency of the photon measured in hertz.

This implies that low-temperature (room temperature and below) objects mostly emit long-wavelength, i.e., low-energy radiation, such as radio waves and infrared. Very hot objects (temperatures measured in tens of thousands of kelvins) on the other hand, mostly emit short-wavelength, i.e., high-energy radiation, such as ultraviolet and X rays.

The quantum theory of matter treats EM radiation not as waves but as discrete particles of energy called *photons*. A photon is, in effect, a particle of light. The energy of a photon is proportional to its frequency: the higher the frequency, the higher the energy of the photon. Infrared photons have relatively low energy. X-ray and gamma-ray photons have the highest energy.

Sensor Technology

A variety of instruments have been developed to detect and measure radiation throughout the EM spectrum, from the longest wavelength radio waves to the shortest wavelength gamma rays.

Large, dish-shaped radio antennas are used to measure radio waves from space. The largest radio telescope in the world is located near Arecibo, Puerto Rico. The receiving dish of the telescope is actually built into a shallow crater some three hundred meters in diameter. The radio-wave detector, suspended high above the dish, moves and changes orientation to point the telescope at different objects.

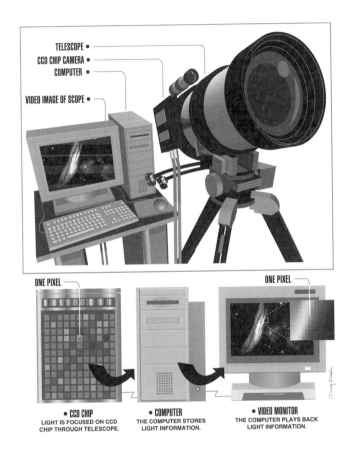

ONE PIXEL

ONE PIXEL

• CCD CHIP
LIGHT IS FOCUSED ON CCD
CHIP THROUGH TELESCOPE.

• COMPUTER
THE COMPUTER STORES
LIGHT INFORMATION.

• VIDEO MONITOR
THE COMPUTER PLAYS BACK
LIGHT INFORMATION.

DOUG DREXLER

Near-infrared through ultraviolet radiation can be gathered and focused by conventional reflecting telescopes. The largest optical telescopes in the world are currently the twin ten-meter Keck telescopes in Mauna Kea, Hawaii.

Solid-state detectors have largely replaced photographic film for taking pictures of distant objects in space. Some of the astronomical photos in this book were taken by solid-state detectors, which are also known as *CCD cameras*. The heart of a CCD camera is a specially treated silicon chip (much like a computer chip) which is extremely sensitive to light. The chip is divided into a grid of *pixels*, or picture elements, each some ten to twenty microns square.

To take an image of an astronomical object, the CCD camera is placed at the focus of a telescope. Light striking the CCD chip generates an electric current in each of the pixels proportional to the intensity of the light. A computer reads out the current in each pixel, and displays the corresponding intensity of the light intercepted by each pixel (see figure). Similar to a newsprint photo or a pointillist painting, the image really consists of tiny separate bits of color: in this case, an array of tiny squares of varying shades of gray. Using a series of color filters, CCD cameras can be used to make full color as well as black-and-white images.

Faster-Than-Light (FTL) Propulsion

In the *Star Trek* universe, a brilliant but eccentric (Aren't they always?) scientist named Zefram Cochrane developed the first practical FTL propulsion system, the celebrated *warp drive*, in 2063. *Space warps* have been a subject of serious scientific research since Albert Einstein created the general theory of relativity in 1915. Einstein showed that matter warps space; in other words, space itself is not "flat" but curved. Just as we cannot directly perceive the curvature of the Earth while standing on its surface, we cannot directly perceive the curvature of space, but it's just as real.

In his special theory of relativity, Einstein demonstrated that nothing can travel faster than the speed of light in a vacuum. As noted above, the nearest star beyond our solar system, Proxima Centauri, is a bit more than four light-years away. Since nothing can travel faster than light, a journey to Proxima Centauri would require at least four years.*

The idea of using "warped" space as a kind of loophole to circumvent the laws of special relativity has been examined by many scientists, but no one has yet developed a practical means of creating a

---

* As measured by an observer on Earth—the relativistic effect known as *time dilation* would lead to a different reckoning of travel time among the crew of a starship traveling at near-light speed.

space warp for propulsion. According to the general theory of relativity, the presence of matter is the only thing that warps space. High concentrations of extremely dense matter—in a black hole, for example—will warp space to an extreme degree (high concentrations of energy can also warp space, since, according to relativity theory, matter and energy are different manifestations of the same thing). Black holes may also be connected to other points in space through *wormholes*, cosmic short cuts through the curved space-time fabric of our universe. The question of how to create and manage space warps through the application of forces we know how to control—such as the electromagnetic or nuclear force—will have to await a fundamental breakthrough in basic physics.

For much of the twentieth century, theoretical physicists have struggled to achieve what many would consider the ultimate theory: a "theory of everything." Such a theory would be a single mathematical formulation that unifies all four fundamental forces in nature: gravitation, electromagnetism, and the strong and weak nuclear forces. The last three forces were combined into a single unified theory in the 1980s, but gravity has yet to be incorporated into the scheme. Understanding how gravity is one manifestation of a single, general force may provide the theoretical understanding that will eventually lead to the ability to manipulate gravitational fields through some mechanism involving the other basic forces. Or we may discover that matter is the only thing that can warp space; if this proves to be the case, "warp drive" may never be a practical means of propulsion.

On *Star Trek*, we assert that in a starship warp engine, high-energy plasma, created by a matter-antimatter reaction, is pumped through a series of warp coils cast from an artificial (and fictional) material called *verterium cortenide*. Verterium cortenide provides a bridge between electromagnetic and gravitational forces. By design, it has the property that when a high-energy plasma circulates through appropriately fashioned verterium cortenide castings, a "warp field" is generated. Electromagnetic interactions between waves of superhot plasma and the verterium cortenide coils change the geometry of space surrounding the engine nacelles. In the process, a multilayered wave of warped space is born, and the starship cruises off to its next destination at hundreds of times the speed of light (relative to "normal" space; within the warp field, the starship does not exceed the local speed of light, and therefore does not violate the principal tenet of special relativity). A more detailed description of the warp drive and other *Star Trek* technologies can be found in Rick Sternbach and Mike Okuda's *Star Trek: The Next Generation Technical Manual*, also published by Pocket Books; Rick and Mike developed the scenario described above for the operation of the warp drive.

Wormholes

What we call three-dimensional space is really a curved surface in a higher dimension. Extensive mathematical analysis of the general theory of relativity has led physicists to speculate on the existence of a variety of strange structures in *space-time*, including *wormholes*. Analogous to the tunnel a hungry worm bores through an apple, wormholes are tunnels in the fabric of space that connect widely separated locations through higher-dimension shortcuts. Wormholes, if they exist, are thought to be transient phenomena; the slightest gravitational flux will trigger the immediate collapse of naturally occurring wormholes.

The most famous wormhole in the *Star Trek* universe is of course the extraordinary transgalactic wormhole discovered by Captain Benjamin Sisko in the Bajoran sector of the Alpha Quadrant. The Bajoran wormhole can take a starship a distance of fifty thousand light-years in roughly thirty seconds. The stability of the Bajoran wormhole is maintained artificially through a "scaffolding" constructed of *verteron* particles. The creators of *Deep Space 9* have also devised a race of aliens who live within the wormhole, outside the boundaries of normal space and time.

Bibliography

For more on the characters and stories of the *Star Trek* universe:

Star Trek Chronology: The History of the Future, Michael Okuda and
    Denise Okuda, Pocket Books
*The Star Trek Encyclopedia: A Reference Guide to the Future, Updated
    and Expanded Edition*, Michael Okuda and Denise Okuda, Pocket
    Books
Star Trek: The Next Generation Technical Manual, Rick Sternbach and
    Michael Okuda, Pocket Books

For more on various fields of science, at a level accessible to the
general reader:

Being Digital, Nicholas Negroponte, Vintage
The Cosmic Connection, Carl Sagan, Anchor Books
Cosmic Wormholes, Paul Halpern, Dutton
Does God Play Dice?, Ian Stewart, Blackwell
Genetic Engineering: Dreams and Nightmares, Enzo Russo and David
    Cove, W.H. Freeman
Kings of Creation, Don Lessem, Simon & Schuster
The Illustrated A Brief History of Time, Stephen Hawking, Bantam Books
The Inflationary Universe, Alan Guth, Addison Wesley
The Lives of A Cell, Lewis Thomas, Bantam Books
The Matter Myth, Paul Davies and John Gribben, Simon & Schuster
The Mind's Sky, Timothy Ferris, Bantam Books
Naturalist, Edward O. Wilson, Warner Books
Pale Blue Dot, Carl Sagan, Random House
The Physics of Star Trek, Lawrence M. Krause, Basic Books
Voyage to the Great Attractor, Alan Dressler, Knopf

Glossary of Terms

accretion disk. A disk of gas and dust surrounding a central mass, such as a *protostar* or a *black hole*.

aileron. Control surface on the wing of an aircraft.

alpha particles. Subatomic particles consisting of two protons and two neutrons; the nucleus of a helium atom.

alveoli. Air sacs in the lungs.

android. A robot constructed in the form of a human being.

angstrom. Unit of length equal to 10^{-10} meters.

antibody. Protein produced in response to an *antigen* for the purpose of inhibiting, neutralizing, or destroying the antigen.

antigen. Any substance that triggers the production of *antibodies* within an organism.

application program. Computer program, such as a word-processing program, designed to perform a specific set of tasks.

assembler. Hypothetical nanomachine designed to perform a variety of construction tasks.

atomic hypothesis. Contention that all matter is constructed of basic indivisible units.

atomic theory of matter. Theory articulated by nineteenth-century chemist John Dalton, which asserts that matter is composed of various combinations of a small number of *chemical elements*, or atoms.

autoimmune response. An immunologic response directed against an organism's own tissue *antigens*.

axon. Fiber-like structure that carries nerve impulses away from the nerve cell body; see also *dendrite*.

bacteria. Minuscule living organisms—some are capable of photosynthesis, but not members of the plant kingdom.

barycenter. Center of mass of a binary star system, or any other pair of celestial bodies.

beta particles. Electrons emitted by the radioactive decay of certain elements.

Big Bang theory. Widely accepted theory asserting that the universe was born some fifteen billion years ago in an immense explosion, which created space, time, matter, and energy.

binary star. Two stars that revolve around a common center of mass.

bionics. Science of augmenting or replacing human appendages, organs, or tissues with artificial implants or components.

biotechnology. Application of engineering principles in the life sciences.

bipolar outflow. Jets of gas flowing in opposite directions from a central source, typically a young star or the nucleus of a *quasar*.

black hole. A celestial object whose mass density is so great that light cannot escape it.

black smoker. A vent on the ocean floor emitting superheated water rich in minerals; a kind of *hydrothermal vent*.

Bok globule. Dark cloud of interstellar dust and gas, potentially harboring a star in the early stages of formation.

Buckminsterfullerene. A molecule consisting of sixty carbon atoms arranged in a geodesic sphere; named in honor of the visionary designer and engineer Buckminster Fuller.

carbonaceous asteroid. An asteroid rich in carbon compounds.

cavorite. Fictional "antigravity" substance invented by H.G. Wells in his novel *The First Men in the Moon*.

CCD camera. Camera that uses a light-sensitive silicon chip in place of photographic film.

cell membrane. Outer layer of a cell that controls the flow of molecules into and out of the cell.

cell wall. In plant cells, a thick covering outside the cell membrane that protects the interior of the cell.

cell. Smallest structural unit within a living organism capable of performing all of the activities associated with life.

central processing unit (cpu). Circuitry within a computer that performs all arithmetic and logic functions.

chemical element. Any substance that cannot be decomposed into more simple substances through ordinary chemical processes; atoms are chemical elements; molecules are not.

Cherenkov radiation. Radiation produced by particles traveling faster than the speed of light in a given medium.

chlorofluorocarbons. Molecules containing chlorine, fluorine, and carbon atoms, widely used in a variety of industrial applications, implicated in the destruction of stratospheric *ozone*.

chloroplast. Plant-cell structure critical to the process of *photosynthesis*.

chromosome. A chain of *genes*; a chromosome is essentially a DNA molecule and its supporting molecular structures.

clone. A genetically identical duplicate of an organism; a delayed identical twin.

Closed Ecology Life Support System (CELSS). A self-contained environmental control system that can provide for all of the air, water, and food needs of its occupants indefinitely.

cloud chamber. Device used in physics laboratories to render the passage of subatomic particles visible.

coal sack. Dark interstellar dust cloud located in the southern hemisphere constellation Crux (the southern cross).

commensalism. Relationship between organisms in which one partner derives a benefit, while the other partner is basically indifferent to the relationship; a barnacle attached to the skin of a whale is an example.

composite. Material comprising several different substances.

constellation. Pattern of stars that represents a person, animal, or thing. Most of the northern hemisphere constellations recognized today were named by the ancient Greeks, and represent characters from Greek mythology.

cosmic maser. Coherent emission of microwave radiation typically emanating from the vicinity of giant stars or deep within *molecular clouds*.

cosmic microwave background radiation. Residual radiation left over from the *Big Bang* that gave birth to the universe.

cosmic strings. Hypothetical ultra-thin, tremendously dense threads of matter that might have played a role in the formation of structure in the universe.

cosmology. Science concerned with the study of the large-scale structure and evolution of the universe.

covalent bond. Chemical bond in which electrons are shared between atoms.

cryonic suspension. Freezing a person in liquid nitrogen immediately after death in the hope that someday medical science will find a way to revive and restore to health the frozen individual.

cybernetics. Science of control and communication systems; it can refer both to machines and to living organisms.

dark matter. Matter invisible to conventional astronomical instruments, thought to constitute a major fraction of the mass of the universe.

delta ray. Fictional form of radiation, extremely hazardous to living organisms.

demotic writing. Cursive form of written ancient Egyptian language.

dendrite. Threadlike nerve cell structure that carries nerve impulses toward the nerve cell body; see also *axon*.

dielectric. An electrically nonconducting or insulating material.

differentiation. In planetary science, the process by which a layered structure develops within a planetary body as denser materials sink and settle toward the center of the body.

DNA. Deoxyribonucleic acid, the biochemical substance of which genes are made.

duranium. Fictional material used in the construction of Federation starship hulls and bulkheads.

dynamo effect. Production of a magnetic field through the circular motion of an electrically charged substance.

echolocation. Acoustic sensing system bats use to locate objects.

ecosystem. Interdependent collection of organisms, atmospheric gases, soil, rocks, and water that comprise a biological habitat.

electromagnetic radiation. Self-propagating wave of electric and magnetic energy; light is a form of electromagnetic radiation.

electromagnetic spectrum. Entire range of electromagnetic radiation, from radio waves to gamma rays.

electron. Negatively charged subatomic particle; a fundamental particle whose mass is 1/1837 the mass of a *proton*.

emergent property. An ostensibly complex phenomenon that arises through repeated, simple interactions among the components of a system.

endangered species. A species on the verge of extinction.

energy shells. Set of discrete energy levels within an atom.

enzyme. A biochemical substance, typically a protein, that affects the rate of biochemical reactions.

eukaryotic cell. A *cell* that contains a *nucleus*.

event horizon. Boundary of a black hole; observers outside the event horizon cannot see or influence anything inside the event horizon.

evolved supernova remnant. Expanding shell of gases in space, created by a supernova explosion thousands of years in the past.

exchange particles. Subatomic particles responsible for the propagation of the fundamental forces in nature.

false vacuum. Ultradense region of space that in some ways mimics a vacuum.

fault line. Roughly linear break in a planet's crust.

fluorescence. Emission of visible light through the absorption of higher frequency radiation, such as ultraviolet light

frequency. Number of cycles per second of a wave or wavelike phenomenon.

gamma ray. Most energetic form of electromagnetic radiation.

gene therapy. Medical treatment that seeks to repair damaged *genes* in cells.

gene. A segment of DNA that determines the structure (composition and shape) of a protein molecule; genes are said to "code" for the production of the various protein molecules that make up living organisms.

geological record. The evolutionary history of a planet as revealed by rocks and rock strata.

geosynchronous orbit. Orbit whose period matches the rotation rate of the Earth; a satellite in geosynchronous orbit appears to remain above the same point on the Earth's surface; also called geostationary or synchronous orbit.

gravitational radiation. Waves of gravitational force propagated at the speed of light, generated by cataclysmic processes, such as the collapse of a star.

graviton. Quantum, or exchange particle, of the gravitational field.

gravity wave. A wave of *gravitational radiation*.

greenhouse gas. Any gas that traps infrared radiation, and can therefore significantly increase the temperature of the atmosphere, even if present in relatively small quantities.

Hawking radiation. Radiation produced by pair-production events near the *event horizon* of a *black hole*.

hertz. Unit of frequency: reciprocal seconds.

histone. Protein compound that supports *DNA* in *chromosomes*.

HLA antigen. Human Leucocyte Associated antigen; protein found on the surface of white blood cells.

Homo habilis. Genus and species of the first true human beings.

Homo sapiens. Genus and species of modern human beings.

host. An organism inhabited by a *parasite*.

hydrothermal vent. Crack in the ocean floor through which superheated water erupts.

hypercube. A four-dimensional cube.

icon. In computer applications, a graphic representation of a computer function or program.

immune system. Collection of cells and other physiological structures that protect an organism against infectious agents.

imprinting. Process whereby very young animals become behaviorally attached to their mothers or a mother surrogate.

inflation theory. Variation on the *Big Bang theory*, which argues that shortly after the Big Bang the universe underwent a short period of extremely rapid expansion, a kind of cosmic growth spurt.

integrated circuit. Electronic device composed of myriad miniature, interconnected electronic components on a single chip of silicon or some other semiconductor material.

interstellar medium (ISM). Dust, gas, and other matter that lies
  between the stars within a galaxy.
intron. Segment of *DNA* that seems to serve no specific purpose within
  a *chromosome*.
ionic bond. Chemical bond created when an atom loses one or more
  electrons to another atom.
ionization. Process of removing one or more *electrons* from a neutral
  atom or molecule.
iterated function. A function that is repeated many times; the output of
  each iteration typically becomes the input for the next iteration.
jovian planet. A large, mostly gaseous planet; Jupiter is a jovian planet.
kelvin. Unit of temperature in the metric system.
lichen. Symbiotic organism made up of algae and fungus.
light-year. Distance a beam of light, in vacuum, travels in one year; a
  standard unit of distance in astronomy.
linguistics. The science of language.
macrophage. One of the cells of the *immune system*; macrophages seek
  out and destroy harmful bacteria and other foreign matter in the
  bloodstream.
magnetosphere. Region surrounding a planet, created by the planet's magnetic field, that traps charged particles streaming away from its sun.
main sequence. On a chart of stellar temperature versus brightness, the
  group of stars that are converting hydrogen into helium through the
  process of *nuclear fusion*; a main sequence star is basically a star
  (like the Sun) in the prime of its life.
mass extinction. Global-scale extinction of a large fraction of plant and
  animal species.
Massive Compact Halo Objects (MACHOs). Hypothetical planet-scale
  objects orbiting the Milky Way and other galaxies; one possible
  form of the dark matter that appears to make up most of the mass
  of the universe.
melanin. Dark pigment typically found in human skin, and largely
  responsible for skin color.
micron. A millionth of a meter.
Milky Way Galaxy. Spiral system of several hundred billion stars in
  which the Earth resides.
mitochondrion. *Organelle* that produces energy within a cell.
mitosis. First step in the process of cell division.
modem. Literally "*mo*dulator/*dem*odulator," a device used to electronically connect computers via telephone lines.
molecular cloud. Massive cloud of interstellar gas mostly in the form of
  molecules.

molting. Process whereby an organism, such as a snake, sheds its skin.

monotreme. Lowest order of mammals; the duck-billed platypus is a monotreme.

motor nerve. Nerve that relays electrical signals to muscle tissue.

muon. A short-lived subatomic particle, related to the *electron*.

Mylar. A thin but very strong plastic material, potentially useful in the construction of solar sails.

naked singularity. A *black hole* stripped of its *event horizon*; essentially a black hole visible to the outside world, not considered likely to exist in the cosmos.

nanotechnology. Branch of engineering that seeks to create molecular- and atomic-scale machines.

neuron. A nerve cell; a neuron consists of a cell body, *axon*, and *dendrites*.

neutron star. Dense core of a star that has exploded in a *supernova*, consisting almost entirely of *neutrons*.

neutron. Electrically neutral subatomic particle; one of the constituents of an atomic *nucleus*.

neutronium. Name sometimes given to a material comprised entirely of neutrons, such as the matter within a *neutron star*.

nova. A star that undergoes a sudden, temporary outburst of energy, shining at hundreds or thousands of times its normal brightness.

nuclear fission. Process whereby an atomic nucleus is split into two smaller nuclei, often accompanied by the production of energy.

nuclear fusion. Process whereby two atomic nuclei fuse into a single, heavier nucleus, often accompanied by the production of energy.

nuclear pile. Assembly of radioactive material used for the controlled production of nuclear energy by the process of *nuclear fission*.

nuclear reaction. Reaction involving the fission or fusion of atomic nuclei or subatomic particles.

nucleoplasm. The *protoplasm* within a cell nucleus.

nucleus. In biology, the "control center" of a cell; in physics, the central part of an atom, consisting of *protons* and *neutrons*.

occultation. Eclipse of a star or planet by another astronomical object.

optics. The science of light; the light-bending components of an optical device, such as a telescope.

orbital precession. Tendency of a planet's elliptical orbit to rotate slowly over time.

organ. Biological structure, consisting of two or more dissimilar tissues, that performs a specific function within an organism.

organelle. Structure within a cell that carries out a particular cellular activity; analogous to an *organ* within a cell.

organic molecule. Any carbon-based molecule (with the exception of some small carbon-based molecules such as carbon monoxide and carbon dioxide).

ozone layer. Layer of ozone (O_3) molecules that protects the Earth from ultraviolet radiation.

pair production. Quantum mechanical process that spontaneously creates pairs of matter and antimatter particles, such as electrons and positrons.

parallel processing. Computational technique that addresses several or many parts of a mathematical problem simultaneously.

parasite. An organism that lives at the expense of another organism, called the *host*.

parsec. Unit of distance in astronomy equal to 3.26 *light-years*.

perihelion. Point in a solar orbit closest to the Sun.

periodic table of the elements. Chart that organizes chemical elements by their common properties.

phloem. Name for the transport tissue that carries sap and is found within plants.

photon. A particle, or quantum, of light.

photosynthesis. Chemical process plants use to convert sunlight, water, and carbon dioxide into simple sugars for food.

pixel. Picture element; electronically generated images, such as those on a computer screen, are composed of arrays of small pixels.

Planck's constant. A fundamental constant of nature that characterizes quantum processes.

planetary system. Retinue of planets, moons, asteroids, and comets orbiting a star.

plasma cell. One of the cells that plays an important role in the *immune system*.

polaron. An electron and the polarized electric field it generates within a *semiconductor* or other similar medium.

proboscis. Strawlike appendage used by some insects to ingest fluid.

prokaryotic cell. A *cell* that lacks a *nucleus*.

protoplanetary disk. Flat, rotating disk of matter surrounding a young star, which may eventually form a *planetary system*.

protoplasm. Liquid substance within a cell that provides a supporting medium for *organelles* and other cell structures; more commonly called cytoplasm.

protostar. Large, hot spherical cloud of condensing gas on its way to becoming a star; a protostar is not hot enough to generate energy through *nuclear fusion*.

psionic field. Fictional field that serves as a medium for *telepathy* and *telekinesis*.

quark. Class of six fundamental particles, the building blocks of *protons*, *neutrons*, and particles called mesons; also the name of a greedy but basically honorable Ferengi bartender.

quasar. Short for quasi-stellar object; an extremely powerful and compact source of energy typically located billions of *light-years* outside our galaxy.

radar. Acronym that stands for *r*adio *d*etection *a*nd *r*anging, a technique that uses radio waves to detect and identify distant objects.

radiation pressure. The small but significant pressure exerted by *radiation*.

radiation. The emission of energy in the form of electromagnetic waves or subatomic particles.

radioactive fallout. Radioactive material, including dust, smoke, and ash, produced in the wake of a nuclear explosion.

radionuclide. A radioactive element.

rays. Term sometimes used to describe a stream of particle radiation.

rest mass. Mass of an object at rest with respect to an observer at rest.

Richter scale. Exponential scale used to measure the intensity of an Earthquake; a 4.0 quake on the Richer scale is ten times stronger than a 3.0 quake.

robot. A mechanical device designed to perform some particular function; robots are commonly used in manufacturing processes.

rogue wave. Wave created when several smaller waves interact in such a way that they are amplified and combined into a single large wave.

Rosetta stone. Stone tablet discovered in 1799, provided the key to translating Egyptian hieroglyphics.

semiconductor. A material that is neither a good conductor, nor a good insulator; semiconductors have found widespread application in the construction of *integrated circuits*.

sentience. Intelligence or consciousness.

solar system. A star and its retinue of planets, moon, asteroids, comets, particles, and fields.

solar wind. Stream of energetic particles emitted by a sun.

sonar. An acronym that stands for *s*ound *a*pplication and *r*anging, a technique, similar to *radar*, that uses sound waves to detect and identify objects under water.

space warp. An extremely curved region of space.

space-time. In Einstein's special and general theories of relativity, space and time are treated in equivalent mathematical terms as a single entity called space-time.

species. Any two organisms that are capable of mating to produce fertile offspring are said to be members of the same species.

spectroscopy. Technique of spreading light into a spectrum for the purpose of analyzing the relative intensities of various light *frequencies*.

spore. Minute biological structures produced by plant organisms for the purpose of reproduction.

sungrazer. A comet that passes very close to, or collides with, the Sun.

superconductor. A material that offers no resistance to the flow of electricity.

superluminal jet. Jet of interstellar material that appears to travel faster than the speed of light.

supernova. A tremendous stellar explosion, wherein a star suddenly produces so much energy that it temporarily shines at billions of times its normal brightness.

symbiotic relationship. A mutually beneficial biological relationship between two organisms.

synapse. Junction between two *neurons*.

T cell. A white blood cell that can differentiate into six different types of cells, all of which play important roles in the human *immune system*.

tectonic plate. A large section of a planet's crust that slowly moves over underlying rock strata.

telekinesis. Hypothetical ability to move an object purely through the power of thought.

telepathy. Hypothetical ability to read the thoughts or feelings of another person.

tensile strength. Amount of tension a material can sustain before breaking.

terraforming. Process of turning an otherwise inhospitable planet into a habitable biosphere.

terrestrial planet. A planet consisting mostly of rocky material, with a relatively thin atmosphere or no atmosphere; Earth is a terrestrial planet.

thermophiles. Bacterial organisms that thrive in conditions of extreme heat.

tidal force. Differential force within a body due to gravitational field gradient; tidal forces can sometimes rip an object apart.

time dilation. Relativistic effect that makes time appear to run more slowly for objects moving at a substantial fraction of the speed of light.

trinary star. Three stars that orbit about their common center of mass.

trinitite. Nickname for the fused sand produced by the blast of the first atomic bomb test, near Los Alamos, New Mexico.

tritanium. Fictional material used in the construction of Federation starship hulls and bulkheads.

vaccine. Chemically crippled segments of viruses and/or bacteria used to stimulate an immune response that will protect an individual from later infections by those substances.

valence electron. An electron in an atom's outermost *energy shell*.

velociraptor. A predatory dinosaur that lived during the Cretaceous period.

vertebra. Any one of the twenty-six bones that make up the vertebral column or backbone.

vertebral canal. The cavity within the vertebral column that contains the spinal cord.

verterium cortenide. Fictional material used to construct warp coils for starship propulsion systems.

verteron. Fictional particle that maintains the stability of the Bajoran wormhole.

virus. Fragments of DNA or RNA wrapped in a protein coat.

voice recognition software. Program that provides a computer with the ability to recognize spoken language commands.

warp drive. Hypothetical propulsion system of Federation starships; the warp drive propels ships over interstellar distances by warping space, producing velocities equivalent to many times the speed of light.

wavelength. Distance between adjacent crests or troughs in a wave.

Weakly Interacting Massive Particles (WIMPs). Subatomic particles of great mass that nevertheless rarely interact with normal matter; one possible form of the dark matter that appears to make up most of the mass of the universe.

white dwarf. A small, dense star at the end of its life, glowing due to residual heat from its time on the *main sequence*; a white dwarf is typically rich in the element carbon, and can sometimes flare into a *supernova* if its mass is increased past a critical limit through accretion from a companion star.

wormhole. An extremely warped region of space that forms a sort of "tunnel" connecting two widely separated points in space.

X ray. High-frequency electromagnetic radiation.

X-ray diffraction. Technique used to probe the structure of crystals.

xenotransplantation. Medical term describing the transplantation of organs from other species into humans.

Index